KRISHNA

AF653885

KRISHNA

MAHA VISHNU AVATAR

Kevin Missal

SIMON & SCHUSTER

London · New York · Sydney · Toronto · New Delhi

First published in India by Simon & Schuster India, 2023

Copyright © Kevin Missal, 2023

This edition published in 2023

The right of Kevin Missal to be identified as author of this work has been asserted by him in accordance with Section 57 of the Copyright Act, 1957.

3 5 7 9 10 8 6 4 2

Simon & Schuster India
818, Indraprakash Building,
21, Barakhamba Road,
New Delhi 110001

www.simonandschuster.co.in

Paperback ISBN: 978-93-92099-92-2
Hardback ISBN: 978-81-94643-03-6
eBook ISBN: 978-93-92099-93-9

Typeset in India by SÜRYA, New Delhi

Printed and bound in India by Replika Press Pvt. Ltd.

FSC
www.fsc.org
MIX
Paper | Supporting responsible forestry
FSC® C016779

Simon & Schuster India is committed to sourcing paper that is made from wood grown in sustainable forests and support the Forest Stewardship Council, the leading international forest certification organisation. Our books displaying the FSC logo are printed on FSC certified paper.

No part of this publication may be reproduced, transmitted or stored in a retrieval system, in any form or by any means, electronic, mechanical, photocopying, recording or otherwise, without the prior permission of the publisher.

This book is sold subject to the condition that it shall not, by way of trade or otherwise, be lent, resold, hired out, or otherwise circulated, without the publisher's prior consent, in any form of binding or cover other than that in which it is published.

Note

What happened after the Mahabharata? What happened to Krishna, Arjun and the other heroes? This always piqued my interest, until I happened to read the Mausala Parva—the last chapter which spoke about the submergence of Dwarka, the fight of the Yadavas. In its truest sense, this is my reimagination of the Parva, while adding all the elements of fantasy, myths and history around it.

Hope you enjoy it. I enjoyed writing it.

Disclaimer

This book is a fantastical reimagining of the Mausala Parva from the Mahabharata. The writer does not claim this to be a scholarly or religiously authoritative representation of the Mausala Parva. It is a work of worship, utilizing the epic as a source of inspiration. Readers are encouraged to explore the original Mahabharata and consult reliable religious and literary sources for a comprehensive understanding of the epics. The book should not be misconstrued as factual or historical representations. The book does not endorse any particular religious or philosophical perspective.

EPISODE ONE

1

"Do you want to listen to a tragedy?" asked the stranger.

Vaisampiya, a chronicler, had been in Dvarka for the last sixty-five days and he had never met someone like the stranger until now.

He thought his night would be an ordinary one. He would come to the tavern. Drink his madira. Listen to the tales of the seamen, the farmers and the drunkards. And go back to his inn and call it a night.

But as he had received his madira and he was about to sip it, the stranger arrived. He had a cowl over him and his face was in the shadows. He had a voice as deep and dark as possible. And his nose popped out from the shade, showing the scars that it carried.

"Listening to tales is my hobby."

"And churning them out with morals is your occupation." The stranger added.

Oh well, Vaisampiya was a proud man. He liked his choice of career. He would travel the world. Listen to stories and tell it to others orally. He knew about everyone and everything. Except for Dvarka. That was an island nation which was shrouded in mystery; a nation that built its reputations of being invincible and indestructible by having the best army in the world.

To pass through customs was tough, but bribing his

way in was his knack. He did so, and he reached here, welcomed by the almighty beauty of the brusque lands, the tall volcanoes and the crystal palaces. This was the island where the god Krishna resided, though he had not been seen for the last five years.

Wonder why, he thought. And when he asked, he got answers plenty. None that would satiate him though.

"Indeed. So what tragedy is this?"

"I believe you seek why the former king of Dvarka disappeared five years earlier?" The stranger asked.

"And you might know?" Vaisampiya added, leaning forward on his chair as the hum of the trumpets blared in the background, the taps of the dance were heard. "Tell me, is it because he fought an Asur and went into Pataal, or is it because he was turned invisible by a Rakshas's Maya? What is it? I have heard so many variations, I have grown tired of it."

"Then perhaps you might want to know one more."

Vaisampiya watched the stranger for a moment, contemplating whether to listen further. But every man who comes with a story, is a man who is selfish. He wants to be heard. But most of all, he wants something in return. "What do you seek if I hear you out?"

"Information that you might possess."

"I don't possess anything."

"Your reputation is of a traveller and a learner, a scholar and a gentry. You have travelled around Dvarka more than the ones who have lived here for years. You must have seen something that matters to me."

"And what is that?"

"You'll know. So should I begin?"

"By all means."

The stranger leaned back. His face popping out of the shade of the cowl. His skin parched and breaking, his lips scorched and torn. An ugly man hidden in a cowl. That answered why he wanted to hide himself.

Or perhaps, he didn't want to be known.

The mystery of the stranger eluded him, and Vaisampiya knew he wouldn't be given an accurate answer if he asked. Because if the man wanted to reveal his identity, he would have introduced himself.

"Do you know the greatest war that was ever fought?"

"Yes."

"What was it?" The stranger asked.

"Happened far from me, but I heard it all right. It was at the Kurukshetra. The Pandavas and the Kauravas fought a war where they both lost, even though one got victory," Vaisampiya said. He was at a small village when it happened, close to Kamboj. He was training to be a sage, which went horribly wrong when it was discovered that he's a Shudra. Oh, that led his entire dream to become a sage go down the drain and he ended up choosing something else he loved other than devoting himself to Mahadev—devoting himself to a path that Mahadev chooses not to destroy: humans.

"It was called the The Great War."

"Indeed. And our great lord, former King Krishna was part of it. A charioteer to the famed Arjun. It was him who made sure the Pandavas won."

"But I know this story. How is this a tragedy?" Vaisampiya paused. "Also, why do you say Lord Krishna, the *former* king? Why did he give up his throne?"

"His stead is being ruled by his favourite son, Pradhyumna."

Vaisampiya had heard of the young, feverishly good-looking boy. His eyes were of sapphire stones and his skin was opposite to Krishna's, a mix of golden and bronze. He had also heard that Pradhyumna legalised madira, gambling, prostitution. He was a progressive king who believed there were no vices, just human follies that should be embraced rather than be curbed.

"I know. But why?"

"Patience. One thing, at a time." The stranger chuckled under his breath. "Do you know what happened after the triumph of that war?"

"Happily ever after?"

"Unfortunately, no. There was a meeting with Lord Krishna. He met a woman, of the opposing side. Her name was Gandhari."

"The mother to Duryodhan?"

"Yes." The stranger nodded. "And she had cursed Lord Krishna for she believed that Lord Krishna could have prevented the war from happening. The curse was simple. His men would die the same way her sons were butchered."

"Men as in? The Yayatis?"

"Indeed. You are right now in a village that comes under the jurisdiction of Sattavahas," informed the stranger. "Now our king was paranoid. Initially, he thought of this curse as bogus, but as his mind cleared, worry began to cloud his judgment and he decided he had to do something. So, using all his power, his might and his divine energy, he transferred his powers to the Yayatis so they remain invincible and indestructible."

The chronicler hadn't heard of this and when he did, his ears turned red. *So that's why Dvarka as a nation has continued to be undefeatable.* "You mean they are protected by magic?"

"Call it what you would."

"But I don't see the tragedy till now." The chronicler added, disappointed. "Till now, it's going merry ho happy."

The stranger waited. A long-drawn pause before he took the bamboo cup from which the chronicler had been sipping all along and drank the madira. Vaisampiya didn't retort. The man's throat might be parched, for he did all the talking.

"Unfortunately, great power begets great ambition. And ambition comes with a price. The price of superiority, of dominance. When one race becomes greater than the rest, they begin to believe they should rule over others. Correct?"

"Indeed. As the myths spoke of—how the Danavs felt about the Devas and how the Devas felt about the Manavs."

"Indeed. People don't talk about the flip side of power. The side which is sad. It's a side which is more or less about arrogance. It's a side where self-indulgence becomes so overwhelming that it shapes the remainder of one's life."

"So what happened? The Yayatis became power hungry?"

"And they began to rebel against our Lord Krishna.

Told him he's no more a god for he gave his divinity to humans. Now he's a mere man. Not fit to rule. They began to fight him. They began to hate the rules that Krishna imposed. They began to divulge themselves into all the carnal desires a man possesses. Seeing this, Krishna realised his grave mistake. In the process of making his race safe, he ended up making them his enemies." The stranger guffawed at the irony. "So he left. Packed his bag and left. Where he is now, no one knows. Realising it was the perfect opportunity, his son took the mantle and never called a search party for him because he was afraid that if his father was found, his crown would be taken back for he has never defied his father. He was a good son." He chuckled at the statement as he continued. "That was five years ago."

"It's been five years since Krishna has disappeared?" A cold shiver went down his spine.

"Yes. And his men have run afoul. The Yayatis are no more in control. They rule their individual steads and don't have any unity. Worse, they do raids in neighbouring islets and lands. Murder women, men and children. Rape and pillage. They are now led by the once good prince and now a defiled king—Pradhyuman. His aim: to make people kneel in front of him, for he thinks he's greater than others."

Vaisampiya couldn't believe he was hearing all of this. From the outset, Dvarka looked harmless. Full of peace. But then, of course it would look peaceful since no one would dare to attack them. Everyone feared them. And the only man who had a chance to silence them, had disappeared half a decade ago.

"I don't believe this to be true," Vaisampiya nodded his head. "Yes. It sounds like a fairy tale. You mean your kind can't be hurt, wounded or anything?"

Another chuckle. Vaisampiya was annoyed, but the stranger didn't wait. The mug he had, he smashed it hard as he could on the table, letting the wooden shards spread across, but muted by the songs and the ballads that were playing in the background.

He picked up one of the shards and raised his other hand, cutting his skin with the weapon he had just made. The serration pierced through his skin and blood trickled from his arms, his veins were bursting and he left the shard in the corner. For a moment, it remained like that until the wound began to heal itself, the cut was being incisively treated by invisible shamans and the blood that was dripping, had cleared. The skin was dry and clear as a day.

"By the thunder of Indra, how did you do that?" Vaisampiya's entire body was shaking.

"Magic." Another chuckle.

Vaisampiya knew that perhaps the man in front of him was a trickster or perhaps the creature of the dark... the one people say one must hide from. The Asur. Or he could be far worse than anything: he could be an honest man.

"If this is true, then the Yayatis have the power for world domination?"

"That's what I fear." The voice didn't mask anything, anymore. It was diligent and laced in worry. "I have done my part of the bargain and as history says, you hold up yours."

Vaisampiya nodded and ordered another madira. Fidgeting nervously he said, "What would you ask me that I know and you don't?" He chuckled to himself at that, stroking his beard, which was his usual call whenever he was nervous.

"I believe you have travelled enough and I think you were mentioning to some soldiers the other day at the tavern that you had seen a man with blue eyes and a silver beard." The stranger asked. "A few days back."

Vaisampiya furrowed his brows. Trying to recall. And then he did. There was a man. An odd, old fellow but quite kind. "He was very hospitable. On the south of Dvarkipur, there's a farm. You'll not miss it for it holds a large stead, red in colour. But what business do you have from a simple cowherder?"

"Cowherder," there was a smirking tone and then he whispered to himself, with a quiet snarl. "He's gone back to his humble beginnings."

"Who?"

"It's funny." The stranger said, and as he did, he pulled down his cowl showing his curly brown hair and his face...oh the face! It had all kinds of scars, but most notably, he wore an iron mask covering one-fourth of his face, hiding his nose and his eyes. The stranger was a boy, a simple looking one but with wisdom beyond his years. "How you wanted to know about Lord Krishna, but failed to know that you have already met him."

"The *cowherder*?" Vaisampiya's body just sprang with horror. "As a matter of fact, he was the one who told me that Lord Krishna went to find the finest butter out there."

"Ah, a charmer."

And before he could say anything more, he felt something tugging at his shoulders and his arms. Realising what was happening, he turned his head to see that men had gathered, the same soldiers with whom he had chatted about Krishna the previous day. They had small daggers hidden under their robes.

"Are you going to kill me now?"

The stranger shook his head. A smile dancing on his lips. "We are not the bad guys, chronicler. You will be escorted out of the island by tonight's spice shipment."

"Why?"

"Because you know where he lives. And no one else should."

Vaisampiya was pulled up and shoved and dragged around, when he staggered and pushed back and asked: "Please, who are you and why were you asking me all of this? I am burning with curiosity."

The stranger smiled. And then he signalled the soldiers to be stricter with him as the stranger said his final words—"Call me Samva. And you just finally told me where my dad has been hiding for so long."

2

When the wicked would rest, so would Pradhyuman.

But today, was not that day. It was the day of the reckoning. The day of the trial. The arena was set and the red earth would glisten under the hot, blistering sun. The coconut trees were in one line, shadowing the place and the murmurs, whispers of the councilmen, the politicians and the administrators of the kingdom were heard.

Pradhyuman remained impassive on his throne. Where the king's seat was, at the arena. On top of the people's arches and at a helm, which was way above everyone else.

He had a way of looking. His eyes were pure, crystal blue like the deepest end of the ocean and his hair was brown like his father's and his brother's. Long locks of curly hair just falling flat on his heavy, muscular shoulders. A man as beautiful as Pradhyuman was unbridled and unrivalled.

Rukmavati, his wife with green coral eyes, was on his side, in a long drape that had diamonds and rubies. Though he paid no heed to her, for Pradhyuman was a man of varied taste and he didn't like to settle. If it wasn't for the political relations he had to create with the Ahira tribe of Yayatis, he wouldn't have been here but with a lustful of wenches drying his naked frame and oiling it, only to gratify him in the end.

A man as beautiful as him should not be kept selfishly by one person. He should be given off to the world. Pradhyuman always believed that.

He looked on his right, hoping to find his ally and his political machinist for the spectacle today, but she was not here.

"Where's Durgajyoti?" He asked Rukmavati.

She shook her head, as she drank her wine. She didn't care much and just rolled her eyes.

Durgajyoti was the scion to the Taljan tribe of the Yayatis, having a firm control of the Vitihotras who were the mutated sub-tribe of the Taljan. They were a bunch of, one can say—monsters. Even by thinking about them, the king of Dvarka had a shiver run down his spine. But Durgajyoti was more than just a scion, she was also an important person to Pradhyuman, a dear friend and someone who wanted to see him rise.

"She's running a little late my lord." He heard a voice and Pradhyuman turned, amidst the sounds of the raging crowd who were waiting for the fight at the arena to begin.

The voice was from the dramatist, a man who wrote plays and stories and made them to be enacted out in public for pleasure.

"Ah, you are here."

The dramatist was a scrawny fellow, he sat down on the lower shelf below Pradhyuman.

"So everything is planned for it to begin?" He asked.

"Yes, indeed." The dramatist nodded, going through

the papers. "The orator will begin the match and the slaves would be brought forth to fight the creature. And then you step forward and save them."

"Does the creature lose its chain in the process?"

"Yes, have checked the chain properly. It'll break with a few jerks. For a moment, everyone would be scared, but no worries, the creature would be stopped by our valorous king Pradhyuman."

"Great." He smiled. Having all of this in place was important because as a king, more than being valorous, the illusion of it was more important. Because here, everyone was invincible, so they won't be ruled by someone who has power, but one who they respect.

"But are you sure you want to use the slaves for this? We have few criminals in the prison." The dramatist asked. "Those are innocent people on the line."

"No. The criminals are Yayatis and they wouldn't die, so the stakes aren't high. The slaves on the other hand are farmers, seamen who had come here as immigrants illegally. If they die, people would enjoy it, because people love violence."

Rukmavari, drunk as she was, said: "And since when have immigrants become innocent?" Then she chuckled.

Pradhyuman sighed. Rukmavati would become very unlike a proper woman.

The dramatist grievously nodded. And then before he could say anything further, the orator came to the middle of the arena and with a loud, booming voice began to speak:

"Ladies and Gentlemen, your Majesty," he bowed to Pradhyuman who boringly raised his arm in support.

"We have come and gathered here to witness a grand event. To see and behold, the great creature of the Indus Valley. Of myths and legends, it has become reality, brought to these lands of Dvarkipur by our great king Pradhyuman."

He raised his arms towards Pradhyuman and everyone jeered, clapped, tears trickling from their eyes. They loved Pradhyuman, they craved him. He was their god, their saviour. He was the blood of Krishna, after all.

But like his father, he was not stringent. He lived freely. And yet he knew, people out there still looked up to his father and if he would ever return, which Pradhyuman would not like, he would be displaced.

"We welcome the contenders to fight." The orator began and from the other end of the arena, coming out of the caves were meagre men and women with swords that were too heavy for them. They were five in number and they looked confused.

The dramatist yelped in nervousness for them, while Pradhyuman with a stoic face looked at the poor souls.

And from the other end, the cave opened and the creature was let out with a chain around its head, and three Yayatis holding spears poking him. But the creature, as it was let out, made a huge shrieking sound, leading the orator to run away as he shouted: "And here we have the Indus Worm!"

The sound made by the fifty feet long worm was a high-pitch shrieking and screaming one. Everyone nabbed their ears in frustration. It then began to move its body, which appeared to be gel-like revealing its inner organs, each as large as a human.

Pradhyuman didn't anticipate this, but it broke the chains as quick as possible, releasing itself, but instead of darting towards the immigrants, it instantly dug itself inside the sandy ground, making itself unknown.

Everyone was screaming in horror, for it had suddenly disappeared.

"I believe right now it's your cue to enter," said the dramatist, nervously. "Also make sure that you don't let him eat you because its saliva is quite poisonous and can burn your skin. Even though you'll survive you'll lose the way you look."

For a moment, those words sounded worse than dying to Pradhyuman.

Pradhyuman nodded, his brows arched as he took the bow and the arrows from his soldier standing beside him. The bow was ornate and golden in colour, with silver lines of hope all over it.

And before he could leap from the king's balcony and enter the arena, the worm sprung out surprising everyone, its mouth opening wide swallowing the immigrants who didn't see the attack coming. The masticated bodies were swallowed and were passing through the transparent, slimy skin of the worm.

Pradhyuman rolled over the arena, and the crowd jeered at his entrance. A smile pasted on his face as he tried to show that the win was already his. The worm turned towards him and made the same shrieking sound, slime snaking out from its mouth.

"Come here, you big old oaf!" Pradhyuman yelled.

And the worm moved as if it listened. Moving with rapid speed, it began to dart towards Pradhyuman who hurled himself in one corner, rolling over, pulling out the arrow and plucking it on the string before swinging the arrows right towards the worm.

But the creature paid no heed to it and disappeared inside the terrain yet again, letting the earth shake.

Pradhyuman waited with his bow and arrow, before he moved straight towards the lamps that were burning and lit up his arrows after dipping them in oil which he had a pouch for.

The creature lurched behind him, and as it did he shot the fiery arrows straight towards the creature, hitting the heart of it, as he could see it thought its transparent skin. The fire burnt and pierced, digging deep inside the organ making the worm cry loudly, as it fell on the ground and crashed, against the pavilion.

Pradhyuman smiled, chuckling as he raised his bow and he could hear the claps around him.

He began to move towards the slave rooms, which were underneath the arches as the claps began to dim behind him, muting with each step of his, spiralling dust as he swirled it backwards.

Pradhyuman reached the slave deck and his men began to take his armour, his weapons from him, and made him wear a robe as he looked at the foreign immigrants who had come to Dvarka, all caged either in iron boxes or in manacles. He paid no heed to them, and he decided to go upstairs yet again where his seat was next to his wife, when he saw a familiar figure with cropped hair, purple eyes and a smile dancing on her lips moving towards him. She had olive skin and a long gown draped over her, her soldiers on the side, distinctively colourful like her, as all Taljans are.

"Durgajyoti? Why aren't' you upstairs?" Pradhyuman asked.

"Because I knew you would come here eventually. Decided why waste the energy to travel upstairs," she said with a smile. But her smile was confusing.

"What happened?" He knew that look more than anyone else.

"As you know, I have spies everywhere," she said.

"Indeed, you do."

"We have a problem," she continued. "One of my spies happened to see your leper brother in the frontiers of Dvarkipur in a small village with a bunch of his loyalists tagging along with him."

Pradhyuman grunted and growled under his breath. "He is free to go wherever he pleases to."

"I know. But the intentions matter, my lord. He is, after all, after something or if I should say...someone."

A chill ran down his spine. "What are you suggesting?" He asked.

And then he saw the lightness of the smile on Durgajyoti's face, as if hundreds of punishments worse than death were running in her mind, who nodded and said, "Let's just first catch him."

3

What a waste of time.

Balaram saw the men that stood in front of him were in absolute disagreement, as they quarrelled and fought and he watched them with boredom.

"He took me wife and got me mead in return," one of them said. "As if my wife is comparable to a drink."

"Well, you sure did choose the drink over her, you drunken buffoon." Another said.

Balaram watched the quarrel and as the Prime Minister of Dvarkipur it was his duty to take out time and settle disputes when it came to citizen matters. He didn't like this part of his job, but he had no choice.

There were other people in line, waiting for the Prime Minister to solve the dispute for the people before them, so their problem could be addressed.

Balaram knew that Pradhyuman was at the arena where the fight with the big creature was on. Last time, there was a sabretooth and now, he had heard a worm was brought in, as large as an elephant and as tall as alpine groves.

"What is the problem, please?" Balaram ran his hand through his bald scalp and leaned forward to listen to the plea.

The betrayed husband said, "It ain't me, the problem.

He took my wife and decided it was just fine. Well, I found them in a pig's farm, butt naked, your majesty."

"No need for the grisly details," Balaram persisted.

"Because he used to hit her." The other one scowled.

"I'm not here to solve domestic issues. I got to know there's more to this story."

"Yes, indeed." The cheated husband added proudly. "Apparently, my father was a heartless person and the land we own, a large apricot field, was given in a will to my grandson. The funny part is, the kid that was born doesn't feel like mine." He turned to the other lad. "But I know it's mine."

"Na-huh!" Shouted the man. "It ain't yours. It's mine."

And they began to quarrel, their voices turning slurry while Balaram just watched them in confusion. It was a property dispute. He turned to see Akoorji, the Commander-in-Chief to the King, coming from the corner of the hallway, passing the people, his axe in a sheath and his thick brown beard glistening with an oily touch.

He leaned next to Balaram and whispered: "Five innocents killed in daylight. Immigrants."

"Pradhyuman?" Balaram shouldn't have asked. He should have already known.

"He plans to sacrifice more for his glory." Akoorji said. "And more for his charm."

Balaram sighed. He looked at the fight in front and asked Akoorji: "Whatever happened to Dharma?"

"It died in Kurukshetra."

The words hit him flat and there was an ominous sense of foreboding.

"Let's go." Balaram said. "We have a meeting to attend."

*

The sound of the staff thumping against the ground was the first thing that was heard as Balaram entered the silent room.

The sound echoed and the bald-headed brother of Lord Krishna stood with a hulking presence. He had the frame of a wrestler, arms that were huge and shoulders that had cuts and crevices. But he had the eyes of a wise man, blue like his brother. The one thing that stood out was his leg. The right one to be exact. It wasn't as muscular as the other, and was suffering from a childhood deformity, a paralysis of sort. Ever since then, he had used something to lean on. This time, it was his staff. A simple, ornate one, with a curved top that could be used as a weapon too in times of dire need.

Like now.

Balaram knew one of the seven people who were in the dark room, lit by the ever-engulfing fire lamp, could be a traitor. There was always a possibility. For what he was doing here was far worse than any sin a man can commit.

It was treason.

An act against his own king. And rallying a coup that would change the face of Dvarka.

He saw the men. All sipping wine and behaving as if it's a social club, even though it was anything but. There were councilmen from Sharyata, Bhojas, Avantis,

Satvatas. Each councilman who had a grievance against the dear old boy-king—Pradhyuman.

The only two tribes from which councilmen were not present were the Vrishnis and the Andhakas. They had distanced themselves from Pradhyuman and built their respective clans close to the Ratvaka Hills. But they had problems amongst them and they had continued to fight. Pradhyuman could easily go there and conquer them, make them part of his empire, but he didn't need to. It would lead to unnecessary tarnishing of his image and he would have to send a lot of people to exile.

"I believe you have started without me," Balaram said, with a grin. "What is the topic of discussion?"

"The recent event." One of the councilmen burst out. "Did you hear how he mercilessly let a few people wreak havoc because he wanted to show himself off? I feel, to destroy him, we should tarnish his image, that's what we have to do."

Balaram had heard it many times, this same plan. The cowardly way to destroy Pradhyuman. Balaram was not a man of such theatrics. He was someone who would go in the forward line of offence and fight till his death. His eyes fell over Akoorji, the commander-in-chief to the king, but a loyalist to Balaram, who had a wispy brown beard and a ponytail in the back, tied like a bamboo string. He was sniggering at the comments.

"The funny part is," Balaram began, "that when I had gathered all of you together in a place—I was under the impression that we were revolutionaries in this corrupt regime we are in. I have begun to believe now that we are merely gossipmongers."

Everyone in the crowd began to whisper amongst each other. Akoorji in the corner was standing with folded arms.

"And what do you propose we should do if not this? We can only plan. If the army is not with us, then we have to do things like these." Someone else said.

"We don't do anything but talk. Talk and chatter and drink wine and go home to our wives and bed them," Balaram blurted out. "You are right about one thing. We do need an army and when I rallied you all, I believed you would bring yours. You all have your lands, your men and yet you don't make use of them."

"They all swore an oath to the king," the councilman said. "What do you propose we should do, if I may ask again?"

Balaram had been thinking about it for a while. He thumped his staff again as he mumbled and contemplated, as he turned and twisted his face, looking at everyone. "When Pradhyuman became king, I was happy. My nephew, my blood was sitting on the throne, wearing the crown. But as he ruled, he began to do things that went absolutely against my brother's wishes. My brother was a smart man, clever as one may say. And he was powerful. So powerful. But he had this vice that perhaps went down to Pradhyuman: he was someone who believed we should relish our flaws. The idea of utopia was not something he believed in, but that didn't mean he didn't want to achieve it. After the The Great War, he tried a lot and now once Pradhyuman rules, it has gone to waste. He doesn't try. I would give the lad a brave clap for he's not pretentious like my brother. But I know the kingdom will perish under his rule."

The councilmen were listening to the story, though thoroughly offended by the last statement he had made for calling them utterly useless.

"Tell me,"one of them said, "if not him, then who should rule? You?"

"No. We should not be unified. We should be separated. Build your own lands and your kingdoms. Unification has led us here. Look at the Andhakas and the Vrishnis. They prosper more than us. Why? Because they don't do dirty politics amongst themselves. They want to better themselves more than anything else."

Balaram would say all of it, though he did agree to the fact that he believed in it. He didn't want to be the king. He never thought of himself as one, a fit king. But it was more than that. He wanted to do right for the soil that he had made his own.

And he wanted to do right by the very man who built it—Krishna.

Balaram had sent several search parties, but it never came to fruition. The man had disappeared—why, he had no idea.

"What a generous soul." The councilman sarcastically added. "Tell us something, so what's your plan?"

"What I should have done months back." Balaram said, moving towards the window and looking over at the wide cast of snow crusted hills. "I should find an army. Create a diplomatic relationship with the Andhakas and the Vrishnis and bring them back to support us and support our cause."

Everyone looked at each other.

"Because they haven't sworn to their king, so might

as well be it." Balaram said, waiting for any protest that may erupt but saw none, because he knew this was a sane idea to go towards. "Akoorji, though, the dear old commander has planted a few spies along the way around your households, so when I'm gone and if I hear there is someone ratting me out because you just don't believe in my idea anymore, you will be stopped and wounded and punished."

The councilmen, some of them sniggered, while others went white with horror.

"You don't trust us, Prime Minister?" The councilmen asked.

Balaram smiled. "Don't feel offended. I have never trusted anyone in this world."

And saying that, he strode outside, with Akoorji following him in the dim hallway. They made their way in silence, walking in the lane, and coming out of the fort that was actually a brothel. Balaram knew this was the perfect place to hold these meetings, because no one would suspect anything.

"Are you sure you did the right thing by telling them the plan?" Akoorji asked.

"Yes," Balaram stopped. He was growing tired of everything, of life. And he wanted to rest but he also had to do the right thing. "By doing this, you'll know who stands on the judgment day and who doesn't."

"But am I going with you?"

Balaram nodded. "My friend, where we are going…I need every trusted person by my side. Because the tribes we are meeting…will give us punishments worse than death."

4

I hate myself.

Samva thought, while watching the reflection of his face in the small pond of water. They were stationed close to where allegedly Krishna was hiding. The camp was set up. The light was beaming. The wisps of smoke were circling and moving for the skies. The sound of the nightingale and the croaks of the frogs, and the hoots of the owl could be heard. There was a narrow ravine that had a twisted and thorny personality of its own, the background was made of a nice pair of snow crusted hills.

"You sure he won't talk, your highness?" Asked one of his three soldiers, who were roasting a butchered chicken. "I'm sure as the sky's thunder he will."

Samva watched himself in the pond again. His face... it was ghastly. He had taken out his iron mask, and the little bulbous marks could be seen. The skin was torn and parched. It was all over the place. He had caught leprosy.

And he was cursed for it. By his own father.

For what he did was nothing, but important. Something far more important. He wanted to tell his father about it. Why he did that. Why he killed. Why he left the corpse high and dry.

Why he murdered one of his father's many wives.

But he never got to it.

Sighing, Samva said, "He could. But who would believe him?"

"We should have gutted him like we discussed." Another soldier propped up with a bleary sound. "What could he have done?"

"Killing is not always an option," Samva said.

"And yet we are on that path." The soldier sniggered.

Yes. The path. Where they were going. Why they were doing what they were. It was all for a reason. Samva had convinced his soldiers. He had told them that this must be done. And they must follow this path or everyone would go into damnation.

There was so much mystery he didn't want to speak of himself and he kept under murmurs and silence.

"What we are doing is for the greater good," Samva said. "We are destroying to build something. Which is greater than all of us."

All the soldiers—petty thieves, butchers and pirates they once used to be, were now under Samva, the iron-masked leper, as he would go on to be called. Some would even say the handsome face of Krishna was hidden somewhere in Samva, and some would say he wasn't even the son.

"I'll call it a night," he said. "And we will draw our mares tomorrow for the west."

"Just one day before we see the Lord God Krishna," one of the soldiers squeakily jumped. He was the youngest of all. With a fat head and a double-chinned face. He had beady eyes like a bear. "I'm so excited. I have only seen him once, when he came out to show himself from the balcony and then disappeared."

"He gave up his divinity for you to live," another solider, a grizzly one spoke. "We are invincible because of him. It's a gift he gave..."

"Which became a curse," Samva snapped in between but with a whisper in the end. A lot of trebles could be felt in his chest and it was making him question everything. But it was all right.

He began to leave for his tent to sleep, but before that he decided he would take a piss. And so he walked downhill and planned to relieve himself when he heard it. It was so quiet, and he felt something wrap around his neck, his throat coming close to shining silver.

It was a blade.

"Who is this?" Samva asked, unafraid but he could hear the breathing of a person near the nape of his neck.

"I could have sent someone who's less important, but I believe the betrayer of the blood should witness the blood itself."

The voice was very familiar.

"Pradhyuman."

"Oh well, remember me? The one who you plan to betray."

"Go away!"

"Oh, that's how you talk to your older sibling?"

"You don't possibly think that you'll scare me with a knife, do you? We are invincible have you forgotten?"

"But it'll surely hurt and it'll take time to heal, because I will stab you as deep as I can."

And then he was about to do it, when Samva pulled him over and threw him on the ground. Even though he was more of a hunchback and shorter than Pradhyuman, he was broader and more muscular. He had a frame like his uncle Balaram.

He looked at Pradhyuman and saw he was in a cowl, which he then took off, as the ravine behind him silently swished.

The wind gushed and his face was revealed, a smile dancing on his lips, the cowl falling back. His eyes were sprinkling with delight and he had a grin that would suffice any woman's loins.

"You know when I got to know where you were heading, I could have sent my army for you. But that would be..." he began to speak, circling around him, "...too passive, too daddy like. He would sit in his throne and give orders. Not me. No." He shook his head. "I thought I'll go alone and bring back everyone, or possibly bury all of you deep underground to meet a fate fit for vultures."

Samva knew that was a big possibility. "I'm doing the right thing."

"By finding father and asking him to return so you can displace me?"

He doesn't know my plan, Samva thought. He was glad that Pradhyuman only knew half of it. Convincing father to displace Pradhyuman was a childish, inane desire only Pradhyuman could conceive of. He was a boy who never grew up, hungry for entitlement and power, who sucked on his mother's milk till the age of five and who would kill a pack of dogs Samva owned just because he didn't receive any of his pups.

"But he wouldn't return. Because if he had to, he would have done so many years back." Pradhyuman said. "We are at the pinnacle of success and prosperity, brother. Why don't you understand? Trade has never been better, everyone fears us, our relationship with Sassanids and the Byzantines is growing like wildfire and Indraprastha has been supporting us diplomatically."

"But just one problem."

"What's that?"

"You are close to the edge, Pradhyuman," Samva said. "You just need a trigger and then you might as well scape a full-blown conquest across the world."

"I can, but I wouldn't. You know we will win. We can't be killed. But I don't choose to use my absolute power. I don't want to rule the world."

"That's what you say right now, but what about the conquest of the Naga kingdom? You didn't have to do that."

"The Manis were important to a few of our allies. I had to sell it to them."

"Human rights. That's the problem. You will end up massacring thousands and I can't stand by and watch that happen."

Pradhyuman sighed, scratching his head. "Progress comes at the cost of innocent bloodshed."

"Says who?"

Pradhyuman arched his brows, his obsidian sword pulling out of his woolskin. "History." And then he hurled himself forward with his blade.

Samva took some time to retreat, his reflexes had gone for a toss and he did what anyone would have: he raised his arms, letting it slice through the obsidian blade. His wrist fell and a searing pain surged through his body.

"Oh, that'll take time to grow." Pradhyuman chuckled, bringing the sword close to Samva's chest, but he just rolled over, blood spurting from his arm, or from what was left of it.

His right hand was his main hand and that was cut off. He was cribbing and cursing under his breath, as he made his way towards the tent where his men were present to protect him. He knew he would not be fit enough to fight Pradhyuman, the greatest warrior to have ever lived. And he couldn't even pick up a sword properly. He couldn't even hold his bow and arrow. He was quite an amateur and he knew that about himself.

He scampered towards the tent, as he heard his angry brother's voice behind him:

"I'm going to cut you up in so many pieces that by the time you'll be getting better, you would lose the hope of seeing father at all."

Hundreds of things were running through his mind at that moment and he seemed to be absolutely flustered and angry. But sad too. He wanted to give up, but he was so close.

He came to the tent, only to see his men—the way he imagined he would. Split from torso. Limbs flown apart. They were all unconscious. They would eventually get better but by then, Pradhyuman would throw away their bodies in different parts, inside volcanoes or at the bottom of the sea.

He could feel the fear inside him rising.

"You can't run away like always, you little ogre. Mother always hated you." Pradhyuman's voice was close as he batted his sword against Samva, who could feel the tears in his eyes. "Father despised you. You are an unwanted beggar born to a royal, beautiful lineage. And I let you live. I should have known you had a dagger, waiting to stab me."

"You don't understand. This is greater than all of us."

Pradhyuman rolled his eyes. "I'll give you a second to pull out your sword. You are making this too easy."

Samva did. He did pull the sword and stood there. His hands shaking. He turned to the side to see a mare, waiting to be straddled and it was positioned towards the east. Pradhyuman came forward and Samva deflected his blade with it.

"Father said, he should have killed you the moment he saw what you hid behind that ghastly mask of yours."

"It was not my fault. He cursed me."

"Bleh. It was because of your karma. You killed his wife."

"No," he said. "It was because of the curse."

"What curse?"

"He punished me. Father." His eyes welled up. "For what I did."

"How did he do that?" Pradhyuman narrowed his gaze. The embers burring in a corner.

"He exposed me to leprosy. He forced me and let the infection sink in."

For a moment Pradhyuman was taken aback. "Why would he do that?"

"Because he wanted me to see the ugliness that's inside me and he wanted it to be seen outside always."

"You killed his wife. What do you expect?"

And then he brought the sword down. There was another crackling sound, as both blades clashed together, underneath the thunderous dark clouds.

But Samva didn't wait long. He had to escape and to do that, he instantly grabbed a handful of mud and threw it across Pradhyuman's face, as it temporarily blinded him. Samva took the opportunity and escaped, grabbing his horse and sitting on it while Pradhyuman tried to see through the mud.

Samva rode. And he rode.

Until he saw the darkness himself.

*

He woke up.

He had slept too long. He had blood all across his mare, but the horse had taken him where he wanted to. He fell from the animal and on to the ground. As he struggled to get up, his body ached miserably. He staggered and looked up, and he saw what he thought was beautiful. He was far away from what had taken place a while ago and in front of him was a nice cottage, the sun was beautiful and orange, and the forests were greener than they usually are.

He tried to come on his feet when he saw his arm was getting better. His face was weak and exhausted, but he moved forward, leaving his mare behind.

He was feeling the hurt of his brother ready to kill him like this, but then it was warranted for.

Samva walked towards the cottage, and he saw a separate farm where there were cows, in hundreds, grazing. It was an empty field. There were stables. There were squirrels.

Am I in the right place?

He turned to look at the horizon, in the empty canvassing field, a man was walking. A simple tunic over him, his grizzly black hair and a thick brown beard visible. Scars adorned his face, but the burning blue eyes were visible. Dark skin, just like Samva and he had a cowherd's stick in his hand.

"Who are you?" The man asked.

He took a while to recognize Samva, even though it wasn't at all tough for Samva to do so. And when he did, his brows arched and his eyes moistened.

"Samva?" It came from a place of shock and then he said, "You found me!" As if he didn't want to be seen.

Samva still smiled. Because his journey was complete. After years of searching, he was right where he was supposed to be.

"Father..." he said. "We need to talk about something."

There was a pause. "Why are you here?" The voice was curt.

"Because..." Samva wanted to say, but the words were hard; painful, though necessary. "I want you to execute a genocide against the Yayatis, your bloodline."

5

There were two people he trusted.

Akoorji, the commander-in-chief and the most loyal person to him in the city and Revathi, his wife and the mother of his three children. And here he was, Balaram, looking at both of them in the confines of his quarters. Here, he felt protected. Here, he felt he was not being judged or being targeted.

"You are insane if you think going away makes the most sense right now." Revathi said, she had those grey, stormy eyes like her father. Her hair was tied in a knot, and she wore jewellery all over her body. "They need you right now, the island of Dvarka needs you."

Balaram clenched his jaw. He glanced at Akoorji, who shrugged his shoulders. For a man, who was older than Balaram, he sure made sure that he looked quite young for his age. He had dyed his hair with colour brought in from the finest shops in Persia.

"What do you think?" Balaram asked Akoorji.

"I feel, it is of importance." He said instantly. "Prime Minister Balaram is doing nothing here but watching wrestling matches, adorning children's birthdays with garlands, and taking out policies which no one cares about."

Balaram felt a particular sting in his heart, but he

knew the words were scornful but true. He rested his frame against the wall, his arms clutching his chest. His face was impassive and quiet.

"And that's where he's safe." Revathi instructed. "In the midst of all this."

"What could happen to me?" He leaned on his staff now, which was long and golden, shaped like a plough. He was a farmer and he had the look and muscles to show. "I'm fine. I'm grand as ever."

Revathi rolled her eyes. "Commander Akoorji, you should have some sense at least. The Andhakas and the Vrishnis are vicious. You know what they do right? They tear intruders limb by limb and spread them across the land. You might live, but it will be worse than death, not even knowing where your limbs are."

It was funny thinking of that scenario, but Balaram resisted a chuckle. "I think I should go. I know the royalty there. I'll figure it out."

"You plan to create allies of sworn enemies? They might share a mountain, but they bloody hate each other." Revathi shook her head. "This is worse than when you thought of sending kids back to Indian soil."

"To not be corrupted by the spoils of Pradhyuman, that's why."

"He's not that bad," Revathi shrugged. "He just needs improvement."

Balaram knew it was an aunt's ideal way of looking at her nephew. She would never see faults in Pradhyuman even though he was worse than any monster. But Balaram did. He was a realist.

"I'm going," Balaram sternly added.

"And so am I then." Revathi stood up from the comfort of her bed and looked at Akoorji. "If you get torn limb by limb, I need to be there with you." She came close smelling of lavender as she embraced him.

Balaram couldn't help but laugh. "You would distract me."

"Oh please, I'm a better politician than you are, mister. Don't you think so Akoorji?"

Balaram turned to see the commander, who was awkwardly standing in a corner, with his hands clasped.

"I hate to agree, but yes."

Balaram saw Revathi cheekily smiling as the light faded in the background, and there was a knock on the door. They were all alarmed, and Balaram gave a stern look to Akoorji who disappeared in the shadows of the wall into crevices where the light from the window couldn't reach.

Balaram opened the door slowly, to his royal guardsman who was his close confidant, who said: "My lord, there is someone..." and he didn't have to say more, for in front of him he witnessed a grand sight—the short-haired woman Durgajyoti was standing there. All fashionable, beautiful and luscious, Balaram knew she was Pradhyuman's right-hand person, and used to be a concubine to a king of Taljans until she came down to riches and owned property, army and most significantly, the dangerous creatures—Vitihotras. How she did it, that too so fast was still perplexing. It was all happenstance and there was mystery, albeit a supernatural one that surrounded her.

Even though she stood all glittering with gold, there

was a sense of darkness and brooding desire of death that loomed on her.

"Oh, hello." Balaram didn't like her and neither did she like Balaram, but they greeted politely. "How may I help you?"

"Can I talk to you for a moment?" She smiled artificially.

Balaram nodded. He closed the door behind him and she found it suspicious, but didn't bother much.

"Yes. May we walk?"

She nodded, and they walked together. Their footsteps trudging and making noises, as they moved from one hallway to another. Balaram's thumping of the staff was heard, as he asked: "To what do I owe the pleasure?"

"I came here to give you something," she said, and from within the sleeves of her robes, pulled out a scroll.

Drenched in blood.

Balaram gasped, but he calmed down internally as he grabbed hold of the scroll and read it. He knew what it was. He knew it very well.

"I believe this was supposed to be delivered to the king." Durgajyoti stopped in front of the Prime Minister's main office which was a large pavilion, with a smaller throne than that of a king.

"Yes," he nodded. "As you know, he wants to be updated but it didn't warrant you to murder my messenger."

"Hard way of learning he was not a Yayati, thought we could punish him but we did well with just a slit throat." She paused. "But I don't think he wants to know his step-mother is getting married again." She added curtly. "She was an abomination and a distraction to the king. She was not healthy. He had murdered her first human, Shambara, for her until she banished him."

"And yet, he still dreams of her, craves her and loves her and wouldn't be able to stand it if she marries someone else. A son's obsession. Sends her emissaries who return empty-handed. I just thought..."

"No, Prime Minister. I know what you thought. You planned to distract him. Make him busy like the child you think he is, into fighting again for his stepmother even though she hates his guts."

That was the plan, sure. Balaram knew, when he heard Pradhyuman's stepmother Mayavati was to be married, that Pradhyuman would get instigated, would get frustrated and would decide to do something abrasive. And he wanted that, so meanwhile he could go to the Andhakas and Vrishnis and form an alliance, and return to usurp and execute a coup.

"You don't know but she does. She took care of him when he was just a baby, lost in a river. She still cares for him and I genuinely cared for the king to update him regarding this." He lied through his teeth.

She watched Balaram sternly as she could, as if her iron eyes were piercing through his soul.

"Well, I am his advisor and I feel he should not be knowing this."

"As you say," he smiled. "That's your discretion. And I don't think our king as petty as he used to be. He wouldn't go out of the way to kill her new husband. In fact, he would send royal garland and riches and fruits as a celebration." He paused. "Though it does beg a question—how is he? Has he returned from his excursion?"

"Yes. He went solo hunting. A meditational art."

"Strange, he went right after Samva was declared a traitor and accused of conspiracy for treason by the officials."

Durgajyoti was surprised, but Balaram had been keeping the numbers on Samva. He had been planning, but not sharing with Balaram. They never shared a good relationship and the idea of exposing Samva to leprosy, was, in fact, Balaram's idea, so the hate Samva had was real and dark.

"Don't tell me you made your king chase after his own brother. How much would you twist him to benefit your goals."

"What goals do I seek?" She narrowed her eyes. "I am a simple woman who believes in our king."

Balaram knew she was lying. "A woman? Last I heard you were an Asur. I choose to not believe in gossip, but then who knows?" He was trying to be funny.

But before she could respond and could fathom what he had said, he saw someone walking in the hall and it was the soldier—the royal palace's one, who had silver and gold laced in his iron armour.

"Your Majesty," he bowed to both of them, "the king summons you both." He was panting as if he had been trying to restlessly search for them for a long time.

"Why?" Durgajyoti asked.

The soldier looked confused.

They both walked towards the palace, leaving Balaram's fort and grabbing hold of the chariot. They didn't speak. They could hear though. The ravens cawed. Darkness was enveloping the place. They reached the palace, which was decorated with lamps. It was also littered with a lot of fountains and statues, pastures and forts made of red clay baked bricks. They dismounted and made their way towards the inside of the palace, and the main hallways, where the king made way with its audience. The throne was like Balaram's, but much bigger, grander and had so many guards with their spears and their helmets guarding it. The ceilings were high and the drapes were red in colour.

The king sat with his goblet, sipping from it, as the wine trickled and fell on the carpet. He was grunting under his breath and his crown was hanging lopsidedly. He had piercings and his nose was pierced too. His eyes were tired and bloodshot. Drunk, he was, it looked like. On the big throne, he looked like a small boy, which he was.

Balaram and Durgajyoti both bowed, and they stood on either end of the throne, as Pradhyuman hiccupped and said, "I heard the news."

"But...how?" Durgajyoti whispered.

"The messenger Balaram kindly sent to me," Pradhyuman said in a sheepish voice with a grateful tone. "Thank you, uncle, though the news is unpleasant, nonetheless."

Balaram smiled and turned to the shocked Durgajyoti.

Of course, Balaram wasn't stupid. He would get two messengers, delivering the same news. If one was caught, another would do the work.

"I know, my lord and I believe there's nothing you can do."

"I have made an offer to her to stay with me," Pradhyuman licked his lips, shaking his head. "She doesn't want to. She hates me. But I keep LONGING FOR HER!" He threw the goblet and stunned everyone. "I hate her too. She doesn't know what's good for her. She used to be treated like a whore when she was with her then husband, the ravenous Shambara. And now she again pledges herself to a man. Doesn't she realise, her son loves her more than anyone else? Would take care of her. She has to be stopped, from making that mistake again. Stopped!"

Balaram couldn't help but smile, but he didn't show it.

"I had a dream." Pradhyuman stood up, hiccupped and stumbled from his throne, as he said: "The dream that to protect my mother, I should kill her. I dreamt of holding her by the throat and choking her, so others couldn't touch her. She was everything to me and she plans to do what I hate. She doesn't deserve to be with whoever she's marrying."

Those were strange feelings. Balaram knew that Pradhyuman's real mother Rukmini was someone who would long for him, but he would long for his step-mother. The one who helped raise him. Who took care of him. He had strange thoughts about her, contradictory even.

"What do you want to do?" Balaram asked.

"Nothing, should be the answer, my lord," Durgajyoti intervened immediately. "We are in a good position and dealing with this, would lead to unnecessary hassle. Don't forget, these are Rakshasas."

"Yeah, so?" Pradhyuman sounded bored. "They aren't as strong as us. They just have their Maya to protect them, their bloody magic."

"But, my lord, we must think this through."

"I have to save her again." He stood up from his throne, declaring and ignoring Durgajyoti. "I have to bloody save her. I hope you all realise that. So I believe, we are set."

Balaram wanted to hear the sweet nectar of those words, clearly as he asked: "You mean..."

"Yes," Pradhyuman nodded. "We are going to war."

6

"No," Krishna said for the third time, as he wrapped a piece of cloth around Samva's hand. "This is not happening."

Samva stayed quiet. He brought up the topic again, but he got rejection again. They were inside the cottage and the hearth was burning, with fire logs igniting it. There was peace here and tranquility. His father's flute was kept in the corner.

"Do you still play it?"

"I uh..." he sighed, "it's been a while." He said, as he looked at the bandage that he had wrapped. "Never thought I would be mending wounds of a son after being attacked by another son of mine."

"Pradhyuman has gone mad."

He sighed.

Samva stared at his father for a moment; there were wrinkles on his face, he had short hair with a beard as thick as his muscles. He looked huge and didn't have the same frame as his son Pradhyuman anymore, but more like his brother Balaram. He could fight a tiger with his bare hands if he wanted to.

"Why?"

"Reminds me of the life I have left behind."

"And why did you leave?"

He closed his eyes. The smell of Ayurvedics was engulfing the surroundings as he came on his feet and moved to the corner of the room. "You know why."

"The regret of seeing your own blood going towards Adharm," Samva said. "I'm here to rectify it. I know how to make them vulnerable."

"And why can't I just reverse the divine powers I've given them?" Krishna asked.

"Because if you could, you would have done that already. You didn't because you can't. You are a mere human and no god. The way you used to be."

Krishna had wisdom behind years, his eyes blue as the horizon dipped ocean. His skin, dark and velvety. "You weren't always a smart cookie. Whatever happened?"

"I grew up."

"Then humour me. What is it that you found, that you think has the powers to make my powers reversible?"

Samva smiled, after a long time, as he went for his rucksack that he had grabbed hold of while escaping from Pradhyuman. He put down a piece of paper, a yellow parchment of sorts and on it was written a tale. "This is a live oral narration written in paper, in Devnagiri which clearly states that the man who wrote, a pupil and a follower to the great sage Durvasa had found an iron ore that has the power to kill a god. To kill you. To kill your power. Durvasa in his journey as a traveller and a sage, had seen this ore, close to the mysterious coast of Dvarka and felt the power and was threatened by it, for it was a harbinger of death. Though, when I went there, there was nothing. I believe the parchment holds lies, some of them to elude, but I believe there is an ore from which weapons can be created that could kill a Yayati."

"An ore? You want me to go with you to find an ore?"

"Durvasa believed in it."

"He was an angry man. He did lot of things that wouldn't make sense," Krishna shrugged. "What is this ore called?"

"Erakas, he calls. No idea why."

"Where did you get this?"

He smiled. "I had been searching for something like this for long. Had a bounty out there, for any information and one of the shamans brought it to me."

"You believe in fairy tales and lies, boy. All of this sounds fake and extraordinarily benign. You are obsessed with ending the Yayatis and you shouldn't be. They should live out their lives and live as long as possible."

"Committing butchery and spreading Adharm? I'm sure this is not the way you had wanted them to be."

Krishna shook his head. "If we do this, we create the very curse I was trying to protect them from. What an irony. But I still don't believe it."

"Then go for me. Go for my faith. You don't have to believe in it. You have never done anything for me. At least do it for me now."

He paused; his eyes shimmering with hurt. "Why me? I'm human. I'm killable. I'm not the right fit for a person to travel with."

Yes, you are. Because I have not told you everything.

"I want to do this with you. Because I want you to

redeem yourself in your own eyes and in everyone else's too. You live out here alone in regret and I want you to change that. For once in your life, I don't want you to feel bad about any decision you took," Samva earnestly pleaded his case.

He looked at him. Starkly. "I had a dream. It was a long night." He crouched on the floor and grabbed hold of the flute from the sideboard. "The dream had a bald man, with sunken eyes and a hairless body. It had a long cape and it walked on its talons, as it made a screeching sound across the window." The sound of the window crunching could be heard in Krishna's ears, but he ignored it. "The man spoke, it's coming. It's coming. The end is coming. You know who he was?"

Samva shook his head.

"Time. Kaal." Krishna replied. "Time brings us to a circle. I used to hunt Asurs. Then I killed my uncle, after which I became a king and formed relations with the Pandavas but, now I am here, alone and now you ask me again. The world for us will be perilous," he continued. "The journey would be hard. I don't think I will be able to make it. I have a good life here. Alone. Just the way I came."

Samva could see he wanted to ask about everyone back home, but he didn't. It would hurt him more, he knew.

And before they could proceed further with this matter, a raven came to the window and began to use its beak against the glass. For a moment, it was fine until it became too much and it started to crack the window.

Krishna's face turned pure white, and the first thing

he did was dash through the lanes of his home and bring forth his mace and chakra with a long rope tied to one end of it. He was gearing up with a breastplate and he looked awkward, wearing all that, a man out of time, it sure felt.

"What happened?"

"Do you remember when I taught you…" he hastily said, "about hunting animals? Why do we hunt them?"

"Yes. Not to take pleasure from the consumption of their meat but ridding them for the forest to be less dangerous, for those who travel."

"Yes. Exactly." He left the cottage, without answering further.

Samva grabbed his sword too and he made his way outside, following Krishna. They moved towards the direction of the forest and the canopies, the shrubs, the twigs, the lemurs that travelled and the baboons that were in abundance. Samva realised, they were being followed. He could sense it.

As they made their way inside, Krishna said: "The raven is Bhusanda, an old shapeshifting sage who had requested my help to fight against Ajakaya, a poisonous scorpion."

"A scorpion? He's afraid of a…"

And from the shadows of the forest, pounced a large creature, Samva rolled back as well as Krishna. The raven cawed loudly, and the creature made its appearance known and Samva saw it clearly from a distance. It was a twenty-foot scorpion, a giant of its species and had a long tail with which it was spitting out poison.

"That's not a scorpion," Samva said.

"Biologically, it is."

"Not realistically though."

"Do you remember how to fight?" Krishna asked.

Samva should have told him that he's still bad at it. But the time didn't allow it, as the poison was flung at him and he hid behind a tree, to save himself. Another spit came and it pierced the tree, letting the log fall on the ground with a tumble and tweed. Samva began to chase further, as Krishna yelled:

"Distract him!"

"With what?"

"With any bloody thing!"

Samva grabbed hold of rocks, as he ran, as the scorpion with its claws made its way further, while Krishna had disappeared somewhere. Samva began to throw the rocks as fast and as soon as possible, hitting him on the head. The scorpion got annoyed and spat more poison—which drenched the life out of the plants as well as the trees and the forest had begun to have this strange, dirty smell of feces. Samva was losing his breath and he knew that even if he wouldn't die because of his gift, he would still end up getting poisoned and hurt for a long time.

The scorpion didn't waste time. It let out its claw close to Samva who dashed under the four legs, took his sword and plunged it deep inside the heart of the scorpion. The scorpion shook it off, then he tumbled on the ground.

The scorpion moved backwards and brought its tail close to Samva, hitting him, as he rolled around, and the tail got stabbed on the earth.

Samva couldn't roll further, as the two legs of the scorpion stopped and he knew its tail was close to his face, poison blurting out of it, ready to scar and destroy his face, whatever was left of it—

When he saw a shadow.

Lurching from the trees, and a huge mace in its hand as he smacked the weapon hard against the skull of the scorpion, breaking it apart. There was a loud cry and the scorpion fell to one side, with Samva taking a breath of relief.

Krishna was on the other end of the scorpion's corpse and he chuckled, as if he felt alive again. Samva too laughed.

They both looked at the raven who was flying up and it cawed, but this time it was softer and melodious before it made its way.

"We should have gotten something in return."

"Silent gratitude is the greatest gift a person can be given," Krishna said, as he came on his feet.

Samva didn't want to stop convincing him, so he tried it again, as he knew the atmosphere had turned more fiery and energetic: "You still have it in you. Don't be reluctant. Join me."

"I have trust in Pradhyuman. He will change his ways. My brother will find a way. Finding Erakas if they exist should be the last resort."

Oh, how wrong he was.

"If you truly believe what you said," Samva said, "I have to show you something."

"What?"

Samva turned grim. "You'll know."

7

They were in a large, draped caravan, sipping wine and discussing their politics.

Balaram was in the comfort of his corner, while his wife was in another and so was Akoorji, opposite to him.

With a small band of soldiers, they had begun their journey towards the goal: Ratavaka Mountains.

Balaram had convinced Pradhyuman that he was leaving because he wanted to create diplomatic relations with Andhaka and Vrishni so they could assist Pradhyuman in finding Mayavati. Pradhyuman didn't want their help, but decided the Prime Minister's use at the battlefield was not necessary. He already had enough men to travel to Rasatala, the Rakshasas' domain and get his mother back.

"He was too easy to convince," Balaram said, eating a grape. "Kind of scares me how distracted he is. Dvarkipur would go in turmoil, for sure. No king. No Prime Minister."

"Don't worry," Revathi patted his shoulders, "we'll be fine. You'll be fine. It's just for a few days and you have a great process and system in place with your councilmen."

Balaram nodded. "It's strange going back to the tribe where me and Krishna were born." He referred to the Vrishnis.

"I am still surprised how Krishna let the Vrishnis leave Dvarkipur. They were his people."

"It was a decision he couldn't have taken," Balaram shook his head.

He remembered the scenario, years ago when Krishna was the king. This was when the Kurukshetra was over and he was still a god, a divine deity. He had not given up his powers. The Andhaka Queen Devamidha had lost her son. Brutally slaughtered. The suspicion had fallen on the Vrishni king Yudhajit and his sons. Devamidha had come to Krishna and asked for justice. Krishna wasn't able to provide it, since there was little proof and he couldn't just go against the Vrishnis. This led the Andhakas to drive themselves away from Krishna, while the Vrishnis were saddened that Krishna thought the Vrishnis could do this—distanced nonetheless.

That day, Krishna lost two of his arms.

"Well, I believe, your majesty, it's the right time to discuss this," Akoorji said, laying out some documents and noting down his points. "We should go through it. How do we plan to form peace in the lands which has seen only violence?"

"What are they currently duelling over?"

"A pig."

"A pig?" Revathi chuckled. "What is going on?"

Akoorji just shook his head. "The pig was in the enemy lines and after that, he wasn't seen again. The Andhakas blamed the Vrishnis, the Vrishnis blamed the Andhakas for creating the ruckus when there was none and they had also recently battled over it.

"They have become foolish with age," Balaram shook his head.

"Can you tell me more about the two clans?" Revathi asked. "I don't want to sound stupid, but Balaram knows that I came to Dvarka after all this happened, so I have no clue what is going on."

Balaram instructed Akoorji to speak, who did: "The Andhakas take their name from the demon Andhaka, though their ancestral blood flows from the veins of Yadu. The Andhakas have this tendency of tying knots around their eyes and not see. They work on their other senses, because in the ancient times, the Andhaka whose name they take from had seen Lord Shiva's wife Parvati when he wasn't supposed to, making the angry Shiva burn his eyes. The Andhaka as a tribe follow that, as a way to ask for forgiveness from Lord Shiva. They are more barbaric in nature and they are known to resort to violence, and work on trade when it comes to weapons. They sell their doubled-edged sword and it's quite popular in the gladiatorial arenas of Rome."

"But there's a flip side," Balaram added. "They sell slaves and buy them too. They are quite into slavery and they make sure the slaves don't have human rights, so to speak. The slaves, are not their own blood, but are immigrants, tourists, foreigners of all kinds leading them to have a bad relationship with a lot of other islanders than Dvarka."

"The Vrishnis on the other hand, are the rich kind. The posh, the extravagant and the charming. Yudhajit is an indulgent man. One can say, he has bedded more wenches than anyone else. He has the best of wine and a kind of flower grows where he lives that's called Black Stone which he trades with the Egyptians—it is used as a spice to create a special aroma-inducing food," Akoorji explained. "But, as with every great tribe, they are quite notorious."

"For?"

"They come from the land of Yayati," Balaram intervened. "You know, the king who embraced his son's youth and gave him old age. The Vrishnis, all of them, have the power of sucking youth out of people. The magic runs in their blood. That's how they kill their foes. They have found a way around killing Yayatis, and escaping the gift that Krishna has given. They take the youth out of humans and kill them with old age."

"So Vrishnis are more powerful than the Andhakas?" Revathi asked.

"But Andhakas are more in number. They are huge because of their slavery system and Vrishnis can't keep sucking life otherwise they would just grow too young and become..."

"A child!" Revathi added. "So there's a flip side to the magic as well and that's why they use it in moderation."

Both men in the caravan nodded.

Balaram began, "I want to start with Yudhajit. I have better relations with him. His youngest son is quite a man. I've heard tales of how he would be a better king than any of his four other brothers."

"What is your plan?"

He wanted to answer but before he could the caravan took a large halt. They all jerked and fell out of it. There were shouts and cries, Balaram heard it and before he could even stand on his one leg, he saw Akoorji with the swiftness of a cat, leaving the caravan.

Balaram did the same and instructed Revathi: "Don't leave."

Fear lingered in her eyes. Balaram was stressed out too and was hoping things would be fine, as he staggered out of the caravan with the support of his staff. He came on his feet, until he realised what had happened—the entire sky had become dark and a thick fog had surrounded them. So deep and dark, it was difficult to see.

His soldiers had lined up the lamps, and Balaram knew that the lamps gave them some help, but they couldn't hear anything except for the hooves of large six-legged stallions.

"They are here." He breathed frustratedly.

His men were there, severed heads flying around all across. There were sounds of cries and wails. Akoorji shoved Balaram in the corner close to the lamp.

"We need to run. We can't wait."

They were here, close to the people who could hurt the Yayatis—whose magic was so powerful that it broke Krishna's gift to the Yayatis. They were the biggest threat to everyone. But they would only be unleashed at certain occasions.

They were the Vitihotras. Creatures of the other land, controlled by the Taljans. No one knew how they were born, where they came from.

And no one had seen them. Only heard rumours that they have six-legged stallions and wherever they go, the mist follows...

Like now.

Balaram helped Revathi out of the caravan and they began to make their way towards the mist. The stallion sounds were getting closer, and became even more audible when a large horse came in front of them and a white-armoured figure appeared with a large blade that swished across them, aiming for their heads—

Balaram used his staff to deflect it. Made from obsidian, it held its grip, but it was tough to resist the shivers from the deflection. The horse disappeared and so did the blade. They went ahead further, the light from the lamp that Akoorji held began to diminish, but they could see some light further ahead...

Until Balaram felt a tug and someone grabbed him by the throat and brought him high up in the air, his staff still in his hand. He was being carried away by the large creature that was the armoured Vitihotra when he saw the face of the creature—it was pure black, with golden slits and it had the face of an animal, but what kind of animal, he had no idea. But they clearly seemed like mutations.

Balaram tried to fight back the Vitihotra, swinging his staff from left to right and by chance, he smacked it on the Vitihotra's head, knocking him out a little and loosening his grip. Balaram felt this was the opportunity and he decided to throw himself on the ground into the mist, when he saw the Vitihotra's careful gaze and he...

There was a loud sound—metallic in nature.

And he woke up. He was no more in someone's grip, but was standing up, over a pool of dark bloody ocean.

He knew it was some mind game, some twisted illusion. Were the Vitihotras originally Rakshasas? They could be using Maya here, but then who knows?

Balaram turned and he saw the white-armoured creature walking towards him. He still had the helmet on which was of a strange design—with large eyes painted on it and big teeth. Balaram realised he didn't see the Vitihotra's face while he was being held up, but this paint that they had on. The kind of war paint, Balaram realised, that the other tribes back in India liked to use.

"Where am I?" He asked.

"You are in limbo." The response was immediate and husky.

"Why am I here?"

"Because you should know." The creature walked up close and was almost eight feet tall. The metallic footsteps were heard over the water.

"What?"

"Amongst the two, one is a sparrow." He said, circling around him.

"You have come here as a messenger?" Balaram asked.

"Yes. It's only me. The warrior Vitihotras didn't come here today."

"And so much explosion and mayhem and death just caused by one person?"

"Why are you telling me this? You work for her, don't you? Durgajyoti?"

"Not me. I want to be free," the Vitihotra said. "She binds us all. And most of them like it, but I don't. I am doing this as a favour because I learnt this from her. Someone told her about this path and it was done by one of the two confidants you have. That someone is called the Ledger."

"So, she let one of them die in the process and didn't tell you who it was?"

"No, she didn't. She did ask me to not hurt both of them and that confused me."

"Why are you telling me this?"

"Because I want to be free from her. Destroy Pradhyuman and take her away. Kill her. Find a way to kill her or trap her. I don't know. But just do something." He seemed frustrated. "I was able to come here and I can kill you, but I don't want to kill you. I want to protect you. I hope I don't regret this."

"No. Thank you for telling me." Balaram sighed, though he had no idea whether he should trust the Vitihotra or not and the metallic sound that was coming from behind it.

"Wait, one more thing?"

"Yes?"

"So, if she has sent you, she couldn't have done so without Pradhyuman's permission."

"Yes. Pradhyuman knows you have turned."

Balaram's heart sunk. He couldn't hide it anymore.

"Apparently, the Ledger spoke. They knew everything."

Balaram shook his head and then the mist disappeared as he was back in the present, where the corpses lay around him and he was on the ground—tied to the earth. He was agitated and angry but relieved that it was over. He was leaning on the staff.

He saw Revathi and Akoorji running towards him and trying to help him up.

"What just happened?" Akoorji asked.

"I think he just went away," Revathi added.

They both were holding him. But there was one who was wrong. Could it be Akoorji, who was the most loyal person he has ever known or could it be his wife, the mother of his children? He couldn't believe either of them, which further opened up a third possibility—

Could it be all a lie as well? A ploy created by Durgajyoti.

There was a chariot that was still in good condition, they all sat in that, as they began to move towards the Ratvaka Mountains—knowing fully well that he can't go back and where he's going—he can't trust anyone.

8

Durgajyoti wasn't as evil as people perceived her to be.

She was, in fact, someone with a purpose, who was trying her best to attain it. Unfortunately, for her, people misunderstood her, one of them being Balaram.

She walked with her short hair and her straight eyes towards the war room where Pradhyuman was, behind her the handmaidens and her guards rollicking along as well. People whispered as she walked, calling her a witch, calling her a demon and such. Durgajyoti was human though.

It was not her problem people didn't believe her.

As she walked in the halls, which overlooked the entrance gates to the palace, she saw the wide array of naked men in the front being paraded and flogged by a slaver. Durgajyoti saw all of them were in fact the executioners of treason, betrayers of the nation and the throne. These were the ones who walked along with the greatest betrayer—Balaram. They were brutally punished and later exiled or imprisoned, or flogged repeatedly until they were forgiven.

She didn't smile, though for effect she left the place, and lett the gazes of the naked men be left behind, who cursed her under their breath. She walked to the war room, where she saw Pradhyuman—

The ever-glowing man. The king. The god amongst men.

He had the same shine and glory which Krishna possessed when he was at his prime. Long locks of auburn hair, blue eyes and a chiselled face. He was partially naked, his squire making him wear the gear while he went into the nitty gritties of opening a portal. He had a man and a woman by his side. The woman was clearly a Vidhyadhara, a magician who would open the gates to Rasatala.

To enter another dimension, it is of importance to have a Vidhyadhara, who can create gates. But entering the gate with an army is tough because...

"The Lokpala would be difficult to deal with," the Vidhyadhara said, referring to the gatekeeper of the portal. Each dimension has a gatekeeper and they are all powerful warriors, who know spells and magic that won't allow people to enter no matter how strong they are.

On the left was Pradhyuman's general, who instructed: "If we break the defenses and you could tell us how we do it, we would love to..."

"The powers Lokpala possesses cannot be broken so simply. He can be reasoned with. He can be challenged. But not be broken."

Pradhyuman looked up to see Durgajyoti.

"And even if we break it," she added, "the Rakshasas would know. And the moment they get to know, Mayavati will escape. We need to be discreet and smart. Do it quickly, so she's not anticipating our arrival."

"I thought you weren't supporting me in this." He said with moist eyes.

She would support him in anything. She believed in him.

"I am."

Pradhyuman smiled. "Is my uncle dead?"

"Saved. The Vitihotra was tricked by him."

Pradhyuman shook his head. "So much for being the most powerful out there."

"Don't worry, we will get him. The Ledger is with them. And I have sent further assassins to tackle him. He won't survive long."

"The Ledger was useful," Pradhyuman said. "So good job on that."

"In politics, one should think seven steps in advance."

"Ah, but I never believed my uncle would conspire such things." He shook his head. "Alas, things change. He did one good thing before going. He told me about Mayavati."

"With ulterior motives of course."

"How does it matter?" He asked. "So what do you think about the entire Lokpala episode?"

"I believe just bashing through the Lokpala wouldn't work."

"Then let's reason with him," Pradhyuman said. "Start the process," he told the Vidhydhara.

"Now?" The woman scowled. "Are you sure you want to meet him *now*?"

He took the glass of wine and didn't say anything further. With his armour, he went back to his chair and sat waiting for the Vidhydhara to do what she was told. The magicians here had limitations, they could only perform so much magic that the order of the world allowed. And the order doesn't allow killing or harming others leading Vidhyadharas to be absolutely useless. They could entertain kings by being jesters or fool around. Nothing more. But there were Vidhyadharas who would indulge in chaos, rather than order and they were the ones who didn't have any limitation.

But chaos cannot be practiced by everyone, except for those who have the potential to hold great hate and anger, of course; delving into chaos would lead to castration of oneself.

Durgajyoti would *know*.

The Vidhyadhara had begun chanting, bringing forth the powers out of the electric currents that were slipping out of her fingertips. Things began to topple and fly around. Durgajyoti was standing in a corner and everyone was afraid, even the general who was more of a man of the fist and less of spells. Things began to shift and the bleariness around the room began to grow further, until Durgajyoti saw what was intended for her to see.

The reddish portal, albeit small, from the wall and from the other side came out a man with a trident in his hand, a big stick in another with short, matted hair and a beard and who looked absolutely like a hermit. He was standing bored there, as if he was called from a waking slumber and wanted to go back to his little cave from where he had arrived.

He wasn't tall or large, even. He was quite small, in fact. He was weak and bony. One could smash him and be done with it.

Though behind the deceiving exterior was a dark

interior, someone who possessed more power than anyone out there.

"Who summons me?" The voice was large. "Puny mortals. Why am I here?"

Pradhyuman kept the wine glass and walked straight to the Lokpala, unafraid unlike Durgajyoti. "How are you, old man?"

The Lokpala didn't flinch. "If it wasn't, the son of Krishna. Pradhyuman. How may I help you? To send across another gift to your beloved mother?"

"No, but an army would suffice." He charmingly disarmed the man.

"An army? You plan to invade a cannibalistic tribe who have found ways to live in peace and not hurt humans anymore?" He asked. "A tribe which has made humanity tremble for thousands of years, battled your uncle and your father, fought the greatest of gods and conquered lands. And you plan to invade them? Good for you, little boy."

"Little boy?" Pradhyuman felt the frustration. He was angry, clenching his fist. Durgajyoti hoped that nothing bad would happen, but then who knows. "I'm not a little boy. I know what I am doing. In that little monologue of yours about the tales of Rakshasas, you forgot one thing?"

"What?"

"They always get defeated," Pradhyuman smiled. "It's good business if I invade them and make civilised gentry out of beasts. It's only good sense."

"Absolute power corrupts you, boy," the Lokpala said. "I sense great fear in you, the fear to live up to the name of your father who you always strive to impress."

"Bah! I don't care." He was embarrassed, but the Lokpala was grinning.

"I can't let evil enter the gates," he shook his head. "It is inhuman and against the oaths that I am sworn to. I can't allow bloodshed knowingly. I can't allow slaughter as well. So, I apologise, but I believe we are done here."

He stamped his staff and the red gates which had dimmed, opened again, on the wall. Pradhyuman was gritting his teeth and as the Lokpala began to move, so did he. He launched at him from behind, out of anger, with a sword in his hand that he had unsheathed and brought it next to the Lokpala's head, when the old man turned around and deflected it with his staff, letting a ripple of energy scream across the lands.

Durgajyoti closed her ears, but she kept looking as Pradhyuman like a child continued to batter his beaten sword against the magical defence of the Lokpala. He continued to ram it and break it, but the sword broke instead and the Lokpala pounded the skull-headed stick against Pradhyuman and for a moment, Pradhyuman couldn't hold anything inside and retched, vomiting on the ground and falling unconscious.

"How dare he..." the Lokpala had embers emanating from his irises now, when Durgajyoti came in between.

"Don't hurt him!"

The Lokpala gritted his teeth. "Move, woman. I shall put him in limbo and let him suffer there."

"No," she said. "He's apologetic and we will make sure he doesn't repeat this again."

"Of course, he won't because he will be..."

"You said you won't knowingly allow anyone to hurt the ones who you seem to protect," Durgajyoti said. "The knowingly part was what struck me as odd. You are ready to hurt him, just not put it on your conscience."

For a moment, the Lokpala emanated the embers and then he looked at Durgajyoti with kind eyes. "You are a smart girl."

Durgajyoti smiled. "The Lokpala are assigned to a realm and there are cases, they do not like protecting the realm, but they are bound by duty. Now we both know Rakshasas aren't the best out there. I mean, they deserve the hate that is rained on them. We just want to say hello and push them to the other side, while you don't have to do anything. We will enter with a gift and you won't know what's in it. You are just letting a gift enter and what happens after that, doesn't exist for you."

The Lokpala narrowed his gaze, glancing at the Vidhyadhara and the general, the feared soldiers standing behind.

"What do I get in return for passing on a gift?"

"What do you want?" She asked. "A Lokpala doesn't need anything. They are fulfilled by what is given to them."

"Not always. We often get bored. Stories often mesmerize us, they make us enjoy our loneliness."

"What stories do you want?"

"Yours."

Her smile vanished. Her past was a secret and could not be revealed. She could hear Pradhyuman groan in a corner and she had to make a choice. For him...

"Yes. All right. Take it. Take my stories."

He smiled, bringing the skulled head stick close to her forehead and tapping it slowly. For a moment, she felt it—all of it that she had buried inside of her.

The early times when she was young, she was an orphan. She would run on the streets. The moment her life changed when she was sold to a man. And then he used to beat her recklessly. She became a woman and accepted something within her.

Or someone.

And everything changed after that. It was absolutely horrific. Her bones had been shattered and the only reason this something would enter her, if she had a purpose—of being in love. And she did. She only loved one man all her life.

It was the person who was on the floor, covered in his own vomit.

And the taps of the stick stopped, realising the stories were all given to the Lokpala who was then grinning.

"Oh, you are a delightful surprise," he said. "Your wish is granted. You have forty-eight hours to turn up with a gift for me to pass on." He began to move towards the gate, and turned, looking at her:

"Be careful, girl. You harbour great evil within you. Don't let it overpower you."

And then he left.

9

Krishna had never felt so awkward as he did while travelling alone with his son. He had never shared this kind of feeling with him. He would always meet him amongst others, but never in person.

But now here he was, riding a mare with him, towards where he had no idea.

Krishna had held secrets from Samva, many of which would hurt him, and seeing him in flesh only brought those memories back.

"How's Lakshmana?" He asked.

"I don't know," Samva said. His face was away and his voice was indifferent.

"You ever found her?"

"No. She just disappeared one day," Samva said.

Krishna nodded. No, she didn't. He knew.

"I didn't kidnap her you know," Samva protested as he always did. He was one of those sociopathic kids who would rationalise everything they did even though it was wrong. "They said I did. But I didn't. We loved each other, more than anyone else, but there were jealous people out there."

Krishna nodded. He had heard this tale so many times, but from other accounts he had heard that the girl he had kidnapped wanted to escape and she was sad. Krishna moved his mare further, as he came out of the nest of his protectiveness and out in the open land of Dvarka, looking at the bright skies, the tall groves and endless pastures. He had come here when it was just an island.

And his thoughts began to waver. He went back in time, the first time, when everything was a wreck. And they had found this land here. Only barren rocks. And nothingness. Ruled by tribes. Dvarka was just one of the many islands.

And Krishna was a boy who had angered a maharaja—Jarasandha—after killing the Maharaja's son-in-law, and his uncle Kans. Krishna's place Mathura was being targeted and Ugrasen, the king of Mathura, instructed him to go and find another place. He had a pregnant wife and he had no place. He searched for long, and when he did—he found it.

"Looks beautiful and grand!" Krishna announced, in front of his two companions, the ones he trusted the most. Durjay and Balaram.

Balaram being his brother was always supportive, but Durjay was his best friend. The scion of the Taljan clan, way before the Taljans had branched out.

"We need to get rid of the locals though," Krishna suggested. "Give them a separate land to stay."

"Don't you think they should be doing that to us?" Durjay asked.

"I know. But we are bigger and better. We would survive longer." There was a hint of arrogance dripping from Krishna's voice. He was powerful. He was omniscient and omnipresent.

Absolute power does corrupt absolutely. Even in the most righteous of hands.

And while what he did was not noble, getting rid of the locals, he did eventually gift them a place to stay down the road, to seek their blessings.

A wise man is not someone who doesn't commit mistakes, but someone who learns from them quickly.

He continued to move with Samva in silence and tranquility, back in the present, when Samva asked:

"Do you really think Gandhari's curse would come into effect?"

"I don't know. Curses can be powerful spells because they come from the worst emotion ever—hate." Krishna explained. "I do not wish to be a target of hate. But I have to be safe."

"What if those were just words by Gandhari? You ended up giving up your powers and giving it up to a bunch of idiots."

"I gave it to those who were my blood," Krishna responded. "If I have regrets, I will live with them. I wouldn't try to change it."

Samva just scoffed, as if it was a hard thing to believe and it was actually foolhardy.

They managed to move towards the land, the sun had begun to go down, and the land was dipping too, as if curving downwards and the grass was ending. The smell of rot was evident and so were the flies. There were so many of them.

Krishna moved further and he saw what Samva had brought him there for.

Corpses.

Hundreds of them.

In juxtaposed positions. The entire scenery that was engulfed in beauty was now transcended into something horrible; gory.

He dismounted from his mare, and made his move towards the corpses, looking at them. "Wha—what is this?" He asked. They were in thousands, some had rotted enough to make skeletons, some had continued to rot earlier.

Samva walked behind him. "This is the result of your actions."

"What do you mean?"

"It's called the Mrithyusthan," Samva said. "The land of the dead, as one can put it delicately."

Krishna knelt down, near the corpse of a child, whose skin had sunk and smelled of death. Krishna, by then, had wrapped a cloth around his face.

"This can't be the Yayatis," he said. "I gave them the power. I..."

"This isn't the Yayatis," Samva said, smirking. "This is what they did after they were given the power. This is a reminder of what happened to them when you gave them absolute power. This is what they did to their enemies."

Krishna shook his head, closing his eyes, letting the tears brim in his irises. He felt different. He felt his heart was torn apart from his chest and tossed in the air. He continued to stay there and pray. Pray to whoever was listening. Regret mounting up even more.

"I didn't want to make you feel worse than you already did, but you should know. Knowledge of pain is powerful, if the outcome of it is favourable."

"Right. We should leave."

"Why? Don't you want to mull over more?"

"No. The land of the dead responds to threats. The dead aren't dead really. They aren't given proper burials, so if they see a threat, like me, who has caused this, they would..."

And they began to rise. All the corpses had light in them and they shook up and came on their feet, next to their fallen swords and spears.

"Why didn't you tell me this earlier?" Samva said, fear masking it.

"Because I thought you would know. But I believe I overestimate you again," Krishna could feel the dead around him. "They are Pisaches. The undead." He brought out his mace. "Brace yourself to escape, now."

And they began to sprint, when more corpses came in their way, especially the one who held him by the feet making him fall on the ground. He felt a sharp pain run through his body, but with his mace he broke the skull of the corpse and staggered on, holding on to Samva's hands and moving forward.

More corpses surrounded him and he broke through them with his mace, throwing and tossing them on the side, his mace as powerful as ever. He had his chakras which he flung across whenever needed.

As he made his escape, his body erupted in flames, causing the pursuing corpses to cease their chase. Samva and Krishna shared a relieved glance.

"I think they can't leave their resting place," Samva said.

"No," Krishna shook his head. "Something is wrong..."

And then he felt it. Someone grabbed him by the tunic and tossed him on the mud, his mace falling on the side.

He looked up to see who it was. Realising...it was a big old, burly man with sharp fangs, pale scorched skin. He looked deadlier than ever. He didn't attack Samva, not even acknowledge him.

Krishna felt a punch and a kick on his stomach, for this man was way more fleshy and powerful than the usual Pisach out there. In fact, he was larger in frame as well.

"I am sorry..."

But the Pisach didn't listen and continued punching him hard, when Samva leapt on his back with his sword with which he began to puncture his head. The creature just grabbed Samva like a fly and tossed him on the side, dust swirling around him.

"I am sorry," Krishna said, two chakras in his hands.

The Pisach couldn't speak. So, they wouldn't understand either. They just knew their enemy was in front of them.

As he came forward, Krishna dodged him, using the chakras to cut the remaining flesh from his arms and legs as quick as possible. The Pisach didn't move further at first, but then instantly hurled at him in a surprise attack, grabbing Krishna and throwing him on the ground, choking him, when Krishna brought two of his chakras again and stuck it in the creature's ears making his blood ooze out, letting it spray across his face.

But it didn't work.

He still continued to choke him.

Two arrows stung his shoulder and it came from

Samva, who was hitting him from far. This led the creature to get distracted a bit and Krishna instantly held a chakra up and stabbed him in his eye. The creature scowled in pain, and fell back.

Krishna leapt over him and with the other chakra, he began to dissect his brain and his eyes, assaulting the flesh and the guts as much as possible, turning him into waste. After a while, the Pisach stopped resisting and Krishna knew he had killed him. Not really... He had put him to rest. The anger the Pisach had towards Krishna was gone.

He came on his feet, feeling guilty as ever, and he looked at the other corpses who were watching him from the other side. But didn't attack. Perhaps out of fear.

Or perhaps, out of disappointment.

The ghosts of his actions were live in front of him, and he felt nothing but betrayed by the people he had trusted, the ones he thought would do right by the power he had vested upon them.

But no.

Apparently, goodness didn't exist any longer. Apparently, the war had mutated everyone into these sinister beings, who needed to be put down.

"Are you okay?" Samva asked.

Krishna didn't respond, wiping the blood and moving towards the mare, as he sat on it. His head was throbbing hard.

"I was two," he began, "when I killed an Asura. I had sucked the life out of her tits," he continued. "After that, I have killed Asuras of all kinds. I have killed the greatest demon, my uncle. Kans. I have fought the worst kind of evil that has ever existed." He looked at his chest, as he tore his tunic and revealed his chest, where the symbol of Shrivatsa was made, the same symbol that is given to the harbinger of justice, of heroes.

Of the Avatar of Vishnu.

"But now, I am in the most difficult phase of my life," he said. "I have to kill my own people."

10

Durgajyoti had known Durjay for a while.

Her husband and a slaver. A man who was so evil that not even one redeeming quality could be seen in him. Durgajyoti knew that there were people who were evil, but with some shades of good.

Not Durjay though.

He was a horrific, fascist and an abusive man.

Perhaps because Durgajyoti was just a wench for him. A whore he would slap around. He had the greatest power in his hands—the Vitihotras, but he didn't know how to conjure them. In the early days of the marriage with Durjay, Durgajyoti would see his book collection which would house information about the Vitihotras and how they were just legends and myths. She always wondered whether they would be her princes and save her from the cruelty of the man she lived with.

Until she met *her* and things changed. She saw a new light. A revelation. Her pupils were dilated and her body got weak, but meeting *her* was important.

Durjay soon died and the mantle was passed on to Durgajyoti, a careless way of passing the title since it should have been given to their son, given the patriarchal system they lived in. But in the dying stage, Durjay had left all the titles and the crown to her.

And she had the Vitihotras by her then, so who would oppose her?

And she set out for Dvarka, in search of Pradhyuman, the boy who she had met when she had married the first time. She was his age. They both were young, but he brought the flavours in her mouth, the feeling between her chest like butterflies springing in autumn.

Durgajyoti was in her room. Knitting. Her favourite pastime. But she had the shakes, as she called it. She couldn't hold something for so long. Her fingers would feel weak, her nerves would hurt. She would feel she was dying, but ever since she was with *her* this was happening. *She* told Durgajyoti it was fine. It was okay. It was just a part of the transition process.

When someone knocked.

Durgajyoti looked up, in a loose drape, and moved towards the door, opening it and looked at the irresistible man standing in front of her. She saw his locks and his eyes and his chest and his muscles. He was standing there, doing nothing, just gazing at her. He looked clean too.

"That was awkward," Pradhyuman announced.

And they both chuckled.

"Well, it's all right," she smiled.

"I thought I can fight him."

"Pomposity is a necessity in a king."

He shrugged. They both had a third member in their conversation—Pradhyuman's guardsman.

"May I come in?" He asked.

She nodded weakly, letting him in, knowing very well, she just wanted to climb on him and ride him, and kiss his mouth and lick his neck. She had to control the burning between her thighs, as the door closed behind them.

The shakes grew worse, and she made herself comfortable on a chair, while he sat on the bed.

"You continue to help me like this. The Lokpala episode was embarrassing to me but you emerged as a winner," he said.

"Not true. You trusted me to be here with you till now. For that trust cannot be understated."

"You think too highly of me, Durgajyoti." He shook his head, pausing and contemplating. "You haven't been married till now, have you?"

Her hopes rose up. Was he going to propose? But then she didn't want to be just his wife. She wanted to be *the* wife. The only one. And he had several right now, the favourite one being Rukmini who was a big slob and a drunk.

"No, I haven't."

"Then that should be arranged," he said.

"I don't need to be married just for the sake of it, your highness. I want to do it on my terms."

He smiled. "The Taljans led by Durjay distanced from me when Krishna left. Durjay believed I was inept, but you returned with Durjay's body. I felt sad for a man who was like an uncle to me but I was happy I grew an ally. That day was quite a day and while the Andhakas and the Vrishnis continue to leave my side, the Taljans will join with me in the enlightenment and the revolution that I plan."

"What revolution?" Her eyes grew large.

"Invasion of Rasatala started as a drunken escapade until I saw what they have. They are, if tamed, one of the most ferocious armies to ever have. We would tap into their Maya, the source of it at least and make our soldiers powerful. Make us powerful. With the Vitihotras and the Maya on our side—imagine the horrors we can inflict on our enemies." He smiled coldly and for the first time, Durgajyoti felt scared of him. His blues eyes didn't have the same passion or warmth, but a hearth that hasn't been warmed for a while. He was hidden in the shadows and his beautiful, carved up face was a revelation.

"So much power would make us blind, your highness."

"Perhaps. Or it would gain us insight, far more than anyone else."

"What do you plan to do?"

"Everyone should have a purpose. I have got mine now." He didn't reveal what it was and perhaps, he was in no mood to even.

She wanted to ask him, but she was afraid of the unknown. The boy king had surprisingly dark eyes and for someone who was the Vishnu's son, he didn't exhibit any sort of dharmic laws that must have been bestowed on him.

He hugged her. "I'll find you a good man," he said.

"No," she responded.

But he didn't listen. He left, leaving the door open and breaking her heart into pieces. She remained there frozen for a while, letting it sink. Doing so much for him, has to release her from something, but she received nothing in return. Durgajyoti sighed and felt a turmoil of emotions, when she heard it—

"You seem to lose hope in him." The voice came. It was like a hiss of a snake or something, but it came from nothing. It was just a voice right now.

"No. I continue to love him."

"The man is an explosive. You'll burn yourself around him."

"No," she said, her fingers shaking.

"Don't be sad, child."

A shadow formed in front of Durgajyoti and she looked at the shadow, as if it was a real person and a hand came out of the shadow which touched her chin and brought her face forward. A woman was seen, a young lass with dark skin, black lips and octopus like tentacled hair on her head. She had eyes of burning embers and it seemed she could stare at anyone with contempt and kill them.

"Baagul," Durgajyoti whispered, "what is it? Why have you showed yourself?"

"Devoting yourself to me changed your life, lass."

"I know. It wrecked it too." She showed her fingers. "It hurts my nerves."

"And it would. You hold a powerful deity within you."

"The Lokpala says you are evil."

"The goddess of black magic? Evil?" Chuckled Baagul. "The Lokpalas are often fools. Don't trust them."

"What do you want?" Durgajyoti sneered.

"Straight to the point. Great then." The shadow moved to the back and made itself comfortable. "We have a problem. In fact, you do."

"What?"

"My worms speak."

"Speak?"

"Yes," she said. "They speak of an awakening on the terrain, of virtue and loyalty, of honour and order."

"Who is it?" She arched her brows.

"Krishna."

"But..."

"Yes," Baagul shook her head. "He's not disappeared completely and he poses a great threat to our hero—Pradhyuman."

"What is his agenda?"

"To end the Yayatis of course. Ah, they are a slimy lot, so don't blame him. But if the Yayatis are killable, then so are you which would make you implode and I can't let that happen. You are the only reason I'm alive right now."

She rolled her eyes. "Of course. And also the other mysterious agendas you have that you don't speak of."

"There is none. I speak of only this," she lied through her teeth.

"If you know, what do you want me to do?" She paused. "Send an army?"

"No. Do something about it," Baagul said, with a smile.

They both nodded. Durgajyoti sighed, saying a spell within and letting Baagul go away. "Hope you go though and stop him," she scoffed.

"Can't. Because of me, you are here, because of me, you are released from the pain of your spouse and because of me you are leading the strongest army. Be careful what you wish for or you stand to lose everything."

And with that, she disappeared leaving Durgajyoti alone.

And for the first time in many years, her hands didn't shake even once.

But she knew Krishna would spell trouble for her and her dreams. He would create havoc and if he had been found, it would be detrimental in her larger scheme of things. In fact, it was she who had planned for him to go and orchestrated such a charade.

She remained quiet and mulled over what to do. She knew she had to do something about Krishna for herself and find a way to do it. She didn't like Baagul, but she was right.

I must find another way.

Durgajyoti decided to leave the room and as she was heading for the cabins of Pradhyuman, she stopped.

Wouldn't it be better if I got Krishna's head from my end?

She could surprise Pradhyuman, make him happy. It could be a gift from her. A way to get into his heart. She smiled, as she conjured a bit of a magic on her fingers, bringing chaos close to her heart and exploding, summoning the man who could bring back Krishna's head.

But he was no mere man.

The Vitihotras were dangerous, evil lurking in the corner.

As she snapped her fingers, shadows had begun to form and the mist had clouded her in the empty hallway, the guardsman too was there.

"You came fast," she said to the Vitihotra.

"Always here. Not fast." The voice was soothing.

She turned to find the creature—he was a long-haired whipped guy, with eyes as deep as soulless creatures and his face had a long smile, that was carved by a knife. His skin was just like the other Vitihotras, pale as marble.

"To what do I owe the pleasure?"

Unlike the other Vitihotras, this one wasn't soulless. He was quite the charmer. He had a personality but he was the deadliest too, the most lethal. That is why she had sent him to Balaram, but he was unsuccessful, which was odd for him. He could not be defeated easily. But he also stirred memories in her that she was not comfortable dealing with. She could feel a moral tug in her throat, but chose to dismiss it.

"I want you to murder someone."

"Indeed, yes. Wouldn't be here otherwise," the Vitihotra nodded.

"I hope you don't do the same thing that you did last time: be unsuccessful."

"They tricked me," the Vitihotra said. "It won't happen again, of course."

"Good." She said and then clenched her fist, letting the Baagul in her rise which only meant trouble.

The Vitihotra instantly started choking and fell on the ground, feeling pain and misery of all kinds. "Because next time you don't return fast and with the right thing, you would feel worse."

The Vitihotra nodded and almost wept.

"Aren't you the master of mystics? So solve this thing for me."

She released the clench and he began to breathe again, the mist around it began to clear.

"Who is it though?" He asked, still exhausted.

"You know him, in fact." She smiled and the Vitihotra's smokes and mist intensified as she continued with glee and wonder. "He used to be your friend, Durjay. His name is Krishna!"

11

The snake was him. And he was the snake.

It moved and coiled and wrapped itself around Balaram, like a pet he would pat. But instead of feeling warm, he felt cold. He felt he would sting the snake, but the snake uncoiled itself before that as if it knew his intention.

Balaram realised where he was, the sound of the dry sweeping land, where the sun was bloody and so were the skies. He was somewhere and nowhere too. But what beckoned and appalled him, was the large reptile that was in front, blocking the sun, having fangs and a hood like a cobra and watching him with disdain and disappointment.

"Where am I?" He asked the snake, as if expecting a reply. "Perhaps a dream, a nightmare..."

And instead, the response was: "You are home."

Balaram was confused, arching his brows, he began to walk closer to the reptile who was ten times larger than him...when something else hit him—

He was walking. Like walking without any support from his staff. Come to think of it, he didn't have a staff at all. His legs were fine.

"I am confused."

"You should be."

"What do you want?"

"To protect you. You are surrounded by enemies." Came the voice from the snake and they were proper syllables rather than just ordinary hissing.

"I know. The Ledger." He paused. "Why do you want to protect me?"

"Because I am protecting myself through that."

He didn't understand and that consumed and confused him.

"The end of the Yayatis is nigh. You must let me consume you. And let me become you. The time has come." The snake leaned forward, its tail rising in the back as the skies turned bloodier.

"No..." he was becoming dreary and delusional. "You are wrong. We still have hope."

"Hoping is an act of ignorance."

And his body began to shake, his legs grew weaker and he fell on the ground as if poisoned. He began to shake uncontrollably and then he looked up from all the shrivelling, with fear now that the fangs were close, the mouth of the reptile was opening...

And it was indeed consuming him.

His eyes opened. Fever had taken hold of him and he could feel his body rocking.

He looked everywhere, confused, sweating when he saw Rukmini patting his head and taking care of him.

"It's all right."

"What happened?"

"We are reaching the palace, to meet the Vrishnis."

He sighed. His eyes darted at the opening of the chariot where he saw the lands had become colder, snow had engulfed them from all around and it felt like they were ascending towards the abodes of the gods. The skies were nearer more than ever, and elks and mules could be spotted, the snow leopard mewled from far and the trees were of red cherry coating.

From far, he could gaze at the Samarra valley which was where the other mountains of the Ratvaka stood tall and where the Andhakas lived. He also noticed tall, iron barricades and realised that the only thing which divided two warring clans was a valley. He knew that the Andhakas came here first for the fertile lands, but the Vrishnis followed. That was also a big conflict between the two. Who does the hills belong to? And it was decided, as long as they don't enter each other's turfs, it would be fine.

Balaram was nearing the gate and he could see the merchants, the farmers, the hunters and soldiers around him. Everyone looked at the tattered and scorched chariot they were travelling in and many whispered after watching Balaram, all ill and feverish. They knew him, of course. His statue stood tall here. He was always welcomed too, but he never left Krishna's side and came here. He knew he could have had a peaceful life.

But while these people seemed ordinary, they all had powers that could suck the youth out of another person. Having this much power could yield problems. Balaram and Krishna didn't possess this even though they were Vrishnis because they were adopted. They were not Vrishnis by blood.

He reached the castle doors, after passing through many houses and rock buildings, where everyone was dressed fashionably and looked as beautiful as a Roman artifact. He saw foreigners here too.

He looked at the castle and he saw the army and automatically shut his eyes, realising he was safe here. A pat from his wife was the last thing he felt, before he dozed off.

*

He wished he didn't dream again.

And he didn't.

When his eyes opened again, he wasn't in some red sky picture, a frame of disgusting reptiles but he was here, in the comfort of cushions.

"Hope your slumber was fine." He saw a young man in front of him, quite young probably because of sucking so much youth. He had curly, blonde hair, dyed of course and grey eyes with a charming smile. Yudhajit was his name and he was an old friend of Balaram's. "How do you do friend?"

"Much better."

"Good," he smiled. "Your wife and your commander are worried."

"Where are they?"

"Resting too. In another place. You have raised eyebrows by entering the city." Shadows irked around his face.

Balaram nodded. "I need to speak to you."

"And speak you shall. Rest for now. Let's meet at dinner."

Balaram wanted to say something. But he didn't. He

closed his eyes and went off to sleep yet again. Resting, exhausted from the journey and from his dreams.

*

Balaram had washed his face, cleaned his clothes and wore the Vrishni drape that was kept near the foot of his mattress. He was done with his daily meditation and came for dinner. Balaram had worn his ornate slippers and his skin looked bronze as ever. His face was chiselled but weak, and he saw a long feast of food prepared for him in the dining halls, where flutes and banjos were being strummed.

Balaram saw Rukmini and Akoorji already at the table and so was Yudhajit, chatting with each other.

"Ah well, the sleeper is here," Yudhajit announced. "Sit down, old friend."

"I don't see your son."

"Oh, he's been quite a rebel nowadays, so he wouldn't be joining us."

Balaram wanted to meet the son. That was the point of him coming all the way. The son had to marry the daughter of the Andhakas and the union would bring him great diplomatic support from both the nations.

"We have been chatting about how you were the only one who could beat a bull singlehandedly," Rukmini added with a smile. She looked fresh and tidy too. Akoorji with his matted hair and beard, was solemnly eating and Balaram was in fact thinking of him as Ledger, as he ate his own vegetables.

"When I was young," Balaram smiled.

"You still are," Yudhajit complimented.

"Unlike you, we have real life problems."

"Come on!" Yudhajit chuckled. "I might look young but I am a hundred years old or maybe more. God, I don't even remember." He was taken aback.

Balaram nodded. They ate and talked and laughed. Yudhajit didn't mention anything about business in front of Rukmini and Akoorji. When the night was still young and the food was over, Yudhajit said: "I would like to speak to Balaram alone if you both don't mind."

They nodded.

"I'll see you in the room," Rukmini said, patting and winking at him.

Balaram couldn't help but smile back at her. As she left, he saw Yudhajit's leering gaze at him.

"Come with me. I shall make you drink some good wine," he said.

They began to move, from one room to another, until they arrived at a room with a massive gatekeeper. But before they could leave, they were interrupted by Yudhajit's soldiers who were bringing a bunch of aged, scarred warriors wrapped and clasped by ropes and manacles.

"My lord, we found you some slaves from the frontiers."

"Ah," Yudhajit smiled, sipping his wine and moving towards the prisoners of war. "They seem ripe and young." He looked back at Balaram. "Just give me a moment, my dear friend."

Balaram didn't say anything. But he saw what Yudhajit was doing. He was bringing forth his hand over the slave and a blue energy was being pulled out by his hand, which led to Yudhajit turning from being young to even younger, as the man in front of him grew old instantly, turning papery white and all wrinkled. Sapped of energy, they fell on the ground as Yudhajit said with a charm: "Ah, felt great as ever. What a dessert! You can have the rest, boys," he told his soldiers and they did as commanded, grabbing hold of the prisoners and taking them away, while the yells and the scornful laughs could be heard.

"Theatrics have always been your forte," Balaram said.

"Oh please. Remember back in Mathura how bad I was at impressing the outsiders when we played?"

Yudhajit was just like any other boy when Balaram, Krishna and all played together. Yudhajit was a shy one. And now seeing him like this, brought back completely different kind of memories.

Yudhajit guided Balaram to the rooms, within other rooms, until reaching a place where there were multitudes of jars and candles.

"I have received the finest of the ale that the Romans would drink," he dipped a cup. "Have it."

"Sure," Balaram smiled. He took a sip and felt exuberant. "Oh, it's very nice."

"Indeed," Yudhajit's lips had turned red, but he drank further.

"What happened with your son?"

"He's a warrior. Young blood, even though he looks older than me," he sighed. "The boy has lost his mind because he wants to fight back the Andhakas, destroy them while I am okay with having an adversary."

"So, he doesn't talk to you."

"Worse, he's disappeared," Yudhajit shrugged, uncaring, callous. "Satyaki is a short fuse."

"Any possibility of truth in his words?"

"No. He's hot mannered," Yudhajit said. "So much like you, when you were a kid."

"I was wise. Krishna was stupid and you were quiet. That's how I remember it."

They both laughed and by the fifth drink they were warmly talking about the old days.

"You didn't answer me though," Yudhajit said. "You didn't tell me why you are here. I've heard stories about what happened. Pradhyuman is going mad and going on a conquest to attack Rasatala. Bad choice to hurt the tricksters." He paused. "But you are the Prime Minister, and you are coming here in haste with a broken chariot. These walls have ears but I have eyes too. What is it?"

"There's been a problem," he said. "But it's all right. I'll figure it out."

"Am I harbouring a convict?"

"Perhaps."

He thumped his back. "All the better! I like to irk Pradhyuman as much as I could. The puny boy is such a pain in the ass. But what purpose did you come here with other than the wines and listening to an old man? Did you have something in mind?

Balaram said, "Yes."

"And that is?"

"Marriage and peace."

"Between whom?"

"Between you and Devamedha."

For a moment Yudhajit looked at him and then chuckled loudly. "And what an absurd thought is that? Those are savages and we are elite."

"There's no class among the Yayatis."

"Well, then you live in a land where people still fought for the throne. Bala," he said softly, "you need to understand the Andhakas are beasts in human skin. Taming them with a union is letting a lion sleep in your bed. You know they will eventually slaughter you."

"I don't think so."

"But why would you want that?"

He was drunk but he didn't want his motives known yet. "Because I want peace across Dvarka. Two powerful nations joining hands is a force to be reckoned with."

'Tell you what, take me to the bed chambers," he stood up and tripped, "and if this favour is done, I shall see to it tomorrow that we can have a sane conversation regarding this."

Balaram accepted the condition, then picked him up by the arm and carried him. Soldiers and maids on the way tried to help but Balaram with his staff on one end and his friend on the other moved like a snail and refused any help, declaring that before they had crowns on their heads, they were friends and they would be the ones to help each other always.

As he laid Yudhajit on the bed, Balaram glanced around the room and his eyes fell on something.

It was a side table and there were letters sprawled across it. And these letters looked yellow, slant writings in some ancient language but Balaram understood it since he was a connoisseur when it came to languages.

He liked to study them as much as he could. He looked at the letters and he could see they were written about Balaram—about how he's on his way, how he's accompanied by his allies.

And it also housed his agendas—about the union between the two nations.

But all these letters had one thing in common.

They were all written by the Ledger.

12

Krishna always thought what Samva would be thinking about during his long bouts of silence.

As a child, he was a quiet boy. He would stay in a corner. He would not talk much. Pradhyuman would love to show off. But Samva was the opposite. Even if he achieved anything, he wouldn't bother to mention it. But then Krishna knew it was his fault as well, since in the early days Samva would show things but Krishna would dismiss them and would care more about Pradhyuman's wins.

There was no bias. It was just being the judge of a person's work. Pradhyuman was better and Krishna would make sure that he knew it. But that led Samva to have insecurity issues and he turned into this degenerate.

His innocence ended when he choked a chicken and left it in the corner of his room.

Krishna knew Samva was a sociopath and he grew up to prove Krishna right, grabbing attention from him and his wife.

Perhaps he's doing that now again. Perhaps he wants Krishna to acknowledge him as a son in need.

But Krishna also was aware that Pradhyuman was more like his son and Samva wasn't. He just didn't feel that way towards him. He never did.

They were on their way to Durvasa. A small village in the arid regions of Dvarka, one that was untouched by the glory of Krishna and his empire. It was a long journey, a tedious one, in fact. They rode their mares in silence, not speaking about the gargantuan fight with the Pisach that happened a few days ago. They wouldn't speak of it because Krishna felt guilty for that.

Did he really let the good son get the worst of him? What happened to Pradhyuman? He wanted to ask these questions, go to him, plead to him but then he would remember why he left the place. He was told to. By Pradhyuman himself. Pled by him that Krishna should exile himself if he ever wanted Pradhyuman to stop living in the shadows.

And there was another reason. Something he hadn't mentioned to anyone.

"We are close," Samva said, breaking the long silence.

"I hope you are right about this."

Samva glanced at him. "I have faith."

"Faith must come from a rational place."

"No," Samva said, dismounting and setting up the camp close to the village to rest, as night had fallen and the chilly waves of wind could be felt on the skin. "Faith is there when not even rationality could be felt. But you just believe it."

Krishna scoffed.

The boy had grown.

*

There was one other secret he hadn't shared.

Krishna had a hard time sleeping.

There were days he couldn't sleep for a long time. There were days he would just drop dead. Because whenever he closed his eyes, the past would come back.

And they would come with the tremors and horrors. Thy would come with waves too. And like the chill he felt under the skies of gloominess, he felt it here when he went back to the memories—when he had won the war. He had distanced himself from the Pandavas and decided to focus on himself. He distanced himself from Arjun because of what Krishna had done to his best friend.

As long as he could remember, he was a regretful man. And living in peace, alone in the wilderness, slowly dying was one gratification he wanted.

But now he couldn't have that.

Karma always returns.

Krishna shut his eyes, bit his lips, tried to sleep under a blanket but he didn't feel anything. He felt worse. He felt like he was drained. He sighed and came out of his tent to start a fire, warm himself. He sat next to the fire, watching it, when a mist began to form around him. Smoke and mist. The fog was dense and dark.

The surrounding was unusual.

Krishna instantly knew what it was, but he remained frozen out of fear. Ever since he had ventured out, he had been afraid a lot.

Of dying, most of all.

When you live like a god for so long, you end up realising that being human has its pitfalls.

Krishna wanted to yell for Samva, but his mouth was stuck, his jaw was frozen and his fist was clenched. He wanted to dive and go for his weapons which was inside the tent, but before he could do that, a person appeared in front of him.

And it looked like a person, even though it wasn't. In a white armour, stood a tall man. The helmet too was white.

It stood there for a while. Silence brewed between them. And then the helmet was taken off, and the face of a pale, glowering man looked back at him, his eyes drawn deep and his long black hair falling till the waist.

But what was disgusting about him was his mouth—he had a long cut across both sides of his mouth.

"Durjay," Krishna sighed, "that's a nice look for you right there."

"Never thought I'll be seeing you again." Durjay sighed, as he began to walk in circles around Krishna, not pouncing at him. "But here we are."

"I believe you have been sent to kill me," Krishna said.

He shrugged. "Yes."

"And you would relish that."

"Of course."

"We were friends once," Krishna shook his head. "We founded the earth we stand on. Together. You and me."

"Before you exiled me," Durjay noted.

"You were creating monsters. Creatures. Experimenting with magic and science. You were afraid of death."

"Of course, I was. I am still afraid of death." Durjay's face showed a hint of worry and sadness. "My mother and father both died natural deaths and it scared me that I would too. I wanted to live. I liked living."

"Well, Lord Brahma..."

"Don't start that again," he rolled his eyes. "I was trying to make us immortal and you defied me. You exiled my tribe, threw me out of the island."

"That was the right thing to do."

"And other things in life have been so right too?"

Krishna couldn't answer that. He sighed. "Well, you got your wish. You are a Vitihotra."

"And I can kill you."

"No, you can't. Because when you play with magic, you have limitations." Krishna walked with a smile, his hands clasped on his back. He could feel he was at the cusp of triumph. "And the biggest limitations of yours is that you knew me. Wonder why I had that small chat? It was to trigger the magic you had used to become the Vitihotra. You can't kill me because you *know* me. Vitihotras cannot hurt the ones they have known. That is their problem. The only problem. Indefinite power doesn't come without loopholes. Don't forget that."

Durjay looked down. Frustrated. "I met Balaram too. I chose not to kill him."

"Piss off, you couldn't. You tried to. So, you must have found an alternative." Krishna came close to Durjay, the mist surrounding him. His eyes looking deep into his old friend's soul. "The problem isn't Durjay that you are really smart, but that you think others are stupid."

Durjay remained frozen. He wanted to raise his arms and bring his blades forward. Attack him. But it couldn't be done. Something was stopping him.

Krishna left his side and moved away from him and as he did, Durjay began to laugh. And laugh loudly.

"What is it?" Krishna turned, his blue eyes widening.

"You forgot one thing."

"What?"

"I might not be able to kill you, but I could influence others to do so," he smiled. "And from what I remember, you do not have any powers left. You are but a mere human."

And the mist began to clear, the smoke dissipated, and the fog was nowhere to be seen.

So was Durjay.

Krishna remained there, as the bonfire continued to burn. Samva scooted out of the tent, and asked in his sheepish, sleepy voice:

"What happened?"

Krishna was shocked and appalled. He had to be on his toes. Revenge is going to be executed on him now. And the journey has become more perilous than he had anticipated.

"Nothing. Nothing so far," he said in response.

*

They entered the village which could be called a wide market of sorts. There was so much happening around them—from dancing to music to people yelling loudly and selling all kinds of stuff. Bouts of sandy winds would come and bug them, but they all wore head gears to cover their faces.

"This is crowded. How do you plan to find Durvasa?"

"I don't, I plan to find the pupil who was here with Durvasa. This was where the parchment had come from and then travelled to me via the many messengers I have scouted around this island. Saba might know the exact coast from where Durvasa had seen the ore."

"What's the pupil's name?" Krishna asked.

"Saba," he said. "Durvasa had taken refuge under a tree and Saba would come and feed him. Though whatever happened to her, I have no clue."

"Didn't the messenger tell you that?"

"Unfortunately, that messenger of mine died of smallpox," Samva gritted his teeth. "No worries though. We will find Saba ourselves."

Krishna had a hard time moving around, pushed and pulled by people and realising there was no chance he could fit anywhere here. There was so much going on.

His eyes fell on a boy at the bazaar, who was selling jars of curd and butter. Krishna stopped, his pupils dilated.

"I might want to have some replenishment." He stopped and Samva tried to ask him what happened, but he bought the jar and began to eat from it, like he had not eaten in months.

Samva turned to see his old father's lips smeared in curd. "Oh god! You are such a baby."

"I have not had this for a while."

"You haven't had curd at your farm?"

"It's too much hard work," Krishna shrugged.

Samva rolled his eyes.

They moved for one of the huts as Krishna pledged himself to finish the curd. Samva with his hood and iron mask on, went in and asked: "I'm looking for Saba. She's a young girl..."

Then he moved from one hut to another. Krishna moved along with him, and began to get weary and exhausted.

By the time they had reached one of the last few places, they were told that there's a small stable where they might find Saba. So, they travelled to the stable, and when they reached they could see there were no horses there. It was an empty stable. They knocked on the door and waited for someone to come out.

An old man did. With weary eyes and a look of disdain and absolute sadness reeking of it.

"Hello," Samva began, "we are looking for Saba."

"Are you one of them?" The old, bald one said.

"Who them?"

"The bandits," he said.

"Bandits?"

The old man teared up as he said: "The ones who took her away."

And Krishna exchanged glances with Samva as they both realised that their journey had just become worse than they had expected.

13

The fisherman was stunned by what he saw. A child. He had just seen a child in a wicker basket being carried by the water, protected by the tides and the sunlight.

"What the..." his face went pale as he grabbed the wicker basket, almost toppling in the process from his reed boat but somehow holding on to it.

Once he got his wits back, he held the child in his arms under the dusky sky and looked at it. "Dear boy, who are you?"

The boy had blue eyes. And it looked regal. Human almost.

"You are in the wrong land, child." The fisherman smiled. "This is the Rakshasas domain and a human being here is just wrong."

The fisherman had large teeth, and a big jaw, and a bulbous forehead, with dark skin and ferocious looking eyes, but even then he had the kindest and warmest face. He began to drive the boat towards the shore and when he reached, he saw other boats there too, other fisherman, all getting their bounties, all the fish and salmon caught in nets. But he had none.

He just had a baby.

"Everyone! See what I got!"

All the other fishermen had surrounded him as the

fisherman held the baby high and showed it around with love.

"I found a human child."

Everyone was in awe.

And then they began licking their lips.

"Let's cook it!"

"Let's stew it!"

"Let's broil it!"

The fisherman nodded instantly at his peers. He was hungry too. A fish wouldn't satiate him as much as human flesh. And he would love to delve into it, eat it, masticate it.

"Let's prepare all the veggies along with it," he said.

And everyone hurrahed, clapped and rejoiced. The fisherman brought him towards the hut, and as he was moving, he heard someone call out:

"Lad!"

He turned, to see a young Rakshasi with black hair and a long black gown. But the difference was, she had ornate jewellery on her, marking her as royalty. Though she needed no introduction. She was, after all, from the palace that belonged to the eastern king of Rasatala—Shambara.

And he knew who she was. A cook, in fact, the favourite cook of Shambara, who would take care of his huge appetite and would come to the fishermen community and choose the fish herself. She wouldn't go for the adulterated or the bad kinds. They have to be the right ones and she was picky, a perfectionist. She would often be here, choosing the good fish, separating it from the bad.

"What you got there?"

"Maya, come on, it's nothing. It's my find. I don't want to sell it."

"You know how much the king loves infants?" Maya raised her brows. "I am not the one who's going to tell him a lowly fisherman who pays taxes to him is stealing from him too, now is it?"

The fisherman growled. "It's not right. I wanted to eat him."

"That's the point of the class system," Maya came forward and grabbed hold of the child from him. "The rich get everything and the poor get nothing."

And she took the child away, as far away as possible, away from the naked eyes. She wanted to take him to the caravan. She wanted to eat it herself and when she prepared to kneel down, to have it, the child held her fingers tightly and didn't let go. He smiled brightly at her.

Maya looked at him for a while, and then she smiled back. The child chuckled and jerked its hands immediately.

"Who are you, my dear?" Maya asked. "You are in some dangerous territories."

The boy just made a slurping sound and then closed its eyes. Maya took him in her arms, carefully, not letting her long nails touch his brittle body and then held it against her chest.

"I hope you are fine," she said. "I don't think I'm going to eat you right now. I just lost my appetite. But don't you dare think I won't eat you later though."

She chuckled. The boy did too.

He closed his eyes.

*

He opened it.

Pradhyuman was on his bed. Panting. He watched the ceiling. For a while. He turned, looked at his wife. She was dozing too, stinking of alcohol. She had been drinking too much recently. He bit his lips and came on the floor, half naked as he strolled across the room to check on his son.

Anirrudh.

He was there inside of a wooden cradle and Pradhyuman made sure, he was kept close by. Anirrudh was growing fast.

He wanted to wake him up and play with him, but that would just be cruel, wouldn't it? Pradhyuman smiled to himself at this thought and his moment of tranquility was over when he heard a knock on the door.

He knew a knock on the door was only possible if there was something urgent. Pradhyuman walked quickly, so the other two members of the room wouldn't be awakened. When he opened the door, he saw his guardsman standing.

"We have a guest."

"Is he here now?" Pradhyuman smiled.

"Yes, your majesty."

Pradhyuman closed the door behind him, as he walked with his guards.

To meet the architect of Rasatala, and the original Rakshas.

*

Rakshasas were immortals by birth. They couldn't die of old age and Pradhyuman had met all kinds of Rakshasas during his siege at Shambara's palace and when he had defeated and killed that pot-bellied monster.

And Mayasur was the oldest of them. The original Rakshas. But he didn't get the respect that he deserved, unfortunately.

Pradhyuman sat on his throne, allowing Mayasur to be treated disrespectfully by some of his guards, pushed and propelled, while his other guards stood alert. In fact, Durgajyoti was also standing in a corner of the throne as an advisor should. He had thought about appointing her as the Prime Minister, but that would be too sudden.

Mayasur, by the looks of it, was a charming fellow. He had long hair, big eyes and a bulbous jaw like the rest of the Rakshasas. He was wearing a tunic like humans, pants and boots.

"You came," Pradhyuman announced. "Thank you so much Lord Mayasur for approaching us."

"You called me," Mayasur smiled. "And I'm here."

"Oh, please. You were found in a tavern drunk. Ever since you were exiled from Rasatala, stopped by magic to not enter, you have been dilly-dallying around Krishna because you got asylum here."

"They should not be treating their elders like this," Mayasur shrugged, his voice shaking. Once upon a time, he was a majestic man but now dusted by time. This is what immortality does to people.

"An elder who made some very questionable entry gates leading to a lot of enemy reinforcements coming and destroying them."

"Well..." he shrugged. "In all fairness, I was not given time. Are you just here to make me feel bad?"

"Not really," Pradhyuman came off his cushion and walked downstairs from his elevated throne, as he moved towards the scraggly old man, circling him. "I'm questioning you about your passion project."

"What?"

"Myths were told about it."

"What is it?"

"Mayasabha."

Mayasur growled. "That's not real, unfortunately. Myths as you said, your majesty."

"Indeed, but I don't believe so. I feel that's where the source of Maya lives. What gives all you Rakshasas the power."

Mayasur darted at Pradhyuman. "What is on your mind? Burn the light inside of every Rakshas?"

"If that's what'll get me Maya, sure."

"It's impossible to go through it. Mayasabha is impenetrable."

"That's not your concern," Pradhyuman smiled. "You will be awarded generously—money, gold, palace, women what do you need?

Mayasur paused. He was uncertain. It was betraying his whole race, his entire bloodline.

"You have already given up too much. You can live your life here with riches. And I'm ready to provide you everything."

"What do you want to do with Maya? It's not for human consumption."

"I know. But we are not ordinary mortals."

"Mayasabha...it...it has too many illusions, it tests you and it confuses you and it'll break you. Only the strong will survive. And get it."

"I know. And I *am* strong," Pradhyuman cited. "I will get it myself. And I will break through every prison for it."

Mayasur clenched his jaw and squared his eyes with the king of Dvarka. "You are serious, aren't you? Oh, by the blades of Raavan, I can tell you, but umm..." he swallowed a lump, "Fine, I'll tell you."

"And your price?"

"Nothing." He shook his head.

"Why?"

"Because I want to live a life where I know I had to do this because I had no choice," he said. "And because you will kill me if I don't."

Pradhyuman tapped his shoulders. "Smart man. Age does bring maturity, I believe. And foresight too, though I would have tortured you and then done the needful. But alas, you can inform my general about it. Thank you so much."

The guards came and took him away.

Pradhyuman walked towards Durgajyoti."What do you think?" The people in the room had dispersed and only the soldiers remained.

"I think you did a fine job of threatening him."

"Wanted to be theatrical. I have to thank father for this," Pradhyuman smiled flashing his perfect set of teeth. "If he wouldn't have given Mayasur asylum, I wouldn't have been here. Talking to him."

Durgajyoti smiled.

"Walk with me."

Then they strolled across the palace and the back entrance—with the guards following them—discussing their strategy, their plan and how to go about it. Their eyes fell on the big elephant structure that was being built. An elephant made of wicker, bamboo and wood.

"This is the gift of all gifts," Durgajyoti said.

"I hope this works," he responded. "But tell me something."

"Yes?"

"If it doesn't work out, me going there to Mayasabha, I want you to go."

"Why?"

"Because you should not stop for anyone. You have to go all out and get it. You have to get it for the kingdom and what we fight for. In front of my mother, I go weak. But I want you to be strong there," Pradhyuman held her by the shoulders. "I hope you wouldn't stop, if something happens to me."

"Nothing will happen to you. You are the strongest warrior to ever live."

"I hope so," Pradhyuman smiled. "But you didn't promise me."

Durgajyoti blinked. She was a little taken aback but nodded. "Yes, I'll go. No matter what."

14

He was surrounded by enemies.

Balaram knew wherever he would go, he would be surrounded by the ones who stand against him and his ideals. And he had no idea how to fight it. The days after knowing Yudhajit's involvement with the Ledger made him realise that any day someone could come and take him away. The paranoia was getting to him. Worse, he knew one of his close comrades was the Ledger. But which one? Both seemed nice. Both seemed trustworthy. Could the Vitihotra play with his mind? It could be.

And speaking of mind, he was dreaming again. Of the snake. The snake wouldn't talk this time. It would just stand like a giant reptile in front of him and hiss. The shadows would go bleaker and so on and so forth.

He didn't speak to Yudhajit too. He would act normal. And seeing Yudhajit behave that way, Balaram didn't realise what he had in mind. Were they just holding him off? Playing with time? Not letting him leave. Was he in a cage but had no awareness of it?

Balaram knew that the only way to know about the Ledger and escape from there, was to offer them an escape. If this was a cage he was living in, the Ledger would say no to him. Disagree that they should not leave. They are safe and they should wait.

He had packed his bags in secret and arranged a chariot for the night. But before that, he made his way to his two comrades.

Starting with Akoorji. When he reached, he saw Akoorji was feeding swans at the backyard of the courthouse that was given to him. The flourishing scenery of lush greenery was around them, as the solid snow cascaded on the ground. The cotton cherry plants were surrounding them, and the white clouds were hovering over them. The sound of the swans, and the bread falling in the water as they nibbled from it was only accompanied with the soft hum that Akoorji made.

"What's that?" Balaram asked, with a drape over his arms and across his bulky chest. "The sound you are making?"

"Never heard me do that?" Akoorji turned, his ponytail and his white beard glistening like the snow he stood on.

"Never."

"A lullaby to the daughter who died too early." His voice softened but didn't explain much.

"I didn't know about the lullaby," Balaram patted him, also keeping in mind that he could be the Ledger.

Akoorji had lost one of his daughters to cholera. It was long before the gift, and while Krishna could have saved her, he chose not to play with the element of death. He can't stop death. He can't prevent it.

"When Krishna didn't allow your daughter to live again, what was it like?"

"I understood," Akoorji said. "Like a loyal servant, I did. I have always supported him. He was right. We are no one to decide who comes and who goes in and out of this world."

"But then he turns around and gifts all the Yayatis the power of life?"

Akoorji was silent.

"Doesn't that anger you?" Balaram chided.

"No. Lord Krishna knows when he wants to do something and when not to."

"Sounds hypocritical to me," he said. Balaram wanted to play around, check his reactions, see if Akoorji was with Pradhyuman and the Ledger, but the old man had a faint smile on his face. "I still remember when Kans had asked me to get him, to participate in a festival of bows. I was told specifically that he's being brought so Kans could kill him, after learning that Krishna was his nephew. I was there to support my chief but when I came across the boy, who radiated with brilliance and charm—I was awestruck, and ended up supporting Krishna over Kans. That boy who became a man had never looked down on me, accepted me and forgave me. When I stand with you Bala, I see him. I see the fact that you both stand for the same ideals and I will protect and fight by those ideals as the sun sets."

Balaram bit his lips and cursed under his breath. With those words of brilliance and sweetness, Akoorji was in fact showing himself as too nice, too loyal and too much of everything. Balaram closed his eyes and muttered to Lord Shiva to give him the foresight to see who the Ledger was and then with a pat on Akoorji's back, he left the place.

To visit his wife. Whose chances seemed slim now.

*

Revathi was holding the bow the right way and looking across the horizon at the aim boards which she planned to hit the reed arrows with. She pushed her foot back and looked in front—then she shot it. It went across the wind and stabbed the board.

Balaram walked forward, with his hands behind him. There were other archers on the field, doing the same, working towards the same goal. His face was impassive. "Your frame was tough, but you need little work on your position."

"Don't play with me, boy," she winked. "I know whatever I do is good. How's it going?"

"I plan to leave," he said.

"Where?"

"To the Andhaka's," he said.

"But why? Aren't you planning an alliance with Yudhajit?"

"I have my reasons," he said. "Plus, I've not met Satyaki and I'm hoping to meet him. He's not been here, and this escapade has not been fruitful. We have been going in circles and I feel I need to be more proactive."

"Satyaki has gone on a trip, hasn't he?"

"I doubt that. I think he's been exiled, or worse—he has left this place for some other reason. Now Satyaki's marriage with Devademma's daughter is at peril. I don't know what to do."

Revathi arched her brows. "Do what's right. You always know what the right thing to do is."

"Do you think I'm doing the right thing?"

"Of course, you are."

Balaram held her firm fingers and held them tight.

"Were you okay with the fact when Krishna made us all invincible?"

"Yeah, of course."

"Barring our children."

She paused. "Yes, it was fine. It was totally understandable." She spoke these words but there were a lot of jerks in her statement. When Krishna had given the power, it worked in such a way that it affected everyone who was there on the island of Dvarka. But Balaram's two children were outside, growing up in Hastinapur, leading them to be like a mortal and not invincible like those who were there in Dvaraka. Revathi asked Krishna to give them the same power, but Krishna declined. He couldn't do so because he had exchanged his own powers in order to make others powerful. Now he had none. Revathi didn't believe him. They had a fight. Those were the final days before Krishna exiled himself.

There were many secrets around Dvarka. Balaram had tried to find him on multiple occasions, but always in vain. He knew his brother. If he wanted to be found, he would.

"All right."

"Should I then go with you?"

"No, I'll leave." He kissed her on the forehead, realising both his comrades had motives but as per the law, he trusted his wife more. She was his family. Akoorji was the one who protected family. "I'll try to find more about Satyaki from Devadhemma. I'm pretty sure her spies would get something, correct?"

"Perhaps. What should I say to Yudhajit?"

"Went out hunting alone. Loves to wrestle some lions!" He chuckled.

"Oh, come on that was just one time." She rolled her eyes.

And they kissed each other.

*

Balaram's chariot was waiting. He didn't inform any of the maids, the handmaidens, the slaves or the soldiers. He moved forward quickly, darting like a pelican, mounting the chariot, telling the rider to quickly move ahead. The chariot did so at the command and the sound of the hooves were heard in the silence of the night. Balaram had no idea what he would talk to Devadhemma about, but he knew he would be able to convince the barbarian. She was a savage, and he had been part of jungle life for a while. When Balaram and Krishna were young, they used to hunt Asurs sent by Kans using black magic. It was fun. He had learnt a lot through these journeys, risking his life.

Balaram decided to close his eyes and take a quick nap, when he was jutted out of sleep and he could hear a distant shrilling sound of the chariots collapsing, the horses neighing and him falling on the ground. As he opened his eyes, he could see the fog, and a darkness around him, forming.

Not again.

From the smoke, came out the Vitihotra. In white armour. But this one had a different helmet, a different design over it, painted in blood. He couldn't make out what it was but Balaram stood on his feet, with the help of his staff.

I'm going to fight this time.

The Vitihotra came forward with its blade and Balaram nudged and dodged, jabbing the staff right against the Vitihotra's breastplate. It fell on the ground, and as they began to stand up, it swung it across Balaram's feet, he somersaulted backwards pushing the staff right against the helmet of the Vitihotra, confusing him. The Vitihotra made a growling sound and instantly darted towards him, attacking him with full fury and toppling him on the ground. Balaram tried to punch him on the face, breaking the helmet and shoving his fist against the iron, denting it, and bloodying his hands in the process.

The Vitihotra fell on the side, moaning, and Balaram came on top of him and smacked him hard, pushing the helmet off his face and revealing the intricacies of the dead man. Yes. It was definitely a dead man, rotten skin and skull, with worms all over it. It was like the armour hid a powerful deceased man. But who was he? What are these Vitihotras? The ones who return from the dead in the ghastliest manner possible.

Balaram tried to squeeze his throat and tried to choke him, as the storm of mist and smoke began to spiral around them in the most abysmal manner.

And then the Vitihotra held him back and lifted him, lifting himself in the process. He held Balaram tightly, its eyes with golden hue looking back at him, with power, with greed and with horror. Balaram tried to escape the mighty man's grasp, but it was getting tough, and he was punching and kicking him, but he could feel the life being squeezed out of him.

He saw the Vitihotra's powerful arms reaching for the fallen blade, the only other imaginable thing that could kill a Yayati...

When all of a sudden something happened.

A quick figure stunned both of them, entering through the thick clout of smog and smoke. His long hair and his fair, handsome face reminded him of someone, but Balarm couldn't place a picture in all the pain and agony he was undergoing at that moment. The figure smacked the Vitihotra with the help of his big stallion and as the Vitihotra fell on the side, the figure asked for Balaram's hand:

"Giddy up!" He exclaimed. "Before whatever that thing is, rises up again."

Balaram didn't think twice. With a jolt of his staff, he leapt over the stallion and in no time, they escaped leaving the mist behind, breaking through the barriers.

"I had been following you and I had no clue you were followed by whatever that is. Mind filling me in?"

"Assassins, but no clue why they are after me," Balaram lied to the stranger.

"Oh please, don't lie Uncle Bala," he said.

"Uncle? Who are you?"

"Have you forgotten?" He grinned, as they left for the bazaar at the dead of the night. "I'm Satyaki, son of Yudhajit. And I'm here to talk business with you."

15

The old man's name was Jagrat.

Krishna and Samva were not served anything and if Jagrat knew it was Krishna himself in front of him, he would have served the best of feasts. But he was drowning in guilt, with sadness, as they sat in a circle and looked at each other.

"Why do you want to meet her?" Jagrat asked.

"She used to serve a sage here, a rishi," Samva responded.

"Yes, there was something." He shook his head. "I have been asking the soldiers to help me, but no one would."

"Why?" Krishna arched his brows.

"Because they are paid by Putana. Bribing everyone around."

"Putana? The bandit you referred to?"

The old man nodded.

"A woman bandit, interesting," Krishna said. "Kidnapped another woman." Something was afoot and he had no clue about it, but he wanted to know more.

"I am sorry I didn't ask—but who are you? I don't have time to mourn, so please get to the business," Jagrat said.

"I am Keshav," Krishna said, referring to the cowherd

name of his which was given to him when he was a kid. "And this is Samva. We are here to help you."

"Why?"

"Because we are looking for the same person as well," Samva added, lying. "Gut her up and take her bounty to the cattle farmer who has hired us, so we search for her."

"She's powerful, a worthy adversary." Jagrat's eyes lit with hope. "And no one can take her down. What does an old man and an ugly boy do?" His words were venomous.

Krishna arched his brows. "There's no need to be hurtful, sir. We are here to help you. So can you guide us and tell us where she went?"

Jagrat paused, tearing up. "I'm sorry...I have no control over my actions. It started with dozens of stallions coming, paving the way with a lot of dust around, as they grabbed hold of my horses as well and took Saba with them. By the time, I could react they were hundreds of feet away from me. I began to search all over and I learnt they were close to the northern dunes. I tried to rally people up, my friends, but none of them agreed to join me, afraid they'll be mauled by Putana."

Krishna nodded, feeling sad for the old man. He looked helpless and Krishna as someone who had devoted his life to helping people wanted to do the same in this scenario. "I understand. We will do our best."

Jagrat nodded, though Krishna could see that he didn't trust Krishna and Samva at all. He had already lost hope in them.

Krishna and Samva bid farewell and left the house,

as Samva who was still contemplating said: "Don't you think it's weird that they took the girl? For no reason whatsoever?"

Krishna looked at him with annoyance. "You always have a habit of mistrusting the words of the elders."

He scoffed in defiance. "If they aren't so mysterious with their habits, I wouldn't have to."

"Mysterious? Do you think Jagrat was pretending to be someone he isn't?"

"I'm just saying we can't take everything by face value," Samva protested.

They both looked at each other in frustration and Krishna could see that they could be talking about Jagrat and Saba, but really they were talking about themselves. About how Krishna was never available for Samva, about how things were kept from him, about how he was just treated as a nobody by his own parent who's supposed to nurture and care for him.

"The sun is setting," Krishna said. "I think we should go."

"Sure."

*

Krishna and Samva had taken a desert mule for themselves and travelled across the tracks and dunes, passing through the oasis, the canyons and the endless dark desert where there was no human sign. And for a moment, everything seemed fruitless if it wasn't for the conversations between them where they both wanted to ask each other something, but were refraining from it.

"Why did you ask about Lakshmana?" Samva asked. "That time."

"Just like that."

"You don't ask things just like that," Samva looked at him suspiciously. "You know when she disappeared, I always thought you had a role in it."

"In making her disappear? Gah!" Krishna guffawed. "You don't trust me."

"You have never given me the opportunity to do so."

"I have always taken care of you, boy," Krishna sighed. "You think too low of me."

"Taken care?" Samva wanted to retort, but something was stopping him. "Don't you start on me with this, you hear me?"

Krishna clenched his jaw. He was wrong on his part and saying that was an opportunity for the snake to bite. He bit his tongue. "Fine. I have not been the best of fathers, but I'm glad you are still here. On this foolish escapade, but still you are here. You want to make a difference."

"What a condescending compliment!" Samva groaned.

Krishna couldn't help it. After all, Samva was the boy who had killed one of his wives. Krishna with a heavy heart had turned him into a leper then. He shouldn't have done it, and after that Samva never talked to him. Was he too hard on the boy? He didn't believe so. He was just and fair. But there were nights he would regret that action of his.

They ventured out, in silence, creeping forward, until it was time for Krishna and Samva to take their midnight rest. They were close to the so-called dunes Jagrat had mentioned, but they were still surrounded by endless nothingness and it was getting to their head. They heated up some logs and cooked some stew, and waited. Krishna wrapped a shawl around himself and closed his eyes wondering why he was even there. He wanted to be in the comfort of his house.

His eyes remained closed and the fire continued to burn, the embers falling on the sandy ground, as he went into deep slumber, not letting any of his thoughts trouble him...

And when he woke up...he saw something in front of him. A sword right next to his face.

There was another in front of Samva, and he was awake too.

Krishna had no idea how much time had gone by, but it was still dark and his entire camp was captured by bandits, all in hoods and masks and paints, with their black stallions circling around their small tent.

A woman with half grazed hair, who was holding a spear in her hand asked: "Your booty please?"

"We don't have anything, dear," Krishna tried to play cool.

"Search their tents." the woman commanded. She was young and had feistiness written all over her face.

"You know, I never understood the point of Yayatis killing each other. You all are invincible so..." Krishna shrugged.

"The blade is dipped in wolfsbane, old man." The girl smiled. "You might be alive, but the venom is quite a hurtful deterrence in your life that continues to run."

Krishna was scared, because he was mortal and he knew the poison would kill him too.

"We are in search of Putana," Samva said. "We don't want to hurt anyone. We just want to ask her about something."

"And what business do you have with her?" The girl asked, pointing the spear at Samva now.

"We are looking for a girl she kidnapped. Saba. She has valuable knowledge about something and I need to know that."

"What knowledge?"

"I think I'll speak to Saba regarding that."

"Fine." The girl stood straight and then ordered her men to make Krishna and Samva wear bamboo masks so they couldn't see where they were going.

Everything turned to black after that.

*

By the time the mask was taken off, Krishna was almost hyperventilating. He hated the dark. He didn't like being in it. He opened his eyes to find himself in a dark cave, surrounded by tribal people wearing all kinds of thick clothing and in front of them was a lady with white paint all over her face, her hair dyed purple which was grazed from one end—just like the previous girl. Perhaps it was a way to enter the tribe of bandits. But Krishna noticed that none of them looked like other bandits. They seemed simple. Scavengers, more likely. And the caves, they had long lanes, small spaces to crumple yourself in tiny rooms that housed people. How to escape from here? That was his first question to himself.

"You seek Saba." The girl in front asked, while the

other girl who had kidnapped them was standing next to the throne.

"Yes," Samva added, who was standing adjacent to Krishna.

"This is a nice settlement," Krishna said. "Must have taken you a while to build all of this—Putana, I presume?"

The girl smiled. "Indeed. And who might you be?"

"Keshav. Cowherder," Krishna grinned with charm oozing.

"A cowherd seeks Saba? Why?"

"I think it's best we talk to her," Samva said. "Directly."

"I think it was best to leave you paralysed with poison back where we found you."

Samva and Krishna looked at each other, then Samva said, explaining the situation: "We are doing a favour to her father. He wants her back. And we also have ulterior motives—we want to know about Durvasa. She was his pupil when he came here and we believe she might have knowledge about where he went, because he possesses some important information."

"So much confusion," Putana shook her head.

But Krishna noticed the girl's pupils dilating, the one who was right next to Putana. The girl who kidnapped them. She seemed instantly unconformable with the question.

"Well, it won't be confusing to you…Saba?" Krishna added.

And the girl narrowed her gaze. "How did you know?"

"I have lived a long time to study the eyes of people," Krishna said. "I believe you can answer our question," he paused. "But moreover, answer, why you joined the bandits who kidnapped you."

"Because we are not bandits," Putana added taking offence. "We are a tribe of people who stick by each other. And Saba is stuck with us because of what she went through at her home. Her father was an abuser and a petty man. He used to hit her and trouble her. He used to sell her off to men, to soldiers for good money. We found her when she escaped one day and we offered her help. But she was so afraid, she wanted to show her father she was kidnapped, so it wouldn't be blamed on her. And so we did what we did. We took his mares too."

Krishna clenched his jaw and saw Samva. He was indeed right about the entire charade and Krishna was avoiding this part about him. He wanted to pat his son in the back, if it wasn't for the ropes that bound them and the spears that were close to his nerves.

"I see. I am sorry," Krishna's eyes softened.

"We don't need your pity, old man," Putana stood up from her chair. "You are an intruder and you ask bizarre questions, so I don't think Saba is comfortable with all of this and we want you gone," she said and paused.

"She doesn't deserve to respond to you. She shouldn't." Putana waved her hands and her guards grabbed hold of Krishna and Samva when they began to struggle.

"We just want to know where Durvasa went!" Krishna struggled and he saw Saba wanted to say things, but she was held back by her tongue and by her position within this structure.

But they were not listened to.

Putana shouted: "Take them to the pits. Let them be masticated by our pet."

"Pet?" Krishna turned to Samva.

"Pet?" His son said the same thing.

And they knew they were in deep trouble.

16

Mayavati had been hiding Pradhyuman under the guise that he was her human slave.

Rakshasas were allowed to be exposed to mortals if they were treated inferior, for mortals have treated Rakshasas inferior all their lives. So, slavery of humans was an important commodification.

She used to show to the world that he's doing chores, but in reality she had been teaching him how to fight, how to be strong, passing on knowledge he should possess and plenty of other abilities that he was learning in secret. Mayavati was more of a mother than Pradhyuman could ever have.

But today's lesson was the most important. She was going to teach him about Maya. The young beady eyed boy Pradhyuman was sitting cross-legged when Mayavati brought her fingers together and snapped, leading to a spark.

"Are you excited to learn about magic?" A blue flame rose in her hands and began to make a wavering sound. "Well, here it is. What do you see?"

"Fire." His eyes widened.

"Touch it."

"But I'll burn."

Mayavati brought the flame closer to him. "No, touch it."

He swallowed a lump and let his fingertips reach for the flame, even though it was irking him to the core—when he touched it, traced his fingers around it, he learnt that it was after all—nothing. He felt nothing. There was no burn injury. It was just an...

"Illusion, isn't it?" She smiled. "You just felt an illusion."

"But how?"

"Maya. The greatest source of magic that persists across the Rakshas clan. We are illusionists, born from the breath of Lord Brahma who ended up eating their own creator," she smiled.

"Can I learn this?"

She made the flames vanish. "Unfortunately, it's only for those who are Rakshasas."

He made a sad face, contorting it.

"But I can teach you a little more about it."

"What's the point of learning something you can't execute?" Pradhyuman asked.

She smiled, her black lips glimmering in the light of the dim candles. "Because knowledge is the greatest strength you can ever have. Not magic."

*

"When will you stop drinking?" Pradhyuman asked.

She and Rukmavati were sitting in the porch of their palace, while the beautiful wooden elephant was in the process of being built. It was almost close to completion.

Rukmavati with her drunken haze, grinned: "You know why?"

"No, I don't."

"Well, you have a pretty solid live example out there in front for you to see."

"What do you mean?" He arched his brows.

"You are here doing all this to get your mother, and your entire life has been dedicated to her." She shrugged. "After a while, you realise you are with a man who has devoted his entire life to someone else and you are just a theatre prop in the corner of the room for him."

Pradhyuman clenched his jaws. He sipped his wine and didn't say anything. He didn't agree with her at all, though. He knew he was not at all hung up on Mayavati but he cared for her well-being. But he wanted to get Maya, the source of all magic and illusions. And this elephant was the perfect gateway.

"Don't think I care about what you think. You are not at all right and you know that." Pradhyuman said. "I bear with you because you are the mother of my child, otherwise you would be ostracised from here."

"And hence I drink, ladies and gentleman." She took another swish of wine and drank like it was water. "And also that bitch...what's her name? Durgajyoti? She's a home-wrecker too."

"What do you mean?"

"You squeeze her around you even though you know she wants to rip your clothes apart."

"She's my confidante and I need one after Balaram left me in the dark."

"Sure you do."

Pradhyuman shook his head. His distaste for his wife was a usual scenario. They would often go on just ranting about what they didn't like about each other. He was about to say something worse when they were interrupted by Durgajyoti. She was sweating and she looked concerned, breaking past the gates and the guards, who were running behind her as she staggered towards their open porch. Pradhyuman's jaws clenched when he saw her and he asked:

"What happened?"

"We have a slight problem," she said.

"What is it?"

"The bloody old man..." Durgajyoti said, cursing under her breath. "He let the Rakshasas know what we are up to. The portal has opened and a band of Rakshasas have entered."

Pradhyuman immediately stood up, knowing what to do. He didn't wait around. He went to call his squire and got himself prepared for the battle. He didn't speak to Durgajyoti because he knew he was embarrassed in this situation. He wanted to say his plan was fool-proof but it wasn't.

And now he had to face the brunt for it.

*

The gates in front were barricaded, but the siege was happening. There was a large illusionary kind of a weapon created of siege engines with which they were trying to break through. There were hundreds and hundreds of Rakshasas and they were yelling and howling.

By the time Pradhyuman in his golden armour had reached, all his men were afraid. Dealing with Rakshasas forthright in such a short notice when they weren't prepared at all was a problem.

But Pradhyuman knew he had to do something before things got even worse. And also, the truth of the matter was, that their fight against the Rakshasas was futile because they knew Yayatis can't be killed, but they can be ingested. And Rakshasas were man-eaters. Pradhyuman knew he didn't want to be a meal, so he ordered:

"Cavalry, make your way further down south, attack when the drums begin to beat. Archers, steady your aim, they are about to break through the gate. We are going to have a hellfire of problems..."

And before he could complete, the gates broke and instantly hordes of monsters began to enter, attacking their people, gnawing their way through. They began to rip the Yayatis' heads off using their talons and their long, incisive teeth to jut themselves inside their flesh and feed on them.

Pradhyuman brought his sword forward and on his chariot he made rounds, using his sword he attacked the Rakshasas one by one, ripping their heads off when instantly a spear flew across the sky and went through the rafting wind and stabbed Pradhyuman in the chest. He was flung back, breaking through the chariot and on to the ground. He was stuck there, feeling the pain when he began to pull the spear out of him and as he did, he felt the pain getting even worse than he had expected.

And he finally threw away the spear, coming on his feet with the strength he had left and his teeth grinding as the two Rakshasas came around him amidst the war cries, the dirty grounds and the sound of clanging metal.

Pradhyuman rolled over, grabbing the spear with the blade having his blood written on it and swung it across the air, jabbing one of the Rakshasas, while the other came towards him and he lurched on him with full force and might—stabbing him in the head. Pradhyuman's strength lay in his ability to be athletic and really flexible. He was quick too.

As more Rakshasas came forward to attack him, he moved with grace, attacking them back with the weapons at his disposal—all the daggers and knives that he was carrying until...

A net fell on him.

Long cobweb-like net that flapped over him as if he was a prey for the Rakshasas. But he was indeed their food. They instantly nailed the net to the ground, while they began to circle around him, laughing at the hunt that they had just made. Pradhyuman was feeling frustrated as he was trying to tear open the net, but it was made of something strong. His muscles were flexing, but he was not able to rip it open at all.

"Finally got the king of Dvarka on his knees." One of the Rakshasas guffawed. "Imagine how our king would feel."

Pradhyuman didn't know the Rakshasas had a new king. He was under the impression there were several small chiefs who now worked independently and Mayavati was one of the elder Rakshas who would consult these chiefs for she lived the longest.

"You thought we won't find out. The Lokpala owes

us big time." Another Rakshas hissed, blaring the teeth. "We have exchanged our secrets with him, in abundance. He has stories to now live with for a long, long time."

Pradhyuman arched his brows. "Who's your new king?"

"You'll know soon. You'll meet him." They both grinned.

And while Pradhyuman would have loved to listen to them gloating about how they caught him, his men got hold of them first and they clashed, while Pradhyuman rushed through the parts where the nails were dug in and he began to pull those out with his might, leading all four-nailed parts to come out and he was free again.

He grabbed hold of a fallen blade and instantly reached out to the nearest Rakshas, stabbing them in the head. By the time the Rakshas fell, he saw his men had managed to gather enough forces of the cavalry, who were using ropes and pulling the bridge up, while fighting with the men too. The archers with fire arrows were burning most Rakshasas and they were retreating too.

Pradhyuman stormed in front, breaking through the shields and the spears, moving with swiftness as he reached the gate and grabbed it with both his arms trying to push it along with the rest of the crew.

"One...two...three—haiyahh!" And he yelled loudly, leading the gate to come on top and fit right where it's supposed to be.

"Kill the rest." He scowled and yelled, leaving the leftover Rakshasas to face his fury. A smile appeared on his face. "I suppose, it is them we are having for dinner tonight."

And his men shouted in enthusiasm, as they began to spill the blood, flesh and organs of their enemies.

*

Pradhyuman was pressing on his wounds, for a while, as he sat in a corner of his room, a private study which he kept for just himself. He was angry with himself. He lost so much manpower over a stupid elephant and now he lost men in the process of making himself strong. He should have not trusted the Lokpala. He should have not trusted anyone. When thinking about this, his thoughts went back to his father who had taught him that in life people often disappoint you.

So never expect from them. Never trust them. You are born alone and you go alone.

Pradhyuman had taken this to heart. After all, his father won the greatest of wars and he was a brilliant tactician. He would often miss his father and a tug would occur in his chest, but he wouldn't say anything. When he was disappointed and defeated, he would come to this room and feel dejected.

"How do you feel?" A voice came.

Pradhyuman turned to see where it came from, breaking away from the thoughts and almost feeling vulnerable. He could see in the shadows, someone was standing. But how did that someone enter?

"What is the greatest illusion ever performed?" The voice of the woman asked and he immediately recognised it.

Pradhyuman was sweating and he was feverish from

the wound on his chest. "To convince the world that there's a war, when there is none."

"Exactly." The woman came out of the shadows. "Hello, son."

"It's you." He looked at his mother Mayavati and felt absolutely numb. He had felt like this after a long time. "How come...wait...attacking me was just a distraction. You wanted to get to me."

"Sneaky, yes."

"Why?"

She smiled. Her black lips glimmering. "You'll know." She spread her black robes and Pradhyuman could see a new world being wide opened. He was immediately drawn to it, and its energy.

"What is this? What are you doing?"

"I am sending you to your trial," she smiled.

And then the light that emanated from her robes became too bright and he was sucked into it, finding himself in absolute darkness.

17

The snake was yet again seen. In his dreams.

But this time it was further from him, in its shape and size of the ten-headed demon, making coils and rolling over on the ground. There was another man Balaram could see who was standing in the further side with chestnut brown hair and brown eyes like the bark of a tree. He had the same look as that of Balaram's on his face. Confused.

"What are you doing here?" He asked. The man in front of him.

"What are you doing here?"

"I'm always here."

"What do you mean?"

"The world will end, but we will not perish."

At that moment, the ten-headed snake began to circle around and look at Balaram, darting its irises at him.

Balaram almost felt threatened. "Why wouldn't we perish?"

But the snake swallowed the man who voluntarily agreed to be swallowed, letting them be one, as the snake replied: "Because we are infinite. Unleash me…"

"No…" Balaram cursed. "I don't know what you are."

"You."

"What me?"

"I am *you*."

Balaram woke up. Sweating, as he did whenever he had these kind of dreams, frustrated at his own anguish. He was on a rickety bed, before coming on his feet. Fighting the Vitihotra had taken a toll on him and he had slept for a long time. But the most interesting part was that he had met Satyaki, Yudhajit's estranged son in the process.

"The sleeping darling is here, uncle," he could hear the footsteps and he looked up to see the ever-beaming Satyaki, "How was it? Had fun?"

"What is going on?"

"You are exhausted." He patted him on the shoulder and sat next to him.

Balaram took his time to scan his environment and he could see he was close to the entrance of a cave where there were many armour-wearing men and women, with stew in pots and soup being served. The place was huge and there were many people, all in silence and all taking care of their own—be it their infants or their older kids. It looked like a dirtier, grislier land from the one he had just come.

"Where am I?"

"A settlement..." Satyaki's playfulness dropped, "of rebels."

"Rebels?"

"Against my father," he grinned.

Balaram pressed his forehead and massaged the back of his bald head, as he continued to look further. "How did the Vitihotra know about my location?"

"Father, of course."

Yes. He had been dealing with the Ledger. The Ledger works with Durgajyoti and so forth. Balaram instantly panicked about Akoorji and his wife Revathi, though he wasn't sure which one was the Ledger among them. But he was still concerned for them. He knew Revathi, who he trusted more, was in fact capable of taking care of herself.

"So that's why you didn't attend our dinners. You had been planning a coup."

"Far from it. I had been taking care of them," Satyaki said. "All of these people who had been tortured by my father. Sometimes I wonder whether Uncle Krishna's gift was a curse or not, because he allowed people to hurt other people and not let them have the peace of death given to them."

Balaram had often thought about it himself. His brother used to do things based on questionable ideas. He had sided with Arjun, instead of Karna even though Karna was right on certain parts.

"You are doing a good thing," Balaram said. "But whatever happened to your father. Why has he become like this?"

"Because earlier he had the power of Yayati, draining life out of people and now he has the power of not getting killed. In short, he's immortal. He'll never die, which will lead to him becoming an absolute powerful ruler."

Balaram could see the genuineness in his voice but still his heart didn't allow it to be accepted.

"I am just so confused."

"Why?" Satyaki arched his brows.

"It doesn't sound like him."

"What?"

"Yudhajit." Everything else too. Him being with Durgajyoti, knowing the Ledger, sending the Vitihotra and now this...he had a rebellion under his nose led by his son.

"I doubt it. I think he's being framed. I know Yudhajit. I have known him ever since we were children, and this doesn't sound like him."

Satyaki chuckled incredulously. "Well, uncle, then I have something to show you."

Balaram got confused; flustered almost.

"Hope you are feeling dandy, because you are coming with me on a ride."

*

Balaram had been travelling for a while on a cart, along with Satyaki and two of his soldiers. They were being driven by a mule and all of them were wearing large hoods that covered their heads so Yudhajit's men wouldn't see them. They passed through the narrow, snow crusted lanes as the morning became purplish in colour and the howl of eagles were heard in the distance.

"How much does your father know?"

"He knows I don't like him."

"But not this? That you are outright performing treason?"

He didn't answer, but just grinned at Balaram. He had a handsome face and he had these spectacularly bushy brows, wavy hair in the back like that of Pradhyuman, just a little shorter.

"Where are you taking me?" Balaram asked again but got no response. He held on to his staff, wondering why it was not taken away from him yet.

"There's something you need to see," Satyaki said. "We had been eyeing a village for a while now. What we do is we rescue those who are in need of help."

"And then what's the plan? Just keep doing good?"

"At least I'm trying."

Balaram remained quiet. As they neared the village, his eyes widened in shock as he saw what was going on. Outside the rims of the perfect kingdom of the Vrishnis, he could see multitudes of women and men being chained against chariots and moving their slavers and landowners in chariots, while many others were nailed to the ground or the walls of their house. There were soldiers of Yudhajit who were flogging some of the other villagers.

"Why is it like this?" Balaram asked, as they stood in a corner and then crouched to remain hidden.

"Because they paid their taxes late. Rebelled, so to speak." He shook his head. "Father has to make sure the money keeps coming from the poor."

Balaram clenched his jaws. Was this really true? Were inhuman treatments being meted out by Yudhajit? He couldn't believe it.

"The Vrishnis come from the blood of Krishna. My blood." Balaram shook his head. "I can't believe this is happening."

"We have become degenerates over a period of time," Satyaki responded. "Our redemption must be met."

"So, this rebel army you are forming is the redemption for the Vrishnis?"

"Perhaps. Perhaps not." He seemed confused, as if he wanted direction and clarity but he wasn't cutting a popular figure. "In all this time, you hadn't asked me why I saved you. I could have let the Vitihotra take hold of you. No. But I did because I need someone older, someone wiser. I need guidance. I need a plan. A strategy. I have the brawns but I'm quite a whack when it comes to ideas." He looked the other way.

Balaram, before even discussing, began to get ideas. He had something in mind he wanted to execute but his emotions didn't allow him to hurt Yudhajit. He couldn't help himself into forming opinions against his friend. But then all the evidence pointed against him, and Balaram knew that he had to do something about it. And while his thoughts began to meander he began to feeel lost for a moment, he saw a young woman trying to run away with her infant, away from the cruelties and towards them, where they were hiding in the snow. The soldiers were running behind her, some of them sprinting on their stallions...

"She got the ration! She stole it!" The soldiers yelled and scowled.

Balaram didn't wait, as the woman came closer, he stood in front and the woman went past him, confused about who he was. He had his staff in his hand and he stood as a wall between her and the soldiers. The sun was setting in the background, and they all looked at each other and then at Balaram, whose face was impassive.

"Leave her alone."

"Who are you?" One of the guards with a betel leaf in his mouth spat it on the ground, letting the redness smear across the snow. "We don't like no intruders."

"I am not the intruder. I belong here." He smiled.

Along with him, Satyaki and his two soldiers also stood, ready to fight them.

"Come at me," Balaram scorned.

And Yudhajit's men didn't relent. They instantly made a rush for him, storming towards them. Balaram had little time to prepare himself, but he limped and swung his staff against one of the incoming guards, smashing him against the ground, while the other soldier came from behind and grabbed Balaram tightly, loosening the fists around his staff. He felt frustrated and angry, but then he remembered the days when he used to wrestle and he shoved himself in the back, pushing the soldier on the ground. The entire process took him some time, but he was able to do so, and the first thing he did after freeing himself was smashing the soldier's face, breaking his collar bone and his nose.

Balaram then went to search for his staff, scampering against the bloody ground of unconscious soldiers. By then, his eyes fell on Satyaki and his men fighting hard, but Satyaki was dealing with it with his sword and was getting overpowered by a soldier. Balaram moved forward and like a mountain and came in between, letting the attacks of the sword rain on him while he deflected it with his staff and jutted the top part of the staff inside the face of the soldier. He wouldn't die, but he would live the rest of his life an ugly man.

Balaram saw Satyaki had fallen on the ground again, the melted snow covering his clothes, as Balaram brought his hands forward. Satyaki grabbed him and pulled himself up.

"Thank you for the kind help, uncle. We should leave before the others come. Our scouting has been done and my team would prepare for an offensive now." He paused, looking at Balaram's confused gaze, contemplating. "But most of all, I brought you here to be convinced, to lead me, to help me."

Balaram nodded. He looked at the scared girl and the infant, who were hiding behind the tree now, ready to find a new home for themselves. "I have an idea."

"What?" Satyaki narrowed his gaze, reeking of curiosity.

"What do you think of..." he paused, "allying yourself with the Andhakas?"

18

Samva didn't like this place. He was afraid.

For it was dark. It was empty.

He was sitting in a cell with his father and the silence between them was brewing. And it had been hours. He wanted to tear through the cell, but all his weapons had been taken away. For that matter, even his father had given up and was dozing like an old man. He was looking around the cage, he was in a small room lit by fire lamps all across the room as well as the lanes, the little caves that they had built for themselves. Samva had seen a few ladders going up somewhere while he was pushed around the cage, and he knew those were the exits.

But he was unable to find out about Durvasa and where he had seen the Eraka's ore. His passion was to burn the entire Yayatis race for their karma. They should die, he thought.

Samva turned to his father and he was silent. There was so much between them, but he couldn't confess. It was not that he didn't want to, it was just that he was afraid he wouldn't be believed.

"What are you thinking, boy?" Krishna asked, now awake. He asked with his eyes closed.

"How did you know?"

"I used to be quite good at these things." He said mundanely. "Now I'm rusty."

"Nothing. Just about how things would have been so much better if you hadn't given the Yayatis this unlimited power."

"We all make mistakes," Krishna sighed. "Didn't know they would exploit it."

"Yeah," he said. "You made one too many, you know."

"What do you mean?"

Samva didn't want to talk about the entire leprosy episode. So, he remained quiet.

Samva ignored him and he looked outside, with his hands dangling from the spaces between the cell doors. He waited for a while, hoping someone might come and as he turned back about to give up, he saw a shadow crawling in the corner of the cage, right outside. He swivelled his head to see the shadow forming and from the corner appeared Saba, with her grazed haircut and confused eyes.

Samva didn't say anything to her. She took uncertain steps and came close to the cage.

"How do you know Durvasa?" She asked. The first thing.

Samva turned to Krishna, who was still leaning against the wall, lying down, being casual.

"We have heard of him. A great, scary Guru," Samva explained, though it was not sufficient. "But he has a habit of learning a lot over a period of years. An immortal sage."

"Indeed. A great man," Saba said. "A refuge for me

during the times of my tyrannical father. When he left one day, I was left ashtray and then Putana found me." Her eyes shrivelled, her voice cracked. "Those were the days I was not happy."

Samva wanted to comfort her, but he was not sure why she was here. "When you heard Durvasa, you were taken aback."

"Those who seek him, are the ones I feel have a great purpose," she said. "He said to me actually. He said always lead the ones to me who want to find me. I never thought that day would come."

Samva raised his brows. "Did he ever talk about the Erakas?"

She nodded. "Amongst many things, Eraka was the one thing he was sure talking about—an indestructible additive to the world of weapons. Once used on any blade…it could make you kill anyone, anything."

"So, it's not an ore?"

"No." She shook her head.

"Where is it? Where did he see these Erakas?"

"I don't know about that." She paused. "But I do know where he went after here. He was talking about it a lot. To find peace. To find tranquility."

"Where was it?"

"Antar Dvipa." She arched her brows. "But why do you seek this information?"

That was the moment, Krishna came on his feet and came close to the cell gates. "What did you just say?" His voice went dark and brusque.

"Antar Dvipa."

Krishna's face went pale.

Samva looked at him. "You know about it?"

"Of course." He shook his head. "It's the first land I found when I wanted to escape from Jarasandha. But it was small, so I found an alternative, though I made that a trade port. But I removed it a long time back, to harbour someone...something." His voice was quiet.

"What was it like there?"

Krishna didn't respond. He was just shaking his head in defiance. "Why did he go there? What was the purpose? What was there?"

Saba couldn't respond to that. She herself didn't know of it. Samva meanwhile turned to her. "So to find the location of the Erakas, we need to find the man."

Saba nodded. "But I don't think you can. Putana doesn't like intruders and I think she will be pretty hard on you all."

"Can you help us escape?"

"I am a part of this brethren. Even though I divulged the information, I followed what my sage said. But I do not have any loyalty or love towards you, so no I can't."

"We are trying to do the right thing!" Samva cried.

"Aren't we all?" Saba disappeared from the back...

At that very moment the guards arrived, not noticing her who had just escaped. They opened the gates of the cell and pushed Samva and Krishna out.

"Putana would like to see you."

*

Krishna was pushed and prodded ahead, as the court of guests had gathered. The room was small and the air was thick with sweat. He could see all the bandits, in the corner grinning, while Putana sat on her makeshift throne, enjoying herself. He wanted to show his Shrivatsa symbol, but he was afraid it would get unnecessary attention. He wanted to keep at it. He also could see many holding jars of ale and cups of wine. They were drinking and they wanted to see a spectacle of the guests.

"We had been thinking what to do with you two." Putana began, as Krishna was pushed on the side of Samva. "And we decided it was best to have a duel. Then we thought with whom? We had few creatures of the dark ready to shoot at you but then it wasn't that interesting."

"Then what is it?" Krishna asked with a blank face. He wasn't feeling too good after he came to know about Antar Dvipa. He didn't want anything to do with that place. There were too many bad memories associated with it and he wanted to stay away from it.

But now, he had to go. The curiosity was burning as to why Durvasa went there.

"Fighting each other." Putana clapped, and instantly Krishna's and Samva's iron chains began to unclasp and fall down with the help of the soldiers who handed them swords, one for each of them. "One gets to leave tonight, one gets to stay here with us and be treated as a pet since we can't be killed."

"I'm not much of a sword person," Krishna said casually.

"Well, you don't have a choice," Putana groaned. "Should we start?"

Samva turned to Krishna, as Krishna asked: "Do you have a plan?"

Samva shook his head.

"I can't do it," Samva said.

"Is that your plan?" Krishna asked and then he whispered to Samva. "I want you to leave. Fight me. Defeat me and then let me stay here."

"No, you are coming with me," Samva shook his head. "We will find a way."

"There's no way. Let me lose and give up."

"You will lose, father," he said. "You just think I won't defeat you, is it so?"

"I don't want you to feel bad about it, but you were never a good swordsman."

Samva flared his nostrils. "I have become better!" He clenched his iron sword. "But you won't see it. You always see the worst in me."

Krishna could see he was a tad bit annoyed that Krishna was offering to give up. "See if we fight, I would be able to defeat you and I don't want that."

"You are quite something," Samva said and then he brought the sword forward which Krishna deflected, clanging hard. "You think I can't defeat you so you make me pity win. I have honed my skills."

"We are on the same side, have you forgotten?" Krishna asked, but Samva didn't listen. There was an unreliable rage in him that was bursting open and he brought his sword once more towards him which Krishna deflected. "I think you have forgotten."

Samva came forward and jabbed it close to Krishna, but this time Krishna didn't pity him and turned around, smacking him on the face and toppling him.

"You want me to not be weak on you? I wouldn't. But brace yourself," Krishna scowled.

Samva came on his feet, getting hold of his wits and himself. "I am." And then without a second thought he stormed towards Krishna and threw him down. Cups of ale were drunk at that moment, and the roars of the people around them were getting louder, everyone was hooting and applauding.

Samva was on top of Krishna and he brought his sword close to his father's face. "You have no idea how happy I am doing this. Beating you."

"Why?"

"Because you don't listen to me. You never do."

"About what?"

Samva didn't stop. He went forward to stab him and Krishna used his big arms to stop the blade from piercing his head and basically killing him. "About the fact that I didn't murder your wife because she rejected me and that I was in love with her. It was because she abused me. Day in. Day night. She would make my life worse, and no one would listen. The abuse continued for years and when I couldn't take it anymore, I stabbed the dagger inside her and let her bleed to death. But you didn't listen. I cried. I told you. But you didn't listen. You thought I was lying. You thought I was..." tears were coming out of his eyes, as Krishna had stopped defending himself and the sword went straight towards his father's face...

Only to miss him by an inch.

They remained silent for a while and Samva cried, as he sat in a corner, not letting himself kill his father. Krishna remained where he was, confused.

Samva had almost forgotten there were so many people out there and that there was a fire that burnt in him. He looked around and was feeling deeply embarrassed. He glared at Putana, who had begun clapping.

"Bravo! Love the drama! Just love it." She got up from the throne. "The fight to death amongst the peers is to see whether they push their grudges out and make it their enemy, leading to their downfall. You both didn't. You fought well, not letting your hatred for each other consume you. So, I congratulate you on that and you are free to go."

Samva nodded, wiping the tears but he could hear Krishna saying: "I don't hate him" or perhaps it was him who was imagining those words for he knew his father wouldn't be so kind to him.

As they came on their feet, realising they were getting to pave their way out, Samva saw Saba who nodded at him. They began to move out of the room, in silence...

As the mist began to circle them, more smoke appeared and a slight wheezing sound was heard as if someone's cough had taken too long a time to come. Samva was confused to see so much mist.

"This is not right," Krishna clenched his jaws. "Not right at all."

"What do you mean?"

"Durjay."

The mist began to confuse Putana, Saba and everyone around them, but as they did—it began to infiltrate their noses, instantly possessing them, making crackling sounds and turning their eyes icy blue and their faces stony.

"What is going on?" Samva asked.

"He has possessed them," Krishna said. And he remembered how Durjay couldn't kill directly, but he could influence others to do so. "Draw your weapon. It's time to fight now."

19

Durgajyoti had been in the war room when all of this was taking place. The war room had a balcony on which she stood and saw the events unfold. By the time it was over, and they had won, she was meaning to meet Pradhyuman but he had ventured deep into his study and didn't leave for a while...

Until they found him early in the morning. Sleeping. He couldn't wake up.

Durgajyoti was standing outside his room, waiting like the rest of the people as the doctor inside was taking care of the nitty gritties. She could see the ones who were outside and who were already whispering. There were the councilmen. At the gate, there was Yuyudhana as well. A charming, jet-black-haired man with a scar across one of his eyes where he had a marble put in place of a pupil. Lost it at some war. But as she had heard about him, he was a really good fighter.

"How is he?" She asked him.

Yuyudhana didn't particularly like her because she was considered a witch by many, considered an outsider, but he couldn't show the distaste for he was still a general while she was the queen of the Taljan clan and the leader of the Vitihotras.

"The same. Whatever got him in the battle has really taken a toll."

Arching her brows, Durgajyoti wondered what it was. She had heard rumours—that he was paralyzed, he was poisoned and what not. But something was afoot, she knew. As her chance came to see him, she stormed into the room and saw him lying on the bed, peacefully sleeping with the doctor and his wife Rukmini beside him. The latter didn't bother to even look at Durgajyoti but just patted her husband on the cheek and played with his hair.

"What has happened to him?" She asked the doctor, rather than Rukmini.

"A coma. So deep into the sleep, that he can't wake up now." The doctor wearing a long gown said. "There's no cure. He needs time. And our hope that he would wake up."

The doctor left the room and Durgajyoti remained there in silence, looking at the calm face of Pradhyuman and wondering what went wrong. She gritted her teeth and clenched her jaws in anger.

"Can't you do your black magic to turn this around, witch?" Rukmini spat on the floor. She wasn't in a haze of drunkenness anymore. Just a concerned old wife.

"I don't know what's happened to him." Durgajyoti was trying to call Baagul for guidance and advice but she was not answering him. Durgajyoti knew there was some supernatural phenomenon at work here, because as far as she knew, he was fine till the time he had returned. So, what happened?

"This unnecessary bloodshed took my husband from me," Rukmini said, her voice cracking up. "I don't want it anymore. This ends here. I'm calling a council meeting." And her eyes flared up looking at Durgajyoti, as if she was a threat to her.

Durgajyoti knew she wasn't welcome there, and so she went out of the room, with an impassive face as she realised things weren't going to be the same and the man she trusted would have her back had gone into a deep slumber.

"What happened?" The voice reached her. It was of Baagul.

"Oh, nice of you to show up!"

"You looked stressed, my dear. What is the problem?"

"Pradhyuman. He's fallen ill and I don't understand what is happening," Durgajyoti spoke to herself as she continued to walk the halls.

The voice came from within. "I know what it is. I could feel it in the air."

"What?"

"A Rakshas has taken control of his mind, taken him to the dream world."

"What? Dream world?"

"Yes."

"How to help you?"

"You can't," she said. "All you can do is wait and hope he returns. It's magic beyond us. It's Maya."

Durgajyoti cursed. She wanted to find a way to help him and it was bothering her that she was powerless. Worse, there was a council meeting and she would have to watch out for that as well.

*

The council meeting happened in the common halls and Durgajyoti wasn't even invited. When she heard it has begun, she rushed to it and stood in a corner, not directing any attention towards herself because anything she would do would create unnecessary commotion.

She could see the hall was filled with all kinds of ministers from economy to agriculture and all kinds of senior philanthropists, businessmen, financiers to the crown. There was also the treasurer. In the middle though, was Rukmini, as well as Yuyudhana who was her confidante and helping her.

"We have gathered here during unprecedented events," Rukmini began. "I hope you all are seated and I hope you all know what has transpired recently. My husband, the king of Dvarka, son of Krishna, waged a war against the malevolent Rakshasas. But things went astray really quickly and we won a fallen battle, though with a cost. This morning my husband has been declared in a coma and we have no idea when he will wake up. It could be tomorrow or next week or the month after or ten years down the road."

Everyone spoke to each other, whispering and thumping their tables.

"Now, all I can say is," she said, "that we have to be smart. I want you all to vote against the invasion of Rasatala."

"But isn't it going against our king's words?" One of them asked and Durgajyoti instantly got excited about the fact that someone was defending Pradhyuman's decision.

"It is and I know, but we saw the consequences," Rukmini said. "It wouldn't lead us to anything. We might be invincible, but our resources aren't and as we continue replenishing our resources we would begin to starve and have economic issues leading to worse situations between each other. We should build ourselves first and not destroy others. Self-reflection is an important step to be taken during these unprecedented times."

More murmurs. Whispers.

"So who all are aye to the decision? I ask because I want everyone to be on the same page. I want you all to respect the decision we take and send out a formal apology to the chiefs of Rasatala."

There was some disagreement at those words for Yayatis were a proud race and they didn't want to bow down to anyone. But Rukmini being the queen was powerful. As people began to say aye to the decision, many said nay as well. Though the majority would win, Durgajyoti knew she had to step in at this moment...

"I don't think it's wise to go against King Pradhyuman," she said.

Rukmini turned to her and clenched her jaws. "I don't think you were summoned, Queen Durgajyoti."

"I represent the Taljan clan and we are allies to Pradhyuman. I have a say if I'm allowed."

Rukmini couldn't contest that of course, and Durgajyoti knew that. She came in between, as she began: "Pradhyuman's life has been devoted to us and he wants us to be the most powerful race out there; formidable in its might because when we aren't powerful we will succumb to the routine of the submissions. And I believe submissiveness is not something we adhere to. Pradhyuman knew that and I would suggest even in his slumber, he would wish us to continue this journey to become a mighty force and find Maya, the source of the Rakshasas."

"But we are already too powerful, don't you think?" Rukmini asked. "We don't need more. Greed of indulgence is wrong."

Durgajyoti shook her head, almost scoffing at this part. "I think we should do what our majesty wants. I leave it up to you but I am nay to the decision."

She left the central place, as the decision and the votes were being made. She waited with nail-biting anticipation for the response and at the end, she looked at the votes. Rukmini was grinning when she was counting, while Yuyudhan who stood beside her was quiet and watching Durgajyoti with deep contemplation.

"I think we have a decision," Rukmini announced. "We are offering formal apologies to Rasatala and recanting the decision made by our dear king."

*

Durgajyoti couldn't sleep that night.

Thoughts were racing in her mind for now and she was cushioned well, wondering what to do. She had to find Pradhyuman, pull him out of the dream world or she could find the Maya herself. She remembered his conversation with her and he clearly wanted her to not give up on the Maya no matter what happened. But this was her love, her life. She needed to go out of her way to protect him.

But which was more important? Do what he said or

save him? She knew Pradhyuman was capable enough to save himself. He was the mightiest warrior out there. And while she wrestled around on the bed, she could hear something. She turned around and instantly there was a figure who grabbed her. Her face had a mask on in no time, and her legs and arms were tied up instantly as darkness blanketed her.

She tried to push and pull and move, but the heavy set of hands grabbed her up and made their way somewhere she had no clue about.

All she knew was she was being kidnapped. She tried to wrestle further but to no avail, when someone hit her in the abdomen saying:

"Don't be fussy, lass!"

It was growling.

She flared her nostrils and she knew what to do. She snapped her fingers, channeling Baagul within her and the light flared, the flames burning across the burlap sack that she was in, letting herself out and she fell in the lane. Standing right there were three people, guards under the royal garb who were surprised at this.

"How did you..."

The Baagul in her spoke. "You three did wrong."

And then she shot energies out of her fingers electrocuting the men and instantly paralysing them. She realised she was in a lane that was opening up to the ocean where she would have been drowned and tortured in the water. They had been about to throw her.

She grabbed one of the guards and asked: "Who sent you?" But the man didn't respond. Instead, he was holding something in his mouth that he was about to spit on her, when a silver sheen came out of nowhere and stabbed him in the mouth, spilling blood everywhere as the guard began to cry and moan.

Durgajyoti looked up and saw Yuyudhan, with his silver sword.

"Why did you do that?" She rasped, her fingers bursting energy as her eyes turned yellow of the Baagul colour.

"Because he had a spice bomb in his mouth that would have made you blind," he said. "They were sent by Rukmini."

"Why are you defending me?"

"Because you were right at the Sabha earlier. We should follow what our king said even though he's incapable of sending other orders, I follow what I follow. But not many believe it and not many will follow it. Though the ones who would—will defend this ideal," he explained.

Durgajyoti nodded. "Thank you, general."

"Do you know what's the next step?"

"I do," she smiled. "I do, general."

20

The boar was let loose freely.

It walked and trampled. It was hungry for grass. It moved like a ravine and it roared like a lion. It had long horns and it had the fat skin of a pig. It smelt dirty and it made these wheezing sounds as if it was coughing. It walked across the environment of the blind. The environment of the Andhakas.

*

Balaram was fiercely watching the valley in front of him from the top of the cliff as his eyes darted at the road beyond him. He had to cross the valley to reach the Andhaka territory. As he wrapped his shawl around, and took a deep breath, the fog forming around his mouth, Satyaka came and stood next to him.

"So you want me to ally with our sworn enemies?" Satyaka said.

"Do you have an army?"

He shook his head.

"Then you have no choice," Balaram said. "We need to convince the Andhakas."

"What do you want in return?" Satyaka asked.

"Why do you think I need anything?" Balaram said. "Hasn't my reputation preceded me?"

"It has and thus I ask."

Balaram chuckled. "I want undying pledge towards me when I go against Pradhyuman, if I help you win the crown from your father.

For a moment, Satyaka was quiet, almost stunned. "Look at us. Fighting our cousins, our fathers and our nephews. We have become monsters. Violent inbreds. I'm sure your brother didn't think this through."

"He didn't think through a lot of things," Balaram said. "So, what do you say?"

"Fine. You have my loyalty," Satyaki grinned like a kid.

Balaram nodded. He waited for him to speak, but they solemnly watched.

"But do you know what has recently happened to the Andhakas?" Satyaki asked.

Balaram shook his head.

*

The boar continued to whine and wheel around the trampled snow which was muddy and dark, when it saw something move in the bushes. It began to move vigorously and the boar's survival instinct made it want to run away. But it began to creep, when it saw a person.

That person had a blindfold on.

*

"The Andhakas hid in the shadows and the snow forests after they were hunted by my father. They fought a lot, but they weren't as strong as the Vrishnis," Satyaki said. "Now they live in secret, while building themselves a fine army on the side to one day combat the Vrishnis."

"So, you mean to say I can't meet them directly?"

"No. They only meet those who they want to meet. I think that is understood," Satyaki smiled. "Devamedha has been careful that her men had not been taken as slaves. Her men had faced things worse than death. You can imagine. My father is quite a gory man."

"Hmmm, yeah. There's a way to lure them out, though," Balaram said.

"What would that be?"

Balaram smiled back. "They have always loved hunting boars. Don't know why, but they love eating it as well."

"A boar? You sure a simple boar would lure them out?"

"It's worth a try. And it would lead someone out at least. Hasn't your father ever tried?"

"He got bored hunting them and went back. Typical him," he groaned.

Balaram nodded. "Then that's what we do, kid. That's what we do. Do you know where to find a boar?"

"One of my men has a farm. I'm sure we can find a boar there."

"Or a pig who looks like a boar."

And they both chuckled.

*

The hunter leapt over the boar with a spike in his hand as he swung it across the gushing wind and smacked it right across the flesh and bones and pierced through it. The boar loudly yelled and cried, but the blind hunter went forward and put the dagger in and began to skin it.

He was tearing it open and trying to wrap it up in the cloth. To take it back home. Take it to his family. Take it to his children and feed them.

There was thunder in the sky, and the atmosphere was dense. The wind was gushing and there was no one around as he began to take his hunt and find his way towards his home.

As another thunder crackled and the snow hefted amongst his naked toes, there was a shadow behind him that grabbed him by the back and held him tightly, tossing him on the ground.

"Don't worry," the shadow of a bald man spoke to the hunter, looming large over him. "I am not here to hurt you."

The hunter didn't respond. He didn't know who it was, so it instantly grabbed hold of his feet and toppled him on the ground. The hunter went for the dagger in his ankle and stabbed him on the feet. The bald man cried loudly.

"I'm an ally!"

The hunter didn't listen. He grabbed the same dagger, pulling it out of the ankle and stabbing the bald man in the chest, waiting to attack on the throat on the next move, when the bald man kicked the hunter between his legs, right in the groin throwing him on the side and then punched him on the face.

"Now you listen." The bald man spoke. "My name is Balaram, a descendent of Yadu, brother of Krishna and I'm a friend to Devamedha. Take me to her. She knows who I am."

The hunter listened carefully. The words rung true. He nodded calmly.

"Lead the way," Balaram said.

*

Where they entered, there was just barrenness and snow.

They walked slowly. The blade was right behind the hunter while the eyes of Balaram watched carefully ensuring he was led right. The blade was, in fact, close to the spine of the hunter and the hunter knew, though he was quiet. He listened to the breathing. He listened to the skies and followed the path with his smell.

Balaram watched as he went. They both walked slowly but steadily. And as they reached closer to the point where the path ended, Balaram found himself right in the middle of the hills, where there was a lot of depth. He saw that the roads had become treacherous. There was a lot of darkness but he walked calmly...

Until it happened.

Shadows began to move. The arrows with poison smeared on them. They were soldiers, and Balaram saw their arrows pointed towards them. Balaram could notice the difference between reaching out to the Vrishnis, who was so welcoming and this savage, beastly kind of welcome here by the Andhakas. It truly felt they were sons of the demon, of the darkness.

And they would surprisingly be his light, his salvation.

Balaram continued to walk further and even the

Andhakas were not doing anything about it. He moved further suspiciously only wondering whether he should have a backup ready with Satyaki if things went wrong but then he was adventurous, he liked risks.

Balaram watched in front of him as the path got cleared and he found amidst the foliage of trees that had just appeared, a woman, high up on an elevated position, and there were more warriors around with spears and swords and daggers. Balaram could hear whispers, murmurs amidst them. They were talking about him.

And then he looked at the top lady, who was on the elevated platform.

"Devamedha, hope you remember your old cousin?" Balaram smiled.

The woman recognised the voice and smiled. "So it is you, Bala. How have you been doing? Also—you can leave, my hunter. We are at peace."

Balaram carefully released the dagger from the spine, as the hunter began to move. He looked at Devamedha who was majestic. She had ashen skin, while her hair was gray. In fact, everyone around had gray hair, blindfolded and ash smeared across their chests. They were savages and they were fitting the part.

"Have you done it?"

"Yes."

"Good, then you should know that coming here has put you at risk," she said. "You barge in when you are not welcome. We have stopped all association with the outside world."

"But I come in peace and I come with the scent of victory."

She raised her brows. "Interesting. And what is this victory?"

"Killing Yudhajit," he said.

She chuckled. "I have less men. I don't want to make them lesser."

"No, but I have a proposition."

Devamedha came on her feet and began to descend, one foot at a time, when he saw she was coming close to him.

"You know what the problem is?"

Balaram waited. He had a feeling he would be told about it and he didn't have to answer this one.

"The problem is, I don't trust you and your kind."

"We are cousins. We are the same kind."

"Not to me," she said. "My son was murdered ruthlessly by Yudhajit and no one helped. Not you. Not your divine brother whose divinity is measured by limitations. No one! And then Yudhajit began his powerful campaign to wipe us out; make us old, all of us. All because of you...and you think that I would agree to it. I am sorry but I won't."

Balaram said, "At least, listen. I can help. We can work together in some way or the other. So don't worry. Just give me the pedestal for it."

"No, I don't think I would."

"For old times' sake." He blinked his eyes and then he kissed her on the cheek as she was coming close. "Cousin? Come on."

Devamedha growled. "You can't make me feel bad like this. You know I have liked you." She smiled with a hardy look and then they hugged each other "It's good to see you brother. I hope I didn't scare you with all of this."

"Na, the acting was top class though," he grinned. "And listen, I am sorry about the luring part..."

"Na, na I understand, you had to do it." She smiled.

As they began to move, she showed him around. It was closer to the edge of the mountain. He could see they were building a new world inside. There were many people and huts for them to live in. There was a world underneath with roads being paved so beautifully.

"What is this?"

"We have been in hiding, but we have not given up."

"It sounds like you."

"So, what about Yudhajit?" She asked, as she found a room for them to sit in. "Is there an offer brewing?"

"Yes, a strong one and I believe you need to listen to it."

"Hmmm, speak," she said. "But you know, but the thing is brother, as much as I like you, I also know you come with ill intentions. So, I'll tell you something—I have learnt from my sources that you are wanted. Now I don't know for what reason, but Pradhyuman has announced a bounty. He has told us if we kill you, we will get asylum. So..." She smiled. "How about that?"

And now Balaram knew she was not kidding anymore, as two men grabbed him from behind and the world went dark.

21

Krishna flung the sword towards Samva who had tipped off his sword on the ground, as Samva slashed it across the zombified bandit's torso, tearing them apart.

Krishna began to move in a breakneck speed as the bandits with blue eyes, and black mouths which made gurgling sounds, began to chase after him.

He dashed beneath their legs, grabbing the fallen sword and slashed the head of the one who came closer.

"We need to escape!" Samva yelled as he was battling multiple bandits coming closer to him.

"Yeah, of course," Krishna sarcastically growled as he turned to see where he could escape from. He could see the ladder that was going above, and he was actually anticipating this. "We need to make for the east."

"How?"

Krishna couldn't answer as a bandit lurched on him and he deflected it with a swish of his sword, tossing the bandit on the ground, who was half torn but still trying to move. They were not dying and they were possessed by magic, the mystic of Durjay.

"There's too many of them!" Samva shrieked and he was at the other end of the room.

Krishna looked at the fire lamps that were burning at each end of the cave's entrance and he grabbed hold of them, breaking the shards of the lamp and throwing the fire in it towards the bunch of bandits who were trying to crowd Samva. The moment the fire hit, it began to burn them and they all began to cry loudly, whining loudly. Krishna grinned, as Samva got the opportunity to slip himself between the zombified bandits and make his way to Krishna.

They both dashed towards the east, where they had seen the ladder and as they made their way, Krishna could see as he passed the room—his mace. He stopped, halting and skidding as the mud behind him sprayed.

"My weapon!"

And he could also see his chakras. Probably, this was the room where they kept the prisoners' belongings. He made his way towards them and grabbed hold of the mace and the chakras, when Samva said loudly:

"This is not important," he said. "The important thing is to escape the bloody place."

"Yeah, my gear is as important as that."

He could hear the groan behind him as Krishna wore his pigskin belt which had the chakras in it, while he juggled his mace.

Samva waited, whistling to himself, as he could see behind them the slow-moving zombified bandits chasing them. "Can we leave?"

"Yes, yes, we can."

But as Krishna was about to turn, Samva could see the bandits' speed had increased and instantly they had begun to move faster than a human, all crumpled with each other in the small lanes of the caves, but still able to break through the entrance and move towards them.

One of them came close to Samva and he instantly fought it, stabbing the bandit on the face, while another came near him…

And got smacked right in the head by the mace.

Krishna countered a surprise attack by the bandit and before Samva could thank him, more bandits came towards them. Krishna put his mace diagonally in between them and Samva and yelled at his son: "You leave. Quick!"

"What about you?"

"I'll be fine."

Samva could hear the confidence in his voice but he was still unsure whether he should leave his father behind. As he made his way forward, he knew he was about to reach the ladder, his face brightening up, his eyes dilating when immediately a shadow crept in front of him and he toppled on the ground with his sword.

He saw who it was. And it was none other than Saba, the woman they were supposed to rescue.

"Oh dear!"

She had crazy dark eyes and a dark mouth. Smoke was fuming out of her and she was moving towards him erratically and not in a very human fashion at all. Samva didn't know what had happened to these people, but his father did mention someone called Durjay that he should have been aware of.

"I don't want to kill you," he said to Saba.

But the girl didn't listen. Like a spider, she lurched at him, he rolled over on the ground and dodged her. She mewled and lurched at him again, which he deflected with his sword. She began to bite the sword, break her teeth, but continued to do so, her anger rising and her saliva spitting out of her mouth.

"I don't want to do this..." Samva cried, and as he did, he pushed her away, shoving her on the floor and with a quick jab, stabbed her in the heart. "I *didn't* want to do this."

Saba's body jerked and then lay there. Samva didn't kill her and he didn't want to. He moved for the ladder when he saw behind him that his father was trying to stop the horde.

He began to climb up, not looking back.

Krishna was still holding on to the lurching bandits with his mighty mace and then as he saw the bandits were trying to jump over and claw at him—he shoved them behind with as much force as he could gather, before dashing towards the ladder himself. As he reached the top, he found someone latching on to him by the leg and he was trying to move it and push himself away. He kicked the bandit with his heels and then used one of his chakras to swing it across the head of the bandit who had come close to him—before leaving and shutting the gates of whatever that was by closing the bamboo lid behind.

He laid on the ground. Panting fiercely. He saw Samva was right there, on the opposite side.

"That was something!" Samva sighed. "What was that again?"

"The mystical powers of a Vitihotra. They can possess others."

"Why is a Vitihotra after me?"

"Because they know about us."

Samva nodded. "Pradhyuman must have sent it. That Durgajyoti…"

Krishna had no clue about the woman. But he knew his son was capable of doing that. "We should leave. We have to let go of his scent."

Samva nodded.

And they both made their way.

*

Krishna and Samva had found refuge in their old tent from where they had been kidnapped. By then, most of their stuff was ravaged by wolves or the thieves. Even those bandits had taken stuff from them, when they had kidnapped them from here.

"Burn the logs. We will camp with whatever is left for the night and hike in the morning," Krishna said.

Samva nodded silently and began arranging the logs, lighting them up after spilling some oil from the jar they had.

"I am sorry," Krishna said after a while, his voice was sombre.

"Hmmm?" Samva turned back, his iron mask glistening under the moonlight. "What?"

"I am sorry about not trusting you. I didn't know that this had happened. The abuse and all."

"I told you. You hadn't listened. But now you did."

"Somehow now I trust you more," Krishna quietly responded. He felt defeated that he let his son go through such excruciating pain of leprosy because he didn't believe in him.

Samva was watching his father and he could see that there was regret written over his face. Samva wanted to brush him off in the snarkiest way, he could have made him feel worse but he stopped and sighed. He didn't want to say anything further.

"Was I too bad a son that you didn't believe a word I said?"

"No, you were just disappointing," Krishna said straightforwardly. "But now you are not anymore. In fact, you make me proud."

Samva couldn't help but smile.

"Where should we go now?" The boy asked his father. "I have no clue. This was the last strand of hope. And from Saba we learnt nothing but the fact that Durvasa left for Antar Dvipa."

"Yes."

"And you know about it?"

Krishna was trying to avoid this and he closed his eyes, as memories from that place haunted him. "Yes, I know about it very well."

"How well?"

"Well enough that we can't find Antar Dvipa using our naked eyes. We can only search for it through the art of magic."

"Magic?"

"Yes," Krishna sighed. "We have to reflect the sunlight against the Naagmani to cast the shadow of the island and only then we will be able to find it."

"That means we need to go to the Naga's kingdom. The bloody serpentines have always crept me out," Samva growled under his breath. "But I thought the

Naagmanis had all been destroyed during the The Great War."

"It was. Except for one. And I hate that person. I don't want to meet him."

Before Samva could ask, Krishna went down on the ground, close to the lit logs and laid down there to sleep.

Samva knew his father didn't want to talk about his past life. Didn't want to connect to the memories for now and he respected that. It was dangerous to sleep again where they had slept earlier, and so Samva decided to stay awake all night while his father snored and slumbered, until his eyes met with some sleep.

But he woke up with a jerk, as if someone had pushed him and he could see his father awake now. He was doing something. He had some of the paste and sprinkles and had a small bowl over which he was grinding something. He continued to do so, while Samva remained sleepy. In his sleep-heavy voice, he asked: "What are you up to?"

"I'm creating a portal."

"A portal."

"To enter the other Lok."

"But you need a Vidhyadhara for that."

"Not unless you know how to open it yourself," Krishna smiled. "And also yes, good morning to you very much."

And he went to the opposite end of the camp, moving towards the far north before he threw the powder that he had been creating. The powder fell on the ground and the moment it did, it began to spiral across the leaves and the dust and the red earth around it, before a purplish kind of hazed energy started to form in front of him. The movement was fast and quick and it was strong.

The portal was opened. It was right there, and it was swishing and swooshing, making all kinds of electronically whirring sounds. Samva walked to it and asked: "Is this to Naaglok?"

"Yes."

And before they could answer—a hermit like man exited from the portal, with a long staff, ashen body and matted hair. He had a coiled serpent around his body that was moving, and a cobra on top of his staff.

It was from the Naaglok, Lokpala, the gatekeeper and the guardian of the land they were planning to enter. Seeing Krishna for the first time, standing bare-chested with his muscled abs and his Shrivatsa symbol, the Lokpala grinned.

"If it isn't the Avatar of Vishnu," he said. "How may I be of service?"

"We want to meet King Kaliya."

"For what reasons?"

"The Lokpala doesn't care to know. We just want to meet him and we come in peace."

"Of course, you do." The Lokpala smashed his staff. "You are but a peaceful man who prevented the biggest war to ever happen to mankind."

Krishna rolled his eyes. "Are we allowed to enter?"

"Please do. If there's any hanky panky business, you know I'll find you."

Krishna nodded and turned to Samva. "Are you ready?"

"Yeah, but um, Kaliya?" He asked. "Where have I heard this name?"

Krishna didn't want to go back to his childhood when Kaliya had taken over the Yamuna River back in India, in Vrindavan, and poisoned the river and Krishna had to save everyone from drinking it and also was in the process of killing Kaliya before letting him lose at the behest of his six wives.

But he had to. Because this journey was slowly becoming more mysterious and important to him.

"If you don't remember, it's good for us," he said. "Because Kaliya has a knack of making people remember it on multiple occasions."

22

Pradhyuman woke up on the red earth.

He could feel the sand on him, touch him and trace him on his skin. He tried to come on his feet but the energy left in him was negligible. He took a deep breath and pushed himself from it, when his vision began to become clearer. His voice was cracked and he couldn't speak properly, feeling a bad taste in his mouth. He could hear stuff—it was a long wide tone and when he looked up it was getting clearer and he could hear the claps, the applause, the best kind of feeling.

Pradhyuman blinked and rubbed his eyes, and as he did he looked around, scanning the environment. He was in some kind of an arena, very much akin to the one back at home, where he had fought the worm. But that was a place where the situation was controlled, while here it wasn't. He looked at the pedestals where the crowd was sitting and applauding for him. But this crowd, they had no faces—just blankness washed over them, wearing different kinds of clothes and clapping away.

He looked up at the red stormy skies that were turbulent and it all looked like a dream. But dreams were nicer—these were nightmarish—he could feel the chill underneath his bones. He looked ahead, and at the top just where he used to sit, was where Mayavati was.

She was still looking ethereal, until something happened. Her skin began to change, her height shortened and she was changing into a...

A stout man with a red nose and long teeth, furry brows and curly hair. He was really short and he was fat. Obese, in fact.

He was standing next to the ledge, wearing a long gown and a big, winning grin on his face.

Pradhyuman knew him. He knew him too well and distinctly so.

"Shambara," his lifelong enemy. "You used Maya to disguise yourself. You are king of Rasatala, even now."

"Of course. Otherwise you would have attacked me instantly. I had to dress up as your mommy and make you go to sleep, so you can be here. In short—How do you do, my boy?" He laughed, clapping.

"But you are dead. I killed you."

"So you did." He chuckled loudly and the blank-faced public began to clap louder. "But you see, I came back. It required a lot of my people coming together, using all kinds of magic and making me who I am. It was fun when I returned and it took years. But the first thing which I did was what I wanted to do the most—create a plan. To destroy you was my top priority."

Pradhyuman looked around, he was confused. He was seeing so much around him. He looked up again at Shambara and he had disappeared.

"Where the..."

But he couldn't wait further, as something came from behind and he felt it—it was a stab on the right side of his back and he swivelled around to see who had hurt him—it was Shambara, who was grinning.

"Hello there."

Pradhyuman tried to pull the blade out and fell back, while the short man circled around him.

"Here I'm invincible," he said.

"What do you mean?"

"Here, I can kill you and I can resurrect you."

And to prove his point, Pradhyuman saw he had healed the wound he had just received.

"But I would rather kill you,"

And then he made the same wound open up and Pradhyuman began to cry loudly. "Oh goodness!" He shrieked loudly. "How did you..."

"Because this is the world I have created for the prisoners I want to keep, for those whose deaths should be worse than the concept of death itself. Purgatory is something I want to give. The world of dreams. The world of mirrors. The world which you can't trust. The world where you can't trust yourself..." Shambara said.

"This is all a dream...it's not real..."

The entire public went quiet hearing his statement. Even the duplicate Pradhyuman, Shambara impassively clenched his jaws. "Now that would be disappointing, yes."

Pradhyuman chuckled. "Yeah, so I would want you to leave now and let me free as well."

"Oh, that's not going to happen unfortunately because you see, you may be right that I wouldn't be able to kill you because, after all—you are in this position, but I would be able to put you in an internal sleep. You will never wake up and continue to be in this godforsaken place," he smiled. "By piercing the blade in you and killing you, you would be stuck here."

"No, that's impossible."

"What do you think you are doing now? In the real world, you are in coma. People expect you to wake up. Imagine you never could. What a sad pathetic life it would be."

Pradhyuman growled and he stormed towards Shambara, trying to grab him but he disappeared. And he appeared behind him and kicked him on the butt and Pradhyuman fell on the dirt. The entire crowd began to laugh seeing this.

"What do you want me to do here? I did the right thing you know, killing you."

"I'm sure you did."

"You tortured my mother. You raped her. You forced her to marry you."

"Indeed, but your mother lied about me. So, she got what was coming for her."

"No, I'll kill you again."

"Oh, you wish."

Pradhyuman tried to stand up again and grab him and as soon as he did, he saw Shambara escape and this time, he was back at the top, from where he had started.

"I will make your life sad. I will make your life terrible."

And then Pradhyuman could feel the tremors underneath the earth and his heart began to pound wondering what was happening. He tried to move around, clutching on to his wound while at the same time, trying to scamper for his blade. He dashed to grab the sword, and as he made his way, the tremors stopped as Pradhyuman could see what was emerging from the earth...

And it plummeted through the sand and went for him, realising that it was the same worm that Pradhyuman had killed earlier. Pradhyuman grabbed hold of the sword and as the worm came towards him, he rolled on the side.

"How did you know I fought a worm?"

"Your dreams, your nightmares are real," Shambara laughed. "My world of mirrors is the reflection of you, my boy. Don't you dare forget!" And he was jumping ecstatically as two women Rakshasis came into the picture, puffing in the air, as if he wanted to show off to them what he was capable of.

The worm began to slide towards him, speeding with great ferocity and Pradhyuman, unprepared unlike last time, waited for the worm...

And he lurched at it, jumping and somersaulting in the air, before digging the sword inside the centre of the worm.

Nothing happened. It pierced. Blood sprayed on his face, but the worm shook him off and he fell on the ground.

The worm made his way towards Pradhyuman again, so big and humongous, its giant shadow cast over him, its mouth gaping open. Pradhyuman could hear a loud wheezing sound as the worm was approaching him and he had no weapons...

And it ate him.

Only to disappear again.

It just puffed in the air.

"Oh, do you really think I've called you here to just die so easily?" Shambara shouted from the top.

Pradhyuman clenched his fist.

"When you have planned for so long to hurt someone, you don't want to get over with it quickly. You want to enjoy it, you want to relish every moment." He chuckled and jumped on the pedestal he stood upon. "Wait until you face the worst kind of monsters from all kinds of realities and you will be always at the edge of falling into slumber forever, and you know what's the worst part? You have nowhere to go. You can't do anything. You are stuck here, in this limbo and in this purgatory."

Pradhyuman didn't wait and he wanted to dash towards Shambara, leap from his place and attack the fat man. But before he could do it, guards came from all sides, dozens of them and crowded around Pradhyuman grabbing him first and then chaining him tightly. He was pulled by a hound and he could not respond to Shambara who was just clapping along with the blank, fake audience that he had created to satiate his ego. He continued to walk further with the guards around him, and he was inside the arena where other prisoners were being trained.

Just like him, he saw other warriors, some Yayatis perhaps and some perhaps of the other race. Pradhyuman wasn't sure whether they were his imagination or they were all stuck in this world of mirrors. And speaking of mirrors, it was mentioned often but there was none. Was it some kind of a riddle? He didn't understand.

The lanes grew narrower, but the men didn't disperse. All of them with high security took care of Pradhyuman.

They moved and huddled, poking their spears at him, so he would be continually at risk.

He was in a singular lane which had cages on both sides. In front, he could see the light and nothing else. He could see many other people in the cages, and they all looked feeble, starved and sickly. Some were sleeping in their own vomit, while some were talking to themselves. The world Shambara had created was strange in itself and he had no clue how to escape from here.

"This is all a dream…this is all a dream…" he continued to speak under his breath, when the guard on his right began to chuckle.

"This is your worst nightmare, kid. You aren't going to escape from here."

"There's always a way to get out."

But the guards just laughed it off, before opening a cage for him and tossing him inside, throwing him on the ground, letting loose his iron chains. Pradhyuman was on a damp ground and he felt defeated, as if he couldn't go any lower. He turned to his left to see the cage where the man was holding the railings and looking at him, with his dirty beard and mucky hair.

"Aren't you Pradhyuman?" The old man in his shivering voice asked.

Pradhyuman didn't say anything.

"If you are, don't tell me. You are a bad, bad person," he said.

And then the old man disappeared. Pradhyuman must have hurt him in some way, and he had no clue how. Though he could see the other people's reactions, who were seeing him with foul mouths and fouler eyes. Pradhyuman sighed, hoping to find a friendly face somewhere and in the opposite cell, he did see one, almost feeling shocked to see the figure.

It was none other than his step-mother, Mayavati.

And this time, it was the real one.

23

Balaram was back here again.

He was in the midst of the colossal storm and he was standing there in the tall grass and in front of him, a storm was brewing. And the same image was there, as he could see the darkness of the snake forming in front and the shadow of the man below him. But not yet swallowed.

"I don't want to be here." He said loudly, shrieking and pushing himself out.

"But you are here. And you are us." The snake hissed at him. Ten-headed. And then it became five-headed, and back to ten-headed again.

Balaram was sweating now and he didn't know that one could sweat in their dreams too. But instead of always pushing himself away, he decided to throw himself in front. He began walking towards the man who would be getting swallowed in some time.

"I want to talk to you. Who are you?"

The man was still a blank face. A long shadow was cast over his face. Balaram could see the curly hair.

"I'm you," the man's voice echoed.

Balaram moved forward and finally reached the man in front of him. He looked at him, who was squared towards him. The person looked back and then his features began to get clearer and he was smiling. Grinning, in fact, showing off his teeth.

"Who are you?" Balaram asked.

"Don't you understand? I'm you."

"You look different. You don't look like me."

"Because I'm you from another time, another era, another yug."

Balaram arched his brows. "No...I'm a reincarnation..."

"It's more complicated than that," he smiled. "It's far more complex and yet at the same time simple."

"But why me?"

"Because we are devotees of our kin. We are devotees of our brother. The brother who is Vishnu. We are born to protect his world."

"But my brother left me..." his voice cracked. Memories began to stir and he could remember all the times he had tried to not cry when he felt so helpless and sad when Krishna had left the mantle. He had to take care of the entire kingdom, by himself for a while before Pradhyuman came and turned everything upside down.

"Our brothers might not take care of us. We do. And that's why we are immortals. Anant."

At that moment, there was a loud hiss of the snake. And after a long time, Balaram could see that the snake was no more dangerous, but friendly towards him. He was the victim, the prey to the circumstances and not the predator.

"Who are you?"

And the name was told. Immediately, everything made sense. The snake came forward and opened its large, fanged mouth, ready to swallow them and as he did—Balaram had a split second of doubt whether he should be swallowed too, but fear got hold of him and he shoved himself back, falling on the ground as the snake swallowed the man in front of him.

Balaram was there, panting. Recalling the name that was told to him.

"Lakshman," he had said, "brother of Ram of Treta Yug."

*

Balaram woke up in a cage. It was a dirty cage that was smelling of dung and battered flies. He sighed. He didn't know what these dreams meant and whether they were dreams at all or not.

But he didn't like the place he was in right now. In fact, it was frustrating. He looked in front and there were guards, blind ones, all holding their spears and ashen skin, waiting to attack if he tried to escape.

Balaram sighed and remained there for hours, meditating, while pressing his paralysed leg which he had a habit of doing. He would hum too and try to remember the days when he was a farmer. He loved farming, especially ploughing and he had not done it in a while. He missed his wife and he missed his general. He missed his brother and even his evil nephew.

It's ironic how time makes you miss the bad and the good parts of your life. In hindsight, they stop becoming the bad and the good, but they become just parts, something to learn from, something to move on from and something to cherish.

As he continued to contemplate and mull, he saw figures coming and they were soldiers.

"You are summoned," the soldier ordered.

Balaram nodded and the cage was opened, while his hands were clasped so he wouldn't do anything funny. He was moved. He could see the other guards and the dungeon like area he was in. He moved further, until he was told to ascend a set of stairs where he was brought to a common hall under the cusp of the hill. It was all created in the inside of the hill and there were many guards, ministers and so forth. All were blindfolded. All were ashen. All looked like savages.

He was brought forward to the queen Devamedha, who he had met earlier but this time, Devamedha looked different. She was older, with white hair, paler skin and more wrinkled. Balaram was confused and his confusion was solved in just a second when he saw the woman he had thought to be Devamedha was standing right next to the woman on the seat.

"You were the daughter," Balaram stated. "How could I have missed it?"

"It's a common confusion. Take off my cousin's shackles please," Devamedha, the real one ordered.

Krittaverma was awkwardly standing in the corner, her loyal general. And so was someone else too—his wife Revathi as well as Akoorji. They were all seated in the guest seats and Balaram's eyes filled with warmth thinking how they found him. Revathi was getting up to embrace him, but she was not allowed to. Balaram wanted to talk to her, know how she came here, but he refrained.

Balaram's manacles were pulled down.

"Oh thank you."

"My daughter doesn't fancy you, Bala," Devamedha said. "Hate to say, she has her reasons. Her name is Sonja since you havent' had the pleasure of a formal introduction."

"Yes," Balaram said. "Thank you for being a good host."

"My apologies when I knew about your entrance, I immediately ordered my men to bring you here."

Balaram shrugged.

"So what brings you here after so many years? Also keep in mind, you are wanted so if I don't find your reasons justified, I can always get rid of you."

"Sweet of you, cousin," Balaram grinned. "I have a justified reason. I have a standing army ready to take your helm at the Vrishni kingdom. Satyaki, son of Yudhajit, plots to take over his father."

"Interesting." She leaned forward. "And why is that?"

"Because Yudhajit is after all a bad man."

"And you realised it now?"

"My friendship with him has often clouded my judgment."

"Great. So you want me to support Satyaki and bring peace between the Andhakas and the Vrishnis?"

"Indeed, yes."

"What if he turns out like his father? A blackmailing murderer, that is."

"I think he has some hindsight. Plus, I'll guide him."

"Like you guided your brother?" She scoffed. "Come on, Bala, I am having a hard time taking this seriously."

Sonja, on the side, grumbled. "I told you, mother."

"Silence, child. Your insolence of presenting yourself as me was not appreciated in the first place and now two adults are talking, so I don't want any chit chat from your end as well."

Balaram couldn't believe how curt she was with the daughter, but then it was well-deserved.

"Satyaki has how many?"

"Hundred or so but most have the power of Yayati. You can use it."

She clenched her jaws. "Has he agreed?"

"Who do you think sent me here?"

"Interesting. And why didn't he come?"

"Because you would have taken him as trophy."

She laughed. "Of course, you are right. Good job!" She clapped. "Let me think about it, cousin. I would love to dig deep into it and think with clarity. I have hated each blood of Vrishni, and partnering up with them is a task I'm not sure I'm ready to jump on to immediately."

"Of course, take your time."

"Till that happens, I would suggest I give you a good room and make you meet your family. They were able to find us without any violent means like you took."

But how? Balaram wondered.

Though he knew he wouldn't get answers now. The meeting was adjourned and he was then guided towards his room.

*

The moment he entered, he found Akoorji and Revathi inside. Revathi hugged him tightly while Akoorji was smiling in a corner.

"What had happened? How did you all come?" Balaram asked. "Didn't Yudhajit suspect?"

Akoorji said, "We happened to find it when we met a sherpa in the middle, who guided us well. Yudhajit suspected, of course, that we came mysteriously and left the same way. He also heard about a debacle that was caused in the streets of his city."

"I see. So, what is he doing about it?"

"He told us to stay," Revathi said. "And while his search party was at work Akoorji found a way to escape. I'm sure he will search for us, but then, it's fine."

"We are playing both sides. It'll be a problem," Balaram said. Though he had one question. "Who met this sherpa?"

He was looking at Akoorji and Revathi, but Revathi nodded. "It was me who did."

"I never thought there was a sherpa in the first place here."

She paused. As if uncertain. "No, no there was."

"I should have gone that route then," he said to himself, still confused. "But I'm glad you two are here."

"So, what's the plan?"

"We wait and see how this works out," Balaram said. "We give it a few days and if it doesn't work out, we instigate and begin to turn the wheels."

They both nodded. Whenever he looked at them, Balaram would get happy that they were here, but at the same time, he would get frustrated that one of them could be the Ledger. And also there was a Vitihotra after him. He didn't know where he was, what he was plotting now.

As they continued to discuss further, there was a knock on the door. Balaram went to open it, and he saw Sonja, who was standing sternly. Balaram closed the door behind him and squared his shoulders. She had come alone, and she looked angry, her fists clenched and her face impassive, yet with his voice, acting sweet, he said:

"I hope you have come for the apology," Balaram said.

"Anything but." She gritted her teeth. "I want to warn you. Do not try to change my mother's mind. We will not work with any Vrishni otherwise you will face my wrath."

"And why is that? Just because of a feud? Satyaki is a good man. I'm sure he will use diplomatic means to solve the issue between the Andhakas and the Vrishnis."

"But my brother was killed by the Vrishnis," she said. "And I don't want to deal with that again. He was young. Barely an age to die." Her voice cracked.

"There was never any proof that it was done by a Vrishni. You all suspected that it was done by them because you hated their guts as they used to demean your tribe."

Balaram remained quiet. That was true. The Vrishnis were a little pompous and they were arrogant. That was their flaw. They used to love to flaunt.

"No, what if I tell you there was proof?"

"Of what?"

"Of the murder. There was an eyewitness. I heard him, before he died of natural causes, damn me."

"What was this insane proof of yours?"

"The eyewitness had seen the murder."

"By Yudhajit?"

She shook her head. "No. By Satyaki."

24

Krishna could feel his stomach wrestle within himself and then he entered this land that he was unsure of. He could feel his insides churning upside down, and he looked in front, his eyes glaring white as he entered the new dimension. He punched his fist on the ground and took a deep breath, letting it roll.

"You have gone old." A voice said from the side.

"If only I got a coin for every time someone would say this to me during this journey," he growled, coming on his feet, "teleportation is a gruesome process, boy."

Samva shrugged. "Not to me. I just feel funny."

"Because the atoms in your body are transported to another place, another land altogether in a wisp of time," Krishna explained. "I would know. I used it often."

"Wow!" Samva ignored him, as he saw the environment around him.

Krishna saw what he was looking at and it was a clear, blue skin unlike the thunderous one back in Dvarka. They were standing on a long, iron bridge. In front there were cottages, and behind it there were many towers and long ravines flowing between those towers. There were ravens flying across the sky.

"Why is this place better than Dvarka?" He asked. "This is Naaglok right?"

"A part of it, yes. Naaglok is quite huge, and we are in the part which is ruled by Kaliya."

"Isn't he the one who you imprisoned in Naaglok?" Samva asked.

Krishna could see the irony in the statement. Dvarka had become Krishna's prison by himself. While Kaliya ended up making his prison a land of beauty.

He was stoic about it and they both walked together towards the palaces.

"We have to hide otherwise people would recognise us," Krishna said.

"I'm sure Manavs are allowed in this prison."

Krishna rolled his eyes. "Unfortunately, Manavs are prohibited."

"So what do you plan to do?"

"Just try to barge in as quickly as possible through the main gate and get the attention of Kaliya," he said, though the idea didn't sound strong enough. He was walking further, brisk in his pace and he was glad that there was no one around them to see. They continued to walk, their sandals making a slapping sound while in the background, there were woods and stony paths that had all kinds of serpents, watching them. The Naaglok was popular for being the residing land of the snakes.

And as they entered close to the palatial lands, they found there were people but by that time they had stolen clothes from the cottages where they were being dried and their faces were hidden under the hood.

They moved past the bazaar, as Samva said, "So these people all follow Kaliya?"

"Yes. His domain."

They could see the Nagas and they looked amicably different from Manavs. They had strange reptilian noses and green eyes, with bald heads and some of them black. They were tall and really slender. None of them were of obnoxiously large size, for some reason.

Krishna walked carefully.

"Do you think Kaliya would greet you nicely?"

"I don't think so. After all, I had brought him here. But then again, I had forgiven him. I could have easily killed him."

"The irony that now you are here for his help."

"I know."

"Do you regret the things you did?"

"I was doing the right thing. He was poisoning the Yamuna River. He was a demon, boy." Krishna growled. He was in a really foul mood because he had to go to Antar Dvipa, the place he was not at all interested in ever entering but had no choice now.

"But not all demons are evil. Some might just be misunderstood. Did he ever tell you why he did what he did?"

Krishna shook his head. He never asked either. He never thought it would be that important. "I just hate the Nagas. They are conniving, snivelling individuals who must be put to death."

"Quite a prejudice."

But by then, they were in front of a young Naga lad who had the face of a reptile but was smaller. He was a beggar, Krishna noticed and had a pouch, requesting for some money.

"Care for an offering in return for a tale?"

"Don't have anything," Krishna said.

But Samva didn't listen. He went forward and handed it over to the boy. Krishna groaned. The little lad grinned and immediately began to speak:

"Oh, it is of the fine and fair of the tale of Kaliya, the good old king, who had done everything right for his people and stood for them at their worst and the best. There was a time, when he had moved from Naaglok to the land of humans and he had to fit in. But the problem was, there was evil everywhere. Worse, the water that they drank wasn't right. They were getting poisoned, so he began using his own serum to use the Yamuna water as his. This led the drinking problem to be better, but for humans, it was poison. And then came the evil Vishnu's son, Keshav, the destroyer of Nagas and he destroyed our livelihood, our homes, but Kaliya instead of fighting back, found a diplomatiac situation and the evil Keshav had to find them a home which he gave."

Anger overcame him. Krishna could see how he was portrayed in their tales and he just rolled his eyes. They moved on from the lad, and Samva asked:

"Did you just do that?"

"It's more complicated than this. You know each culture has a different interpretation of the same incident. That's how history has always worked," he said. "So, you don't take it seriously..."

"What are these Manavs doing here?" There was a loud sound.

They both turned and they saw a butcher with his cleaver shaft, and an apron looking at them. The bazaar people all gathered together and their eyes met.

"You are mistaken. We are travellers," Krishna said gruffly.

"Manavs are not allowed here," said the butcher. "Because we eat them," he grinned.

Along with him, a few soldiers joined in too and instead of solving the commotion, they lurched forward.

Krishna and Samva nodded at each other, and they both took separate enemies. Krishna had his mace and he instantly bashed the head of the butcher who came towards him with a cleaver, as the teeth spat out of the Naga and he fell on the ground. While another soldier came from behind and grabbed him, making him loosen his fist over the mace and the weapon fell. Krishna used his power to throw himself back and the man behind him crushed underneath him. He came on his feet, grabbing the mace and began to smash him right on the face, till it became pulp.

"Now isn't that a beauty?" Krishna grinned.

He turned to see Samva, who was shrieking a lot and shouting at him, "I need some help here, man!" He was being held by two of the men on either side and as Krishna came close to them, he used the mace on one person and swung his chakra across another one. It broke through the skulls of both and he was able to get rid of them. "Should we run?" Samva asked meekly. "I think we should run."

"We should definitely run."

And they began to move in the opposite direction, when they saw more soldiers, cavalry and archers right there, waiting to attack.

"We should stay," Krishna said.

"We should definitely stay."

*

Krishna and Samva with manacles were brought to a dinner table. Krishna was getting used to the manacles that he was being made to wear. In fact, he would be even expecting a cage soon after, because it was getting redundant. Just getting caught everywhere, since they wouldn't come up with a plan.

Krishna saw the dinner table in front of him, and they were lavishly setting up the table with all kinds of feasts. From apples to boars to what looked like human meat even. Krishna knew he wouldn't have that. There were guards on all four corners of the hall. And the main table was empty for now. But he knew who would join them.

They were made to sit down.

"Well, that's a nice service he has prepared for us," Samva said.

"Yeah, that means he has something in mind."

And before they could discuss further, a voice boomed and echoed: "Why do you always second guess my intentions, Keshav?"

Krishna turned to find a man with his hands clasped back, with his bald head and browless eyes as he began to walk towards the main chair and then sat on it.

"How are you? Very surprised to see you here."

Krishna could see the thing he had come here for. And that was Kaliya's mani on top of his forehead that was gleamingly blue. It was staring at him and shining brightly.

"Yeah, we just thought we should meet you and greet you since it's been long," Krishna sarcastically said.

"Who's he?" Kaliya ignored him and talked about Samva.

"My son."

"Oh, interesting."

"If you don't mind me asking," Samva said, "don't you look like someone who has ten heads or something, like a big serpent?"

"That's my alternate form, my angry form. I don't choose to show you here." He smiled. "Please have the food that has been prepared for you."

"We are not hungry," Krishna sternly added.

"Don't be such a party pooper, come on!" He clapped his hands. "Have the food."

"How do I know it's not poisoned?"

Kaliya sighed and then took a part of the boar and ate it himself. "See, everything is fine. Have it."

"What if it was poisoned for not you, but us?" Krishna asked.

Samva added, "I trust you, I'll have it." And he took the boar piece and ate it. Krishna was hesitant but then seeing Kaliya, he also did the same.

Kaliya sighed. "Then tell me what are you here for or I might just send you directly to the torque chambers? I just thought that I would send you after you have had a nice meal."

Krishna knew he had foul intentions. He was at the devil's trap right now, but Krishna had faced so many devils in his life that he was not afraid anymore of anything. He knew he had to be straightforward with

Kaliya, so looking at the blue mani he said, "I want the mani."

For a moment, there was a pause and then a loud chuckle, before he said: "This old thing?" He pulled out the mani from his head and looked at it. "Now why might you need it?"

"Because it has magic and I need magic right now."

"Don't we all?" He chuckled. "You know, I can give you this, you know I can." He was contemplating. "You want?" He handed it over to Krishna.

He paused. He knew there some catch. "What do you want in return?"

"Oh, just a simple favour to be honest. But it's good you knew I would ask you for something." He smiled. "I want a very sincere and honest apology."

"For what?"

"For sending me here."

"But I was not wrong."

"No, but you were. I was a good man and you chose to send me here, to a prison. I'm stuck here."

"You seem to be enjoying quite well," Krishna said looking at the jars of ale and wine that were kept in front of him.

He shook his head. "I want an apology, Keshav."

"But you can't have that. I'm not apologetic."

"Your ego is a big deterrent in this relationship." He stood up and clasped his hand. "How about that? I have something in mind."

"What?"

He grinned and his incisive snake-like eyes, emerald in colour shone. "You'll see. It's fun."

The guards came closer to Samva and Krishna and stood with their spears pointed towards them.

Krishna knew that coming here was indeed a big mistake.

25

Durgajyoti was kneeling on the ground. Her straight hair was all over her face. Her mouth was filled with bruises and she could taste the saltiness of her own bitter, blood. She was staring into the nothingness of the room and it was dark, with the shrilling sound of the raven's caw coming through the window. Durgajyoti had something in front of her. It was red. It was fleshy and it was dark like the room, but it shone even in the blackness.

It was smearing and trickling blood, when Durgajyoti said: "I present you my flesh. Accept it as my offering."

"Are you sure you want to do this?" The voice asked from the darkness.

"Yes."

"You would be risking everything. I could never leave you and I won't want to."

"I don't care." Durgajyoti shook her head. "I want the abuse to end."

"And it shall, because you wouldn't be an ordinary woman anymore."

Durgajyoti almost felt a burst of joy inside, but she didn't show it. "I don't want to be. I want to strive for greatness."

"Good."

And a large talon of dark flesh came out of the

darkness and grabbed the flesh away from the door. She could feel the pain in her thigh from where she had cut herself to present this offering. She waited as she could hear the munching of the creature, of Baagul.

"It's so delicious. I can feel you," she hissed. "Now I'll be yours and you'll be *mine*." The last word was so malicious and dark that Durgajyoti felt something in her stomach, in her spine moving and then a beam of energy left her, a puff of smoke out of her mouth and nose. She could feel she was ready for it.

She was ready to take down Durjay.

*

Durgajyoti was on her horse, under a hood, alongside Yuyudhan as they both travelled to the outskirts of Dvarkipur, where the valleys met, where the skies were less turbulent and there were no long towers and buildings, just greenery and lush canopies. She moved in silence and as an intruder to the kingdom that she had built along with Pradhyuman.

"Would someone question your absence?" Yuyudhan asked.

"I've told my handmaidens to inform everyone I'm ill but my support rests with the Rakshasas. If they attack and not listen to peaceful solutions, my Vitihotras await. The rest of them have been sent to Balaram as well as to other places." She said quietly not trying to let them know that Krishna was found because that would totally change the entire game for Yuyudhan. All the people of Dvarka were still ardent followers of their earlier king

Krishna, and part of the reason why Pradhyuman was respected was because of his father.

And unfortunately, the Vitihotras were less in number, so she could not use it. She also had to leave some behind because they would control the situation if her act was caught.

Her hand continued to shake as always, but she refrained from thinking about it. She could feel she was being imploded terribly.

"Good, you have come prepared."

"I am prepared. I always am. Where's this team of yours?"

"It's small but effective. Though we could have used a Vitihotra."

"I don't like to take them on such important missions because they can go out of control." She hummed. When she had created the Vitihotras along with Durjay, there were so many machinations attached to it. They couldn't be tamed initially. They only listened to orders that made sense to them. But she wrapped her charm around it and used magic to bind them. This journey which she was on—she couldn't risk being in trouble because of a Vitihotra because if they unbind themselves, she would be choked to death, her soul being pulled out of her mouth.

"All right."

They move close to a peepul tree away from the villages and the towns, in a barren kind of an area where there were almost ten people sitting. Some were chewing on apples, while some were chatting and sharpening their blades. They all looked rugged and not at all cleaned up. Not at all soldier-like, but more like the people who were born into the blade.

"So you got me bandits?"

"Mercenaries would be the right word to use. And there's a Vidhyadhara too, if we have to open the portal." He signalled to the girl in a purple gown and some very dark shade of lipstick.

"Great."

"They are true loyalists to Pradhyuman. He used to assign them the dirty work for the empire," Yuyudhan explained. "They will never backstab him and that means they wouldn't backstab us."

Durgajyoti nodded, even though she wasn't so easily convinced. "Shall we begin?"

"Sure. Lead on."

Durgajyoti dismounted from her stallion and made her way towards these people, most of whom after looking at her, stood straight, while some didn't. Some remained the way they were. "Hello everyone. Thank you so much for coming on such a short notice."

No one responded.

"We have gathered here today to do right by Pradhyuman, your king, our king," she said. "I wish I could bring my army and we could infiltrate the bloody gates of Rasatala but our queen has signed a peace accord, so my men couldn't be seen. The Rakshasas should not know how we are entering and when we are going back. We enter so smoothly and take what is ours. Understandable?"

They all nodded in unison.

"Good. Then the first call of action is to get Mayasur," she said.

"And where would he be?" The Vidhyadhara asked.

Durgajyoti had no answer to that. After the last meeting with him in the court, in the common halls with Pradhyuman, she had no clue where her king had sent her off.

"I know," Yuyudhan came forward. "He was stationed by Pradhyuman in a guest house and given the best kind of security."

"Then we should go there," Durgajyoti insisted.

"But if we attack it, they'll know," Yuyudhan protested. "Rukmini would have an idea."

"No, they won't," she added. "The mercenaries would blend in. It has to look like a kidnapping."

Yuyudhan was not convinced but he also knew that there was no point arguing. Durgajyoti was behind this. She said it and so they had to follow it.

"Let's go then!" Durgajyoti announced.

*

Mayasur had a palace.

Durgajyoti couldn't believe he was given that, but then Pradhyuman was indeed someone who would give away stuff like this just because he had to return a favour. She had ordered her mercenaries to take their moment and then ordered them to attack. While they did, she stood far in the green pastures and looked at the darkness ahead of her with Yuyudhan, on her horseback. There were a lot of cries and wails as the mercenaries attacked, the spines of the soldiers were being smashed and their eyes were pulled out of the socket. Durgajyoti waited for it.

"Are you sure about this?" He asked.

"Yes, I am," she said. "And what's the point of asking?" She chided.

Durgajyoti waited and then as the loud horn was heard, she made her way on the horse, her face was covered by a hood as she entered the palace. Her face was red, as she saw immovable bodies. Their faces were dark. Their faces were covered with blindfolds.

Her dagger with a sheath on was with her. She knew if someone pounced, she would just stab and break through their flesh and bones.

"What a massacre. Good idea, weblindfolded them."

"The mercenaries are strong."

"Of course, the best. That's why they were hired to do the dirty work."

She was impressed. As she entered the palace, after dismounting, she saw who was in front, with his manacles on and his face covered in a burlap sack. Durgajyoti also saw that there were others who were there, especially the women he had for himself. All naked and looking luscious. He was having the time of his life.

Durgajyoti squared next to Mayasur who was grunting and who was a wee bit drunk.

"What is the meaning of this? Why has it been done? What is going on?" He was yelling out loudly. "I'm protected by the king. You are doing something very wrong. Don't you understand?"

"We need to learn about Mayasabha," Durgajyoti asked.

"Again?

"No. We want to learn where it is in Rasatala."

"I'm not telling anything!"

Durgajyoti sighed. She pulled out her dagger and instantly attacked Mayasur with a blade, slitting his wrist as he began to bleed all across the floor and he couldn't do much about it as he was tied up.

"Now tell me or you'll die in the next couple of minutes. You don't have that much time."

"Don't do this to me please!" He cried loudly.

"Tell us," she coldly rasped.

"I have a family," he cried.

"No, you don't," Durgajyoti arched her brows.

"Okay fine, I don't," he said. "But still, there is more to life than this. Mayasabha is not worth going on... okay fine, I'm bleeding too much."

"Where is it in Rasatala?" She asked again, coldly. "Where is it?"

Mayasur paused and then he spoke again, "It's not there."

"What do you mean?'

"It's not in Rasatala," he explained. "It was never in Rasatala."

For a moment, she was confused. How come the source of magic could be not in the very place where the magic was being used. But then, Mayasur cleared up the confusion as he said, "It's in an alternate plane which only I can access. But for that, you have to make sure I don't bleed too much, so can you please mend me?"

Durgajyoti grunted and then ordered one of her men to do so, tying up the wound instantly.

"Thank you," he sighed. "There's a separate dimension. There's a separate plane that I have created for this. There's no Lokpala to it, but it's a world of just illusions and if you are able to pass through the illusions, you'll be able to get to Maya. You understand? It is the most dangerous place you can be in and you still want to be there?"

"Yes."

He growled. "Fine. But only one person can have access to it."

Durgajyoti arched her brows. "What do you mean?"

"It's um…it's like your consciousness will travel to that plane and I can only help one of you to do it. It takes too much energy but by the end of it, you will know what Maya is, what is the secret of it and how to take control of it."

Durgajyoti was tempted but she was also wondering whether he was lying or not. She remained stoic for a moment, trying to think that perhaps it's not the right thing to do. Going alone, in the word of illusions, the world of mirror was a bad idea. "Fine. I want to do it."

"You are an idiot then."

"But I don't understand one thing, if you know the secret of Maya, why can't you tell us?"

"I can't because I've forgotten it. Don't you understand? I'm the creator and I'm afraid of entering that place. That place brings the worst in me and will bring the worst in you. So, are you sure?"

Durgajyoti clenched her jaws. She could see the earnest eyes of Yuyudhan who she didn't want to disappoint but most of all, she didn't want to disappoint Pradhyuman.

He was her lover. He was the one she wanted to be with…

“Fine,” she said. “Let’s go to Mayasabha, then, shall we?”

26

Balaram knew he had to tell the truth.

This was the right moment, the right time. But he had to choose—who to tell? The loyal servant or his wife. What was really biting and clawing at him was who was the Ledger. But he had to trust someone. Worse, he had been with the Andhakas for a while now and he was waiting for Devamedha to tell him whether she's agreed to the meeting or not. Satyaki would be getting desperate.

But there was something even worse than that. There was, except for this, a new problem. Devamedha's daughter, Sonja. He had to calm her down.

Balaram was in his room, getting bored as he looked outside the window and instead of seeing the world of skies, he saw the insides of the hill where a large bazaar had been created, long bridges that went on top of each other, and there were levels within the mountain itself which had different kinds of people living in them. They all lived in huts and small homes and the most beautiful building was the palace that belonged to Devamedha which he could see at the highest level.

"Devamedha has still not responded. I should have involved Krittaverma. He knows me well."

"But he has been with them for as long as possible.

Born a Vrishni, he chose the Andhaka route and wore the blindfold to support Devamedha," Revathi said. "But there's something else that bothers you."

"There's something I want to share with you, but I'm uncertain whether I should place my belief in it." He turned to find her lying on the bed. The memory of the sherpa's revelation and how his wife was aware of it weighed on his mind. The Ledger held information about the Andhakas' whereabouts, and the sherpa's claim could either be a falsehood or his wife's honesty. He was torn, but as he gazed into her teary eyes, he felt he could confide in her.

"What is it?" she asked.

"It's about the Ledger," he said.

"The what?"

He paused. "Where is Akoorji?" Suddenly remembering the trusted commander.

"I've sent him on an errand," Revathi grinned. "Hope you don't mind."

"What errand?"

*

Akoorji was moving really fast, following Sonja for the third day. There was a time when he would just do this—follow people around and then inform his leader about them. Akoorji was a spy. He would blend in. But amongst the blindfolded people, how could he? He had no clue. So, he had to be silent.

Akoorji had noticed the pattern that Sonja had. She would go on multiple raids outside, hunt for food, talk to her soldiers and then disappear for the night.

Except for today. Today she was walking on the lower level and she was walking without her soldiers but she wasn't wearing the bracelet that would tinkle and tell people that a royalty had just walked past. Something all of Devamedha's highest nobility would wear, so the other class people would know it's them.

He was told to get dirt on her, but she was clean.

He followed her outside the caves, through the exit they were out of the hill and onto to the snowy canyons where there was less crowd. She once turned back, but he instantly hid behind one of the walls and climbed on one of the top structures, to have a bird's eye view. He continued to briskly follow her, his footsteps silent.

And then he saw who she was meeting in the middle of nowhere. It was a rocky structure, the snow was dense, but Akoorji could see who it was in front, who she was meeting.

Krittaverma. The general to the Andhakas.

And before he could make any presumptions, they both kissed.

*

"Do you think you can trust him?" He asked her. "With the dirt part."

"He better should. He's good at it."

"I have a feeling we shouldn't," Balaram was torn. He was frustrated.

"What is it?" She came off her bed, hugging him from behind and asking him again, "Tell me, my love or you'll get a slipper on your head."

He chuckled, even though these were dire situations. "It's this...I was told amongst you two, there's a Ledger who works for Durgajyoti and Pradhyuman and has come here to create problems amongst the two, spoil my plans."

She raised her brows. "And you think it's Akoorji?"

"It can't be you. You are the mother of my children."

She smiled. "What if that person could be playing with your mind? Bala, don't trust anyone."

Balaram nodded. She was right. How could he even dare to mistrust his trusted commander who has given himself up for him. He went forward and hugged her tightly from the front, kissing her on the cheek, when there was a knock on the door. They remained like that as Balaram ordered the soldier to enter:

"What is it?" He demanded.

"It's the queen, my lord." The soldier bowed. "She would like to see you."

"Why?"

"She has made her decision about partnering up with the Vrishnis." His tone was snide, but he said it, as if he had no choice in this matter. "And she would like you to hear it."

*

Akoorji was shocked by this and remained stable for a moment. Krittaverma and Sonja are in love. They were exchanging words, but from the top, he couldn't hear them. Akoorji leaned forward, almost tripping from the ledge, as he heard:

"We need to raid the Vrishnis," Sonja said. "Don't wait for mother's decision. She's passive."

"But I can't go against her," the general said. "I have devoted my loyalty to her."

"And to me as well. I'm the queen, the next queen."

"But not now. For now, she's the one," he said. "I'm sorry, my dear, but that is not possible."

For a moment, Sonja was angry and she even tried to push him away, but there was restraint in her voice, as if she was vulnerable in front of him.

"I will do it myself then. You know I have a lot of loyalists at my end. I'll make sure I'll do it."

"You'll be stupid, because then I would have to side with your mother and it would lead to us fighting. Let's not do this. Be patient."

"I had the bloody eyewitness, Kritaverma! Don't you understand? He had told me Satyaki was the one who murdered my brother and now you want me to go and be friends with them."

"Your mother wouldn't side with a Vrishni."

"She doesn't even believe the eyewitness thing. She doesn't want to believe. She thinks I'm making it up because I want a reason to fight with them."

"But she will be inclined towards believing you," he said. "But it's not about she said, he said. It's about the bandwidth of fighting with the Vrishnis. We can't lose our resources, our home right now."

Akoorji was listening intently, when he got held by the collar from behind as someone grabbed him and shoved him.

"Who are you? Why are you spying on our princess?"

It was an Andhaka soldier, and he was perhaps kept by Sonja to make sure no one was following.

Akoorji found a blade coming towards him and he instantly rolled over, pulling out his twisted dagger and stabbing the soldier in the thigh. He bled profusely and there was a cry. He fell on the ground, alarming Sonja and Krittaverma.

"No, no..." Akoorji cursed as he pulled back and began to climb on the opposite direction to hide himself.

*

Balaram noticed something as he entered the palace. It was an empty room, which had one bridge with no ledge, and there was infinite darkness as well around them, in a circle. There was a statue of a bald man, with a black robe on. Balaram knew it was of course, the demon Andhaka who they all worshipped during the time of Narasimha.

Devamedha was sitting on her throne, with her two hands on the arms of her chair, her face deepened by the wrinkles, and her soldiers were all around her.

"How can I help the queen?" Balaram asked in his cheeky voice.

"I have been thinking."

"Indeed, you have," Balaram smiled. "And any good news?"

"I would hear Satyaki out. If we are on the same page, I am in agreement with doing what he wants if he agrees to one thing."

"And that is?"

"An hour with his father," she replied sternly. "I want to know the truth."

Balaram froze. He knew bringing the man for an hour in the room would mean a ruckus if he blamed his son, leading Devamedha to spoil relations with Satyaki. And his point to create diplomatic relations would fail too.

"And in return," he said, "I would want you to pledge for me against Pradhyuman."

She nodded. "As you say. We both clans will be with you."

Those words sounded nice to him, but he knew there were a lot of problems herewith. He was worried. He was stressed. Balaram tightened his jaws and then let go of the moment, as he decided to leave in search of Akoorji.

Hoping he had found something.

*

Sonja was packing her bags. Frustration was getting to her, and especially since she heard about the entire fiasco with her mother and Balaram. She had agreed! How could she? How could she forget that the Vrishnis were evil and despicable? They were horrible. She had thought about it. She knew she was doing the right thing and that would be kidnapping Satyaki and making sure this meeting doesn't happen.

"Where do you think you are going?"

A voice came from behind her.

Sonja turned frantically, to find the bald-headed betrayer of the person in front of him. He was blowing his well-trimmed nails and he looked larger than anyone out there. He was, after all, a powerful man, brother to Krishna and he had a smile on.

"How did you enter?"

"Everyone knows who I am here. They respect me more than your mother," he said.

Sonja nodded. "None of your business, where I'm going."

"It is, but."

She didn't say. She was ready. She had packed everything and was leaving, when she saw Balaram had closed the door behind him.

"If you think you can escape with your motley crew to do something stupid, hear me out," Balaram reasoned, with a softer voice. "If Satyaki is really guilty, I'll make sure he's punished. But don't screw this meeting for the sake of it. Understand?"

"You are looking at your own intentions and that's the problem," she said.

"Aren't we all? But what you are doing is, you are being impulsive. Devamedha's and Satyaki's meeting is a historic moment in everyone's life on this side of Dvarka. Let it happen please."

She shook her head. "Over your dead body."

"Then I have no choice but to tell your mother about you and Krittaverma."

For a moment, she paused, frozen and afraid. How did he know? She asked herself. And then there was a frightening realisaiton. He was the one who had sent that person who was spying on her when one of her soldiers had attacked him. "I don't think she will mind."

"Oh, she would, since of course, the royalty at Andhaka is supposed to live a celibate life. Wonder how she's going to behave the moment everything goes down."

Balaram didn't want to blackmail, but he had no choice. He was feeling bad and like a villain in someone's life, but he had to do it.

"And you think this would stop me? Disappointing my mother?"

"Yes," he said impassively.

She came close to feeling defeated, she could feel it. But there was an urge, an awakening of not giving up. "You are right," she continued. "But you see, you think of me as someone..." she walked towards the door, opening it, "...as someone who is afraid, but you are wrong. I'M NOT!"

And then she banged the door behind, locking him in, as she saw the light in front and the victory closely within her grasp.

27

Krishna woke up.

He didn't remember what he went through. He didn't remember what was there earlier. The last thing he recalled was that he had been around the feast, on the dinner table and he was eating and then the guards had come. Everything went black after that. Now he scanned his surrounding and he could see the serpents on the ground, and he was in a cage-like structure, while in front, he saw none other than Kaliya who was on an elevated position. He was grinning at him. At the other end, opposite to him, was Samva, and he was hanging upside down with a loose rope that was held by two nagas who were on a large ladder.

Krishna felt paranoid when he saw where he was being hung upside down from. There was a vat of green poisoned acid like container. Krishna could see skulls and bones in the bottom of the acid and he knew if Samva were to fall in it, he would disintegrate, his flesh and skin torn apart

"How does it feel being in a powerless situation, my dear friend?" Kaliya asked loudly thumping his hand.

"It feels grand, to be honest," Krishna sarcastically smiled even though he was scared out of his wits. He had no clue what to do, and he often would use humour as a defence mechanism to hide his fears. "So tell me, why are we here?"

"To basically making sure we are in a position to judge you since now I have the ability to do it. You have gone away all your life doing nothing but judge people."

"I think you got the wrong person here," he shrugged. "I never judged anyone."

"You have judged them on the scale of Dharma. Who is dharmic and who is not? But have you ever thought about yourself? Whether you are dharmic?"

"My intentions were always towards dharma," he sternly added. "And you don't have to involve Samva in this. He has no role in this."

"But he has, you see."

Kaliya snapped his fingers and his men loosened the ropes leading Samva to come closer to the vat of acid. The heartbeat increased, as Krishna could feel his adrenaline pumping hard. But he couldn't show it because Kaliya would try to do this again.

"Oh, I have spies everywhere. Snakes, you see, have a tendency of listening a lot and staying under the ground. And I learnt that you didn't care about your son. Those marks on him, oh well, they are of something you gave him."

Krishna felt a clench in his chest. He didn't like to be reminded of that again. "I am apologetic about it."

"Well, apology wouldn't erase the past, would it now?" He asked. "Now tell me, shall we begin?"

"Begin what?"

"Why we are here?" He smiled. "We are here to commemorate your trial. The trial of Krishna. And any wrong answer, anything that would make me feel it's not genuine, I would put Samva closer to being burnt off. And if you answer well, and you are earnest and true, instead of faking it, you might get what you came for—the Mani."

Krishna was enticed but he didn't like playing this game at all. He was always someone who played with others. He was frustrated, but then he had to let go. "Fine. Continue."

"All right, so the first trial is about your lady love. Someone you cared dearly about, but then it didn't work out. For whatever reason. Now, I was told by my little friends and spies what had happened. Care to know who we are talking about?"

Krishna was confused, clenching his jaws. "Who is it?"

"Oh well, it was of course, Radha," he gleaned forward. "Do you remember her?

The days of Vrindavan came back to him in one big shot. He began to recall all those days he had spent with her. She was his first love, in fact his only love. But it didn't work out. There was frustration. He didn't want to remember anymore, but he knew about one thing and that was—you remember the love that you shared, not the obstacles as time went by.

"I do," he quietly responded.

"Oh well, and how does it make you feel? Her memories."

"I don't know," Krishna shook his head. "But what wrong did I do to her that you put me on trial for her?

"Such defence mechanism. Don't you remember or do I have to make you remember?"

"What?" He spat.

"You left her behind at Vrindavan to leave for Mathura."

"I had no choice. I had important matters to handle," he said. "Mathura needed me."

"Yes, you chose your duties more than the love you had for her. She hated you for this."

"We were young. We were infatuated," he was lying.

He shook his head and snapped his fingers. His men dropped Samva immediately and grabbed him right before he was about to fall in the vat of acid. There was a loud cry and Krishna shrieked, but as he decided to leap from his box of trial, he was hampered by Kaliya.

"Don't you even think of saving him. By the time, you are there, he'll be inside the acid."

Krishna remained there, taking deep breaths. "Fine, fine. Yes, I know I left her and I'm sorry. I'm genuinely sorry. After I killed my uncle, I went back to Vrindavan." As he spoke, he began to remember the last dance he had with her. It was so good, right under the tree, underneath the turbulent skies. And then he had looked in her eyes, she looked back and they both smiled.

"It's true what they say about love," Krishna mulled. "You can't choose the ones you love. No matter what you want. It's not my fault, I left."

"But do you think your life would have been different if you would have gone with her? All the things you did, after that, don't you think you were selfish?"

"Perhaps."

"And a liar."

"I'm not a liar," he said through gritted teeth.

"You said you went for her again, but you didn't, did you?"

He sounded embittered. "Uh…I…I was born here to restore dharma, to be on the side of it and being with Radha made me get away from my purpose."

"So you agree that you left her for yourself? Because you were distracted from your ulterior goal?"

Krishna nodded sadly.

Kaliya nodded back and then he snapped his fingers. For a moment, Krishna thought Samva would be thrown, but he wasn't. He was pulled back.

"A moment of sincerity is always appreciated," Kaliya said.

"Thank you," Krishna sighed. "Are we done here?"

"Far from it," Kaliya smiled. "What about the time when you went in search of Dvarka and you ended up taking the locals out just so the Yayatis could settle?"

Krishna knew this was coming. He was not really happy about this. It was one of his moments of guilt, what he had done was wrong. "I had to think about the survival of my people."

"And yet again, you feel it's justified to betray other people for your own people? Do your people have a higher purpose than the rest? Are they more important? Isn't the great Lord Krishna, the most welcoming of all?"

"I'm just a man."

"No, my lord, you are wrong. You are a god."

Krishna sighed.

"And then," Kaliya added, "you didn't even let them fight the Kurukshetra war. In fact, you made them stay at Dvarka. They had no participation while all the tribes were there. Why is that? Because you were selfish, or you worried about their sustainability?"

Krishna knew he didn't allow them. He didn't want them to participate. "It's about survival. I thought for my people." And he expected Samva to fall again, but Kaliya didn't snap his fingers. He remained stoic and a wide smile formed on his face.

"I am actually happy you were honest. I didn't expect such honesty from you."

Krishna shrugged. "You aren't giving me a chance to lie?"

"A lie that would destroy others, it's not a lie. It's a cataclysm towards destruction."

Krishna agreed. He had done a lot of things in his past, but this was one of them that he was afraid to conquer and there was one more, which he knew Kaliya would bring up soon. Because that directly impacted the person within him.

"When the Pandavas," he began and Krishna lowered his head, "wanted to make Indraprastha, what did you do? What did you suggest?"

"To create it in the woods."

"And who lived in the woods?"

"Takshaka."

"My kin, my brother. And what did you tell the Pandavas to do?"

"Get rid of them," Krishna answered, feeling the guilt shadow him. "It was a slaughter and a massacre as the Nagas were murdered brutally by the Pandavas. I know."

"Do you regret that too? Or does your regret only extend to humans? Aren't we Nagas important? Aren't we Nagas just and pure? Don't we have a heart and soul just like you? Then why such prejudice?"

Krishna pursed his lips and remained quiet. He felt there was no point talking any longer, because this was it—it was over. He had done so many things that were questionable that he couldn't face them now. And Kaliya was indeed making him do it.

"I know I have done wrong. I know I am not perfect," he began, with a slow gurgle of the sound in his throat. "I know I might have destroyed hundreds and thousands of lives. And there's no justification for it..."

"And yet it sounds like you are about to give me one?"

"No, I am done," Krishna shook his head. "I'm a man of honour but I have done dishonourable things. I am a horrible person. I am a wickedly dark individual. I am not a god. I am the man of illusions!"

"Good. Accept who you are."

There was something in his voice, his fingers, as the earth around them began to shake. All of the people around the room began to feel it and fear masked their eyes. Krishna looked up, eyes flaring. Kaliya was about to order Samva to be thrown before he was killed by Krishna, but Krishna calmed himself and the earth stopped shaking and they were fine again.

"I am sorry," Krishna said. "I got carried away."

"And I thought you had no powers," he incredulously stated.

Me too.

He was confused for a while. But then he saw Kaliya coming down from his elevated platform, and then he rested on the ground next to him.

"You have passed with flying colours," Kaliya said. "And as much as I can go back on my word, I'm not like you and that's the difference I wanted you to feel. You sent the wrong man to prison."

Krishna remained there, impassive as he saw Kaliya pulling out the stone from his forehead and handing it to him. Krishna took it in his hands and held on to it. "Thank you and I'm sorry. I feel this journey has made me see what I've done wrong and the repercussions of it."

"Good. You should."

Krishna looked at his old foe and he felt what he often felt: the chance to go back in time and change things. But perhaps, things happen for a reason and everything was predestined. He also saw Samva being pulled up and brought to the ground, he was panting hard and sighing with relief.

"I think we will leave now," Krishna said softly.

And for the first time, he didn't feel anything but numbness.

Krishna remained there for a moment, as Samva was being pulled out of the tank, when something happened. A mist began to gather around them, alarming Kaliya to the point that he questionably watched Krishna, a look of concern forming on his face. The mist grabbed hold of the two Nagas who were holding Samva and Krishna knew what this was.

Durjay.

He had been wondering why he hadn't showed up till now but he was waiting for the right time. And as the mist began to cowl around the Nagas, it sucked them in and slit their faces and their necks, leading them to leave the rope that bound Samva and he fell...

Deep into the tank.

What followed was one of the cruelest and most painful cries of a man ever heard.

28

Pradhyuman didn't know what to say to Mayavati. He was still confused whether there was something to even say. He had not seen her for a while and it had begun to haunt him. He remained in a corner and bit his nails. She looked at him, and they both were in opposite cells, while Pradhyuman could hear all kinds of slurs from his cellmates.

"They sure as hell hate me," Pradhyuman chuckled, trying to strike up a conversation with his stepmother.

"You have managed to irk them more than anyone else."

"Didn't know so many of my enemies were here," Pradhyuman shrugged. "How are you, mother?" He was soft, gentle with his voice.

Mayavati smiled, her black lips being pierced by her fangs. "Can be better."

"How did you end up here?"

"When Shambara rose, he made sure he found a place for me. Little did I know that this was my place."

Pradhyuman was not surprised since it was Mayavati who had conspired against Shambara and Pradhyuman had cut his head off.

"How did he rise, if I may ask?"

She froze for a moment and didn't want to speak. "You look well." She responded instead.

Pradhyuman could see she was hiding something about Shambara. "What is this place exactly?"

"A prison made by Maya. He is too powerful right now because we are in his dreamland. And he had brought the consciousness of a lot of other people here."

"Indeed."

"I sent you so many gifts," Pradhyuman said, "why didn't you ever respond?"

She paused again. Looking down. She didn't like to be confronted. The leaking from the cell doors were heard, from where water dripped. She was quiet. "I didn't know what to say. You had to move on from us. We both don't belong together. I had to hold on to Rasatala and you had to take care of your father's kingdom."

Pradhyuman nodded. He knew that was the truth, but he would have liked his mother to be around. He was about to say something else, when one of his cell mates loudly shouted:

"If I ever get out of here, you are the first one I'm going to gut."

Pradhyuman rolled his eyes. He looked at the shrewd-eyed man with a brown beard who was in the corner, burly and huge like a rock with a penchant for chewing something. For some reason, Pradhyuman could recall him from somewhere. He had done something to the guy, though he had no idea what.

But he ignored him, as two soldiers walked across the narrow lanes of the cell and reached Pradhyuman's cell, barging it open and letting him out, pushing them.

"Your turn."

Pradhyuman knew he hadn't slept, and how could he? He was already sleeping in reality. He pushed himself, his body weak as he turned around to see Mayavati who was watching him with a lingering gaze. Pradhyuman swivelled his head and then moved towards the same arena he had come from a few hours back and he noticed it had not changed. It remained the same, as random people were clapping and they had blank faces, their eyes and their clothes were all a blur.

Pradhyuman was handed a weapon and it was a weapon he didn't like. It was a small dagger. Things to make it worse. He wiped his sweat, as he trudged over the red earth, ready to face Shambara, wondering what he would have in store for him.

"How has it been, my dear friend?" The voice reached him, though the body wasn't present anywhere around. "Hope you had a nice sleep!" And then there was a cackle of laughter.

"Where are you?" He soberly asked.

"So you can attack me again? Oh no, please, don't let me fall into that trap again, now will you?"

Pradhyuman grimaced. He didn't answer him this time, showing that he wasn't bothered, but then Shambara did show himself up. He was right there on the elevated platform where the king would ideally sit and he was loudly clapping for himself, grinning as he went, saying—

"So here I am."

"And me too. What do you want me to do? Dance for you now?"

"Perhaps that would be quite a sight to my sore eyes." And then he snapped his fingers.

Pradhyuman could see that the entire earth he was walking on turn into a bed of coals; of embers burning hot. Pradhyuman instantly began to jump and leap and tried to get a hold of this feeling, but it was getting to him, leading him to intense pain, his feet blackening and his throat yelling with the screeching sound of a whimpering man in pain.

Next moment the ground became normal and he fell on it. He didn't like what he had just faced and it was bothering him. He was a puppet and he could sense it. He was feeling embarrassed and hurt and most of all shamed by a short, fat man who had insecurity issues about himself.

"You are a vicious man," Pradhyuman sneered at him.

"I made you dance, something you haven't done much. You should be thankful, I'm making you do stuff that you haven't experienced," snarkily Shambara added. "Now tell me, are you ready to fight for your life with your contender?"

Pradhyuman had a feeling he knew who he was about to fight. He got his dagger ready and waited for it. It was of course that bearded man from the prison, who hated him. He waited, and then he saw the shadows in the opposite end coming and his enemy, being shorter than Pradhyuman had anticipated, even more handsome than him and...

Familiar.

The boy was familiar.

He had a band around his thick curls and his eyes were lined with kohl. His face was impassive, and he held a chariot wheel in his hand as a weapon, a sword that was already bloody in another and he was a young boy who wanted his parents' love. It reminded him of Pradhyuman when he was young.

And of course, he knew who the boy was...

"Abhimanyu," he breathed.

The son of Arjun, his protege, the one he had trained before the Kurukshetra war. Abhimanyu looked as lively as possible in front of him, but how is that possible?

He was dead. He was killed at Kurukshetra.

"But you can't...you are alive..."

Pradhyuman tossed his dagger and instantly with streaming eyes, full of devoted spirit, sprinted towards his protege to hug him, when Abhimanyu stabbed him right in the stomach and he fell on his back—in an appalling shock. Pradhyuman struggled on the ground, as Abhimanyu loomed over him, taking his sword out and directing it to his heart, as he said: "You left me alone. You didn't come with me to the battle. You would have had my back."

"I was...I was told by my father not to," Pradhyuman said in a weak defence.

And their moment was broken, by a quick stab of his weapon towards Pradhyuman's heart, him knowing that it would lead him to a coma, when he rolled over and lurched for his dagger.

"Now, now, a mentor and a mentee, fighting, what a dear sight it is," Shambara shouted from the top. "Never expected this, did you? A blast from the past. Someone who you had given up on, someone who had trusted you and you had betrayed that trust, well now is the time to confront those."

Pradhyuman couldn't help but look at Abhimanyu who with a static face was moving towards him. One of the many reasons he didn't like his father was because of this—he was told by him to not participate in the war. For whatever reason. He wasn't allowed. So, he travelled with his uncle Balaram to an ashram for a pilgrimage little knowing that his mentee Abhimanyu was there. When he learnt of his mentee's fate, he cried like an infant and wondered if he would have been there for him, things would have been different.

And he had never forgiven his father for this. Perhaps going through that made him realise that it was better to be cruel and heartless, than to be warm and loving.

Abhimanyu reached for his blade and struck towards Pradhyuman who deflected it with his dagger, albeit with difficulty. He kicked him on the chest, since he was taller, but Abhimanyu didn't take it lightly. The young lad stormed at him and hit Pradhyuman on the nose with his broken chariot wheel and it threw Pradhyuman to the corner.

"You left me," Abhimanyu said.

"And you are not real." Even though he knew that, he was having a hard time fighting the boy because he couldn't face him, the face and the body, it was so real and uncanny that it hurt him. "You can't be real. You died."

"Because of you!" He rasped and the blade came towards Pradhyuman and struck him in the chest and he felt it poke across his flesh and bones as he cringed and cried. "You made me suffer. You are the reason..." and then Abhimanyu's rage went deeper.

Pradhyuman snapped at him, "I'm the reason you survived the war as it is. I had trained you and I had protected you. I couldn't be there because of my father and I don't know, things would have been different, you didn't deserve it and more than ever, I'm sorry. I have never been so sorry as I am right now."

Abhimanyu didn't stop.

"And I'm sorry for doing this too..." Pradhyuman added, as he pulled the blade from his chest, yelling and scowling in return as he twisted the boy's hand and took his blade, plunging it deep into his chest. There was a short, stabbing pain before Abhimanyu fell over his body.

And they both were bloody, they both were covered in gore and Pradhyuman hugged the corpse of his mentee, as he saw the figure disappear and turn into smoke.

"Oh, that was boring!" Shambara clapped loudly and all the audience members went quiet all of a sudden. "I thought it'll last longer."

"I knew his left hand was weak," Pradhyuman sighed. Once you know the weakness, it's easier. He was hugging the smoke that had become just wisps by then. His mentee was done for good.

"How does it feel?"

"Can I leave?" Pradhyuman felt defeated.

Shambara didn't have to say anything, as tears fell down from Pradhyuman's eyes. He was pulled by the soldiers, his dagger taken away from him, and he was shoved across the arena when something hit him.

Just like how Abhimanyu had a weakness, Shambara might have one too. Last time Mayavati had to poison the demon so he would sleep while Pradhyuman would cut his head off. He never got to know his weakness per se, and he knew who could tell him, for someone who had been with him for a long time would know such a thing.

Mayavati.

29

He had the same dream again. And on that day, he had talked to someone about it.

Little did he know, who he talked to was Devamedha herself.

Balaram had been travelling with her in the caravan, leaving behind his general and his wife. He had begun to believe that the Ledger conspiracy was just as he had thought—a conspiracy. Balaram had been silent along the way, but his breath had been uneven. He was stressed, for sure. He had a quivering lip.

"Are you concerned about Sonja? She's an impulsive girl," Devamedha said. "Give her space. She'll be fine."

Balaram nodded and as he looked, the caravan was followed by hundreds of her soldiers, all walking like ants in a huddle on the frosty grounds. They were all moving to the designated choice of a place when it came to a truce, a meeting. It had to happen close to the valley that divided the Vrishnis and the Andhakas.

"It's more than that, perhaps," Balaram said softly.

"What?" Devamedha leaned forward, her pristine red bandana across her eyes glistening.

The sound of the wheels and the thumping of the hooves were followed.

"I have dreams."

"We all do."

"Not like this. These dreams perhaps communicate to me," Balaram responded.

"What do you see in them?"

"Despair and gloom, and yet somehow I see myself." He explained, pausing and realising he was being too mysterious. "It's about a snake. The seven-headed or maybe ten-headed one, it's so inconsistent and it speaks to me, to accept me."

Devamedha nodded. "I've heard about this snake all my life.

"Really?" A beacon of hope slathering across his voice. "Who is it?"

"Shesh Naag, the snake that belonged to Lord Vishnu. What does it say?"

"That I must protect..."

And then he realised. His brother was the avatar of Lord Vishnu, and he was his snake...that's why. It was clear. He had to be there for him. The snake wasn't bad. It was good...or perhaps it wanted to destroy him.

I must confront it the next time I dream about it.

"Do you believe about the eyewitness regarding your son's death?"

"I don't," she murmured.

"Why?"

"A long time ago, when I had anger fuelled in me after the death of my son, I had tried to motivate a lot of people around me and no one would listen and so I got some charlatans to spread lies to motivate them. Little did I know, that lie would catch up with my daughters."

He raised his brows. "That was a lie?" Of course! He knew Satyaki was not capable of it.

"Yes. I thought it would rouse the public and when I saw my daughter being the victim of my actions, I instantly stopped it from happening. Lies are used for the greater good, and sometimes used for the worst of blasphemous actions."

There was a lot of regret laced in her voice.

"I am sorry. I know I sound horrible." She shook her head. "And now she's on her crusade. But don't worry, I wouldn't let it spoil the meeting that we have scheduled today."

She sounded confident. And so, he was too. He remained quiet for the time being, looking at the road ahead and wondering what life would have been without regrets.

*

The valley was flourishing. As discussed by the truce agreements, both parties brought in respective members from their end. Both had ten soldiers to their disposal and promised that they wouldn't be carrying any weapons along with them.

Balaram came out of the caravan, hearing the gushing of the valley swooning in the background. Devamedha came out too, dismounting from his horse. The Prime Minister of Dvarkipur saw Satyaki from far and nodded. He looked happy. They had both established a large sitting area where both parties would discuss the matter.

Balaram with his staff made his way to one of the chairs and made himself comfortable, while his eyes darted across the landscape in search of anything fishy.

He was worried that she would attack them; that Sonja would come. He was trying very hard not to think. He remained silent.

Devamedha sat next to him and so did Satyaki, at the opposite end.

"It's nice to see you Aunt Devamedha, after a long time," Satyaki said humbly. He had long hair, tied up nicely in a ponytail. "I am glad we are here. And I'm glad you chose to listen to me."

"If not for the mediator, I wouldn't be," Devamedha said.

Balaram continued to watch, he could see Krittaverma on one end who was solemnly standing, obedient and erect. Krittaverma must be considering multiple things and Balaram was glad that he chose not to be around Sonja's choice.

"I understand Uncle Bala has his own intentions," Satyaki added.

"Indeed," Bala responded earnestly. "I want you both to shake hands and do right by each other."

Satyaki raised his brows. "And I'm fine with it. Are you, your grace?"

Devamedha hesitated. "I have a few questions."

"Please shoot away."

"Why would you want to stab a knife on your father's back?"

Satyaki began, "Because he's a cruel man."

"No, why? Why does it personally bother you?"

"Because he troubles a lot of civilians, makes them feel terrible about themselves, have abhorrent forms of..."

Devamedha raised her fingers. "Why?" She asked again in a lethal tone. "You give me such utopian ideals and reasons and yet I can't feel convinced. The one thing of binding cloth around my eyes, is that it has made me more perceptive towards the other senses and I can sense your heartbeat, your voice, and I know for sure, you are hiding something."

Satyaki shared a glance with Balaram who chided him to speak the truth, afraid that the truth might scour away or gain a new partnership.

"There's nothing..."

"Don't lie. If you want this partnership to start, you should make me trust you."

Satyaki flared his nostrils. "You don't have to. I can do this by myself then. I think this was not the right move, Uncle Bala."

"Just hold on..."

Satyaki came on his feet, furiously tossing the chair in the back. "I don't like to be questioned like this."

"I just asked a simple question," Devamedha smiled and shrugged.

"It's okay, calm down," Bala tried to intervene, attempting to soothe Satyaki into not saying anything rash. "Believe me, when I say this, but we are in the right process. All right? Just be honest with her. Just tell me. I'm sure you must have a legitimate reason."

He saw the colour on the young lad's face change to red and his eyes streaming with pure hot hatred as well as sadness laced in it.

"I fell in love," Satyaki responded in a glum voice. "She was of low class, not someone who fit his ideals and I was deeply hurt when I got to know that he had shipped her to be mauled by a bunch of foreigners. I never saw her again and the hatred in me has been ever since then. I hope you got your answer."

"Love makes you do crazy things," Devamedha sighed. "I see. And now your heartbeat is brilliantly concise. Why hide such things?"

"Because I don't want to blame my cause on some triviality like love."

"Love is not trivial. It's the second greatest form of emotion to ever exist," Devamedha said.

"What's the first?" Satyaki asked.

"Pain." She shook her head. "It is of deep sadness and I still remember, my son was murdered right here. By a pack of wolves. By a pack of Vrishnis."

"I'm sorry," Satyaki said softly.

"I am ready to hold you and support your men, but in return," Devamedha said, "I would be requiring you to give me alone time with your father. I want to torture him. I want to hurt him till he tells me who killed my son."

Satyaki's face froze and he was basically being told by his enemy to hurt his father. And he nodded with such ease that Balaram felt comforted even though they were talking about Yudhajit, his old friend. Though seeing all of this, for Balaram it was important to figure out what his priority was and he was beginning to feel that due to the same, he would lose himself, but he had to support his brother, he *had* to support him.

Balaram looked around yet again, hoping for Sonja to turn up but nothing happened. And then with solace he saw Satyaki and Devamedha shaking hands, then embracing and Balaram couldn't help but smile. He was right where he wanted to be and his plans were coming to fruition.

*

The camp had been turned into a celebratory dinner by the end, where people came together in solace. They had begun to dance and cheer and discuss strategies. A fire was lit and men from both sides circled around protecting the camp.

After a long time, Balaram had been drinking his mead and was enjoying while his mind would be scampered into the dull nights of the Vitihotras, especially the one who had attacked him. Surprisingly, he had not seen the creature for a while now and it puzzled him. Why not? Even Sonja for that matter wasn't here. Why not?

The questions kept cropping up and he could have contemplated leaning on his staff, instead he rested and didn't bother. The mead was getting to his head and he was enjoying the mood, the triumph that was closing in. He knew he was doing the right thing by siding with Satyaki and Devamedha, two good people.

And while he enjoyed the lullabies, he was away from the camp and he was watching the stars when a familiar voice called out:

"You shouldn't have done this." The voice declared.

Balaram turned to face the bearded Krittaverma and he was looking solemn as ever, sad with his head lowered. He had no drink and it looked like he was going away, on his way to his horse perhaps.

"And why not?"

"All I can promise is, do not lose your humanity in the process of gaining something greater."

"How do I plan to lose humanity?"

"There's a reason why the Andhakas and the Vrishnis were head-to-head for a while. There was a reason. Because both of them just don't sit well together, because both of them have done some really horrible things to each other."

Balaram thought about it. Very often, he would wonder if he was losing himself in the process of doing this. Of serving his brother and then there was this single greatest urge of asking the snake in his dreams for guidance, in case that would help him. But why not? He asked again. Krittaverma had left and he found another figure cosying up to Balaram and it was Satyaki, feeling triumphant and charming as always.

"Aw great, it is," he smiled, "what a lovely time it was. Thank you, uncle."

"You do right now. We plan a rebellion, and we have to plan it well."

"We shall."

They both cheered with their goblets.

"I thought Sonja would show up, but she didn't," Balaram said. "And now I wonder where she is. So, stay on your toes and hope she doesn't surprise you."

"Oh, don't worry, she won't." He confidently shrugged it off.

And then he moved away from Balaram, when he called out. "What happened? What did you mean by that?"

He smirked. "That she came and attacked and we defeated her. Then I dropped her in the ice-cold water and froze her to death or whatever can be worse than death."

"But..." Balaram's eyes widened and his blood ran cold. "How could you?"

"She was a problem to us, uncle. And problems need to be eradicated, always remember that. Just like Devamedha's son and how my father had to make sure that he had to be put down because he got to know about my father's plan to ruin the Andhakas."

It was Yudhajit. He indeed killed the boy.

But Satyaki smiled.

"Are you going to do the same?" Balaram asked, even though he felt he was so wrong and he had been such a fool in believing Satyaki. The boy was a monster and he had just sided with the wrong person. "To Devamedha. Get rid of her after the job is done and you take the crown?"

There was a sheen in his eyes, a glisten of frantic coldness that Balaram hadn't seen in him for all the years he had known him. "I don't know. I'm quite a spontaneous fellow. So..."

He left.

And Balaram was left there with another regret in an already long list.

30

By the time Krishna had brought Samva out of the tank, he could see Samva had already drunk the poison. Luckily his skin didn't disintegrate, but he was unconscious and the mist had cleared. He wanted to yell at Kaliya, and at Durjay, but he was just holding his boy on his lap and caressing him.

"What just happened?" Kaliya asked.

"What you instigated. You should have never done this entire charade."

Kaliya scowled. "I did it for a purpose and that has been served."

"We were chased by a malevolent entity and now..." his heart was paining. "This poison, how dangerous it is?"

"It kills your organs one by one, burning your skin in the process. You hardly have time, to be honest."

Great. Krishna growled under his breath. He didn't know what his options were, but he knew Kaliya would have some. In an instant, he lurched at the snake king and threw him on the ground, hitting his head against the earth. "Tell me, what I can do for my son. Tell me! I dare you!"

Kaliya's eyes were masked with fear and for a moment, he was taken aback, until he revealed: "There's a way. Okay? Calm down."

"What?"

Kaliya began to choke as Krishna's arms were around his throat, slowly he loosened his grip but still towered over him, so there would be a sense of threat looming.

"Naraka."

Krishna narrowed his gaze. "No. It can't be."

"The Somas, the last remnants of it were taken by your enemy."

"Narakasura," he shook his head. "I hate that monster. That's one regret I don't have."

"I don't know the story but ever since I've been here, we talk, there's gossip. And Narak has been built into this plane of existence where you can meet Narakasura if you pass his trials. He has the Amrit but for that, he would ask you to do stuff. I don't know what. No one ventures there."

Krishna knew that each loka, a plane of existence has a separate world and Naraka, just like earth, belonged to that existence ruled by someone or the other. Naraka though was far more insane, because it was, in short, a torture chamber with blood and fire and rage all around. Narakasura, on the other hand, was a malevolent king that Krishna had defeated a long time ago with his wife Satyabhama after he had kidnapped many women and kept them captive.

"The Lokpala to the Naraka is good friends with the king. He doesn't allow anyone till you accept the trials and he would definitely not accept you. You are his enemy."

"But there's no guarantee he would give me the Amrit?" Krishna asked and by that time, he already knew the answer.

Why would he? Unless he would play the games.

Krishna wanted to kill Durjay and be done with it, but the Vitihotras are the undead. You can't kill the ones who are already dead. But he had to get rid of him. How? He would figure out after saving his son.

"I need your help then," he said to Kaliya, still clinging on to the mani which was given to him. "I need some ingredients to open a portal."

*

Krishna had done all due diligence and armed himself by the time he was planning to open the portal. It was, after all, a lengthy process and Kaliya had helped him surprisingly. He had thought the snake king would get rid of him, saying it's not his job, but perhaps he felt sad for Krishna.

By the end, as the portal had begun to open, he looked at Kaliya and said:

"Thank you." He paused. "I was wrong about you and I believe I should have heard your side of the story the day when we first met. I was young, foolish and impulsive."

"What are you now?"

"The same, except the young part."

They both shared a slight chuckle.

"I hope you take care of my boy till I return."

"Don't worry."

Krishna shared one glance with Samva again and then looked in front as the portal had opened, with swishing and sousing of purple, blue shades all mixing with each other. Krishna could see someone was exiting the portal as it always happens and it was none other than a hermit looking person, the lokpala with matted hair and a staff, just like the one from the Naga kingdom.

"Ah, interesting place, I have been summoned..." and his eyes lay flat on Krishna, "and interesting people calling me."

Kaliya was behind with his men and Samva on the ground, over a cot that had been put on him.

"I want to meet Narakasura. I have an important and urgent meeting with them."

Killing these Asuras has a downfall. Even though Krishna clearly remembered severing the Asura's head, he had been able to survive and stuck himself into the land of the dead and the underground world. No one dies here. They all go through torture.

"Don't we all?" said the hermit. "But why would he want to meet you, is a bigger question?"

"It's because he knows me."

"Everyone knows Narakasura. We founded the land on him." The hermit chuckled.

Krishna had no patience. "You can't deny me entry if I have pure and peaceful intentions and I do have that. You can sense it."

"Oh, I do, but I also sense a lot of restlessness and I'm worried it could lead to..."

"No, it won't."

"You prove my point."

Krishna gritted his teeth and told himself to calm down. He remained there stoic and was about to even further protest more, when the Lokpala moved aside, surprising everyone, even Kaliya who gasped.

"You may go. I have a feeling, this would be an interesting encounter, though meeting Narakasura, our king and the one who rules our land, is not that easy. For that, you must pass a trial and that trial would entail you to do few things. You may enter and know what it is."

Krishna raised his brows but he clung on to the mani, the mace and his chakras as he entered the swishing purple door, finally making his way through and finding himself in a broken land of broken kingdoms. The sky was red and so was the earth, and there were a lot of dilapidated buildings around him, while the bridge was created by a smoke in front of him.

Krishna began to walk on the cloud-shaped bridge, and as he moved further, he heard the voice, amongst the emptiness and the loneliness that this place had to offer.

"Welcome to my domain, Lord Krishna. It is after a great many years, I have seen you."

Krishna didn't know where it came from, but he continued to walk. "Yeah, well, it's not really a social visit."

"Indeed, I believe you have come here for a reason." The voice echoed.

Krishna could see the corpses and the bodies falling out of the sky and volcanoes bursting out in the background. It was all so damp and dark around here. He remained stoic and tight-lipped. "I am here for the Amrit," he blurted out honestly. "My son is in danger and I believe we both can show a bit of a maturity and you can give it to me instead of me chasing you for it."

"You don't have to chase anything."

And in front of him, a smoke formed and out of it, appeared an apparition, in white. It was, after all, Narakasura, with his handsome chiselled face, a light stubble over his cheeks and white hair, frizzled from the sideburns and the side heads. He was a handsome fellow, other than the fact that he was a ghost.

"If you want it, it is right here," Narakasura smiled, as he presented the vial in front of him and that was the only thing that looked real on him. "It has the last surviving Amrit and you may have it."

Krishna knew there was indeed some trick. "Aren't you angry I killed you?"

"I was a cruel man, what can I say? I have been here and atoned for my sins, repented and now I am changed. I do not want to hurt anyone, but just..."

"Why aren't there more people in Narak? The ones who follow you, the ones who worship you here."

"Because you were coming and I wanted no disturbance."

Krishna was trying to figure out his foe and realising he had never thought that this travelling across portals, fighting old foes would be a thing with him. He always wanted to be at his home, but he was here and he couldn't believe it. He came forward, briskly moving to get himself the vial, when the apparition disappeared in front of him and appeared behind him.

"Oh, not so fast. You do have to do something for me."

"What?" That was the trick.

The man looked elegant and not slimy like Kaliya. He was tall and majestic.

"Tell me about Satyabhama. Where is she? She's usually with you, isn't she?"

Krishna pursed his lips. "She left me and settled in the forest with the rest of the girls we had saved from you. She wants to do nothing with me."

"And why is that, hmmm?"

"I...erm..." he didn't want to remember but he knew the vial was dependent on this information. "She knew I loved Rukmini, my first wife. She knew no matter what she did, she could never be able to match her and thus, she gave up and left."

"Do you miss her?"

"Of course."

"You both were a good team." The apparition floated in circles around Krishna. "What a team, I would say. Both of you were out of the way going and you had defeated all my fortresses and killed me. She was quite a girl."

"I know. She was brilliant."

"Did you ever love a woman as purely as you loved yourself?"

"I don't think I love myself."

"A narcissist would say that, for sure." Mundanely the apparition sighed. "Perhaps, there's still hope for you. The last time I met you, you were quite an angry, pompous man and now you are someone who's defeated and wants to go home. What changed?"

"My past. My actions." He honestly responded as if it was an interview.

"Good." And the apparition in front of him stopped, handing him the vial. "You may go..."

And as he grabbed it, Narakasura brought in his other hand, which had another vial. It was a different kind of colour—green and reddish it seemed.

"What is this? Some kind of trick?"

"Yes, indeed. The left palm of mine holds the Halhala, a powerful poison that was spat from the throat of Lord Shiva. The other one holds Amrit, the celestial drink of the gods. To get either, you must have both and ingest one."

"What do you mean?" Krishna raised his brows. "I can't ingest the Halhala because it'll kill me, but if I ingest the Amrit, there would be nothing left to give to my son."

"Well, technicalities have never been my forte."

"You have always been a trickster." Krishna wanted to choke the living daylights out of Narakasura, but he was a ghost, a spirit. "You want me to kill myself."

Narakasura shrugged. "It's your choice, what decision you would like to make for yourself. If you take the Halahala, the Amrit would be given to Samva since you would have time to return but the Halhala will grow and it'll slowly kill you."

Krishna knew he had to save his son and it didn't matter, whether it would risk his life. He was already dead a long time back. Without thinking twice, he took the Halhala poison and drank it. He knew that by doing this, he had limited his life span, but it was enough for him to go and save his son and save Dvarka and hopefully reach in time to do everything. As he drank the Halhala poison, he was enamoured by the entirety of it and he felt weak, his stomach hurting and burning at the same time.

Krishna held the other vial which had the Amrit and with it, he turned around, the portal's work was done. He looked at Narakasura and asked: "How much time do I have?"

"It depends on your immunity and your will power. Perhaps you might die now or a day from now or a month, but you would die. And it would be uncertain. You have, after all, signed a deal with death."

Krishna nodded. And then, he entered the portal, knowing full well that his time in this world was limited.

*

By the time, he had arrived, he saw his son's body was slowly going purple and his mouth was foaming. Kaliya was still there, sitting worried and so were his soldiers like before. The portal closed behind them, and Krishna rushed to his son, kneeling next to him and forcing him to drink the elixir, trickling it in his mouth as Kaliya asked:

"What did he ask you to do?"

"Nothing. Just nothing."

"What did you do? I have a feeling you did something wrong to save your son."

Krishna didn't bother to answer. If it wasn't for Kaliya, he won't have been in this situation in the first place. His son coughed and he was back to his senses, the colour of his skin getting better while his mouth's foaming had become all right. Krishna hugged him tightly, knowing full well he was suffering from leprosy but he didn't care. He had just done something right after such a long time and it had made him feel alive again.

Yes. Alive. That would be the right word to describe him.

"What...happened?" He coughed and asked, his son.

"Nothing. It's going to be fine."

But it wasn't.

Now he had to rush to get to Antar Dvipa and find Durvasa and learn about the Erakas. But Antar Dvipa held a great mysterious and darker past of his.

Was he ready to face it?

Perhaps.

31

Durgajyoti was lying down, in the middle of the dilapidated palace that she and her mercenary people had managed to hunt down and destroy. She was lying on a rock slab, while the burlap-sacked head Mayasur was towering around her, even though he was a short, feeble man himself.

Yuyudhan was holding her hand, and awkwardly enough, she felt warmth in it.

"Are you sure about this?" He asked softly.

"Yes, quite so." She sternly added. "If this is the only way to get Maya, then I might as well do it."

Yuyudhan nodded.

"If the chit-chat is done, shall we begin?" Mayasur growled. "I don't want to be blind forever, you know."

Durgajyoti sniggered and allowed it to start. All her people were standing in a circle, and Yuyudhan left her place. Mayasur began to chant and kept her palms rested next to her forehead, as blue, zapping energy began to pass electric currents.

"I want to give you a heads up," he said.

"What?" She snarled.

"Many people have tried to attain the Maya as a source, and none have achieved it. It's not some heist you can perform, and there's no treasure chest either. Maya is a word, a thing and an object."

"You don't make sense."

"And that's exactly what Maya is." He gritted his teeth. "Now I don't know you, lass, but I do know one thing. Women in general have failed miserably, let alone men. They have woken up mad or they haven't woken up at all. Their brains have been fried."

"Thanks for scaring me. Any helpful tip you can give me?"

"The tip is do not enter Mayasabha," he sighed. "But I believe we are past that. Remember, clearly then."

"What?"

"Don't trust anything. And don't be afraid of your fears. Mayasabha has a charm for taking control of what haunts you the most." He paused. "And Maya shall be obtained, once you learn what it wants to show you."

Durgajyoti grimaced. That didn't feel good. There were a lot of things she feared. There were a lot of things she hated too. But then her mind raced back to the time that reminded her why she started this endeavour. She was haunted by the coma-stricken body of Pradhyuman and how happy he would be if he woke up and saw what she had in store for him. What she had done for him. It was a gift of happiness, a gift of eternal life. Durgajyoti wanted to do this for Pradhyuman and the love she had for him was insurmountable. She wanted to have a picture-perfect life, a life where she could be happy. She wanted to share that life with him because for her, he was the one who could give her happiness, who could make her feel content. Who gave her strength and the motivation to wake up every day, otherwise she had lost herself in the terrible arms of Durjay, the insatiable and horrible husband of hers.

But there was darkness in her life.

And she was about to face it.

The energy zapped in her, her forehead bursting with a billion colours and a trillion sounds of all kinds as she yelled loudly...

*

Her reality changed and when she opened her eyes, she didn't find herself with any pain. In fact, there was a sense of calmness and satisfaction that she didn't have earlier, a warmth that she could be craving for the rest of her life. Only to realise, that she had woken up in a forest. There was greenery around her and a spot of sunlight just dancing over her eyes, a smile forming in her face.

Where am I? Was her first question.

She sighed and came on her feet, hoping to scan her surrounding and try to register where she was—and it was a dense forest, a fairytale-like place. There was nothing scary or extraordinary about it.

She began to walk and she heard the caws of the ravens that fluttered across the skies, the baboons sucking their thumbs and watching her from the trees, and the trudge of the crumpled leaves her sandals were making. She came close to a lagoon, after passing through the clearing and saw what a beautiful waterbody one could have in this area.

"I think I'm beginning to like this." She grinned to herself. "Baagul, what do you think?"

"I feel I can't trust anything." The voice within her

answered in a hissing tone. "But I'm quite excited to see what this Maya has."

And that was when she heard it. Loud steps. Quick ones too. It came from the south. Her ears were ringing and she saw amidst the bushes and the wooden tendrils, the branches, there was a young girl rushing towards her, in rags and loins. Her eyes were turquoise-coloured, just like Durgajyoti but her hair was not short like her's. Her face was oval and she was in a hurry, running as fast as she could until she circled around Durgajyoti.

The girl came behind Durgajyoti and tried to cower.

"What are you running from? What happened? Is everything okay?"

But the girl remained quiet. There were a few other individuals appearing from the clearing and they had swords and shafts in their hands. The man in the middle though, was in fact taller than most and had curls. He wore a large helmet which covered his face too.

"Why are they after you?" Durgajyoti asked the girl.

"Don't trust anything," said the voice within her. And then she instantly realised, this is all an illusion. None of it is real.

But she could feel the little girl's fears and her eyes watering and her face just getting all pale and scared. No matter how much Durgajyoti would try to convince herself that it was not real, it did seem real to her.

"Give it to us, woman." Rasped the soldier. They were in a strange armour and had long swords with shields. "She belongs with us. She's our master's favourite."

Durgajyoti looked at the man in between, who they were referring to as the master. "I don't think so," she finally said, feeling protective for some reason, probably because she was herself in this situation once upon a time. “Get lost.”

“Oh you mess with the wrong lot,” the soldier chided and stormed at her.

A strange energy began to leap out of her fingers, and of a white and pale variety, she shot electric currents across the area, hitting the men on the chest and another on the face, burning them and killing them. She felt different, finally killing someone for a change since most Yayatis were immune to death.

Was she not on a makeshift, illusionary Dvarka anymore? It seemed like it.

The main master remained calm as he brought his hammer and moved slowly towards Durgajyoti. She began to muster the energy of Baagul, her eyes growing cat-like and her face exploding with multiple colours...

And she threw that energy towards the man who was coming at her, but he deflected it with his hammer.

“This has never happened before.” Hissed the voice within.

He came forward with the hammer, and the moment he attacked, Durgajyoti pushed the girl aside and brought her own hands forward, producing a certain energy in front to deflect. There was a shield that she had crafted for herself.

“Who are you?” She yelled. And as she did, she pushed and shoved him behind.

The man stepped back and Durgajyoti asked the girl to run. She did so, as they began to run behind, while the man with the hammer remained where he was.

*

Rain had begun to pour, and they had found a cave for themselves. Durgajyoti had brought in logs and warmed up the fireplace by the zap of her fingers. She sat, warming the young girl and asked her:

"What's your name?"

The girl looked at her and smiled. She was dirty and she looked like she had gone through a lot.

"Silence," she responded.

"Silence? Who gave you that name?"

She signalled at herself.

"And why is that?"

"Because I like to be silent."

Durgajyoti felt sad. She could see herself in her. "What did this master want from you? Why was he after you?"

"He wants to consume me."

"Consume?"

"Yes." She was shivering and scared. "He wants to hurt me."

A voice within her said. "Not real, Durgajyoti. Do not be hassled by the power of illusions. It's all fake."

But it doesn't seem so. What if the illusion was the fact that it's supposed to look like an illusion but wasn't really?

That could be a possibility.

"Well, don't worry, you are safe with me."

"I want to protect myself."

"And you shall."

"How?"

"You have me. Don't worry."

The little girl blinked. The colour of the eyes, the

face, the lips, Durgajyoti realised there was something very uncanny about it. She looked around the forest, and then at the fireplace, then it began to hit her. She had been here before. But she was not the person she was now. She was the little girl. She was...

"You are me." She whispered to the girl.

Mayasabha wants to show me something. But what?

Memories raced back and she could remember the time, she was small and she was running from the people of Taljans who wanted to bring her back. They wanted to take her as a sex slave and hurt her. Because she was liked by everyone, for her eyes. Her eyes were what attracted everyone.

"It's trying to show you something." The voice within hissed.

"Yes, but what?" Durgajyoti responded, under her breath.

"Hmmm?" The girl next to her asked. "Is everything fine?"

"Yeah, yeah."

Durgajyoti had to find the lesson behind what was being shown to her. Or it could be just one of the miseries she was being portrayed as. It was strange and eerie to see herself like this, in this position and to see herself.

"Tell me something. What did the master look like?" Durgajyoti asked, if her memories were being corrected.

And before she could answer, in front of them, she saw a figure. The person had arrived. And it was huge, amidst the rain and had a mammoth hammer in his hands.

"He never gives up, does he?" Durgajyoti said through gritted teeth.

"Please save me," the girl cried and hugged her.

"Don't worry."

Durgajyoti entered the rainfall, her fingers buzzing with energy, her eyes with smoke tendrils coming out as she continued to channel Baagul.

"Whoever you are, leave us," she said, even though she had a hard time knowing the identity, she could have figured out who it was. Durjay, of course, the man who had tormented her.

The hammer came forward and she deflected it with her powers and as she did, the hammer struck away from the man. But the man didn't stop as he went for a punch directly towards her. She felt the punch against the cheeks and she could feel the blood in her mouth.

Durgajyoti smacked her powerful energetic hands towards the master's chest and he fell on the ground, as she went to take over and began to bring forth the rocks around it, using her telepathic powers to strike the rocks against the man's face and hitting them directly again and again. It tortured and destroyed the person. Durgajyoti then decided to choke the man.

"You have been troubling me and destroying my life ever since I was a kid. I was a small child when you took interest in me and it hurts me that you continue to haunt me. No more shall I be pressurised by the likes of you."

The choking from the Baagul's energy was causing a gurgling, helpless sound and the last breaths that were coming out of the man could be heard.

Durgajyoti grinned and wiped the wet hair from her

face, as she pulled away the mask. Looking at the face, she instantly threw herself back with horror and shock masking over her face. She looked back at the girl from the cave and she had disappeared by now. In fact, the man whom she had just killed disappeared too and the reality around her was crumbling.

For she knew, the man that she had seen today and killed ruthlessly, was none other than Pradhyuman.

32

He was told she was here.

It was clear as day, though the mountains in the background looked darker.

The soldier, like just any other soldier, began to move towards the snow-crusted land. The wind was hefty and thus he had a large coat over him. He had fur as a way to protect himself. The flakes fell from the sky and got mixed with the land of the ice and blueness around him. His footsteps were heard and so was the trinket that he had.

He was given very clear instructions by the person that he would find it here. And he had to take off his bandana from his eyes and see it. He had never done it. He was told to culturally wear the bandana always. It was a task to do so, and he would take it off but it was a religious practice they would follow.

But here, he was given the freedom to do so.

He made his way through the snow and out of it, until he found he was stepping on a glass-like ground, which was brittle and scary to walk on. His walk became less focussed and he was more inclined towards holding himself here. He was afraid of falling down in the cold water. He was standing on thin ice and he could feel it. At this moment, he pulled at his bandana and he saw the life around him, with plenty of colours and a lot of movement. In the far end, he could see the elks who were watching him, perhaps wondering what a fool he was that he had been traveling on this ice. He walked a few paces ahead, and as he reached closer, he saw what he had come for.

What the person the Ledger had told him he would see.

It was, after all, the frozen body of his queen Devamedha's daughter, the princess and the scion to the Andhaka clan. The soldier's lip began to shiver and his eyes turned frighteningly horrific. He saw the lifeless eyes of the woman, underneath the water, probably drowned and suffering from hypothermia. She could be alive, but she had gone through too much. He wanted to run back and tell everyone, but he had to save her first.

He should save her, if there was a point of it at all.

*

Balaram had seen how things had changed ever since Satyaki and Devamedha had become power allies. They had both joined camps, and the initial camp that was settled grew larger and more noticeable with Revathi and his general Akoorji also joining. But seeing all of this was drowning him even furthermore in guilt, for he was siding with a murderer—Satyaki. He should have known better.

For now, he was standing outside Devamedha's tent and he was waiting for her to see him. Satyaki was there, joined with a careful grin and his ponytail glistening under the morning sun. They remained in silence while the humdrum of camp life was going on behind them, the sharpening of the swords over a whetstone or perhaps the lullabies the soldiers sung to each other.

"Are you angry with me?" Satyaki asked softly. He didn't have the same drunken attitude that he was showing before so recklessly. "Believe me, I only did it for the betterment of the land and of the people who I strive to protect."

"You could have imprisoned her."

"She had fire and we live on ice. She could have melted me if I would not have punished her, or kept her where she could not be known."

"But she is known. I know where she is."

"And did you do something about it?"

Balaram shook his head. He had only told Revathi and Akoorji about this. He couldn't keep it in his stomach because it made him wretched.

"We are as good as the partnership if we keep our mouths shut, uncle. I hope I can trust you with the discretion. I don't want a civil war."

Balaram nodded. Did he have a choice? "You said your father killed Devamedha's son and now her daughter is missing. If she finds out..."

"We make sure she doesn't, all right?" He chuckled as if it was a joke.

Balaram could see he was talking like a sociopath and had no empathy left in him. He could see Krittaverma on the outskirts, sitting next to the bonfire and being by himself, probably wondering where Sonja was.

"I need to take vengeance for the one who deserves

the vengeance. My father must be punished and he must be punished brutally. Whatever I do, I do for her." He sincerely added, trying to mask the fun he had punishing Sonja.

Balaram didn't bother saying anything as Devamedha allowed them to enter and as they did, they could see she was sipping her ale and was chatting with her soldiers. They were in a war room situation where maps were laid down, where figurines were kept. They were planning a battle and Balaram was participating in it.

"Where are we at?" Asked Satyaki confidently as he poured himself a glass of ale.

The tent was red and low on light, and it was tough to see, though Devamedha was touching the figurines and the maps to figure out how the plan was shaping up.

"We are stuck at the southern gate and eastern gate nonsense. What should we do regarding that? Should we attack both?"

"We attack all four gates," Satyaki explained. "We need to destabilise him and surprise him. Go with full force and let him not see us coming from a mile off. And it's a straight battle."

"Ugh," Devamedha sighed, "I wish Sonja was here. She's good at this stuff. I've gotten too old for this." She shook her head. "I don't even know where she is."

Balaram and Satyaki shared a glance, with Satyaki grinning to himself as if it was a joke.

"Believe me, your grace," Satyaki added, "we are right where we are supposed to be. What we need to do is, to get some of the chariots, use the cavalry..."

Balaram coughed in the middle to divert the attention.

They both turned to him and he remained stoic as he was, when he said: "That won't work."

"Might I say then, please enlighten us what would?"

"Yudhajit is a pompous man," Balaram began to circle the two allies of his. "We need to use that to our advantage. We need to fool him."

"How do we do that?"

"The thing is, attacking his entire army would be a fool's errand because he's too big. He has too big an army and a lot of people respect him. But if we imprison him from within, he wouldn't have the same power anymore. People wouldn't fear him and Satyaki can take his place."

"How do you plan to do that?" Devamedha asked, with interest.

"Satyaki brings in you, Devamedha, to the gates saying that he has caught you and that you will be imprisoned. Of course, that would be all a big hocus pocus, and the moment you are in the room with Yudhajit, you attack him. Meanwhile Satyaki's men begin to attack the palace guards and take them out, bringing a small bridge for your people. Devamedha comes and becomes a part of the raid as well. The moment you are done with Yudhajit, get rid of him and voila, you have the fortress to yourself. But do not show your presence too much. You remain the prisoner, just for the sake of it, and we show that Yudhajit has died or something. Satyaki remains the king and then later on, in a month or so perhaps there'll be a truce between the Andhakas and the Vrishnis, ensuring people also follow that without any hassle. Otherwise, you might have a rebellion on your hand if you shake hands with Devamedha immediately. Don't forget the historical enmity you both have."

As he explained, they intently listened and continued to nod. They were surely enticed, and Devamedha raising her brows said: "How do I know, Satyaki won't go back on his terms when he has the crown, and he holds me as his makeshift prisoner?"

"Oh, come on!" Satyaki protested.

"Don't worry about that, Devamedha. You are here, allying with him, because of me. You trust me, and I trust him," Balaram flared his nostrils, lying through his teeth.

"All right then, the idea seems fine," Devamedha said. "It would require less resources of ours and I'm more than happy about that."

Satyaki agreed as well. Devamedha added, "I would like to speak to Bala for a moment, if you don't mind, boy."

Satyaki nodded and walked out, leaving a threatening gaze lingering behind as he left the tent. Balaram waited for Devamedha to instantly speak as he left, but she poured herself another glass of ale and sighed.

"Do you know where Sonja is?" She asked instantly.

He licked his lips. "No."

"I was told you were the last person she talked to."

"Yes."

"What did you talk about?"

"About her being supportive in the cause of yours to ally with Satyaki."

"And she ran away, I heard that."

The bloody servants would have been eavesdropping and mentioning these details.

"I worry. I feel she's in danger," she said. "And I don't know why, but I feel this boy had something to do with it."

Balaram arched his brows. "Why do you feel that way?"

"Because I was told," she raised her brows, keeping things mysterious, "I had sent a scouter to search for her where she was last seen."

He had no response further even though she was waiting for him to say something.

"You are being too concerned and worried." Balaram came close to his cousin and held her by the shoulders.

"I trust you, cousin. I hope you won't break it. If you truly and genuinely vouch for this boy, then I would trust your judgment and go along with it," she said.

Balaram nodded. He didn't want to lie and it was bothering him that he was, but he had no choice. He had to think about his own interests as well. So, he nodded and said with gritted teeth, "Yes, indeed, I do trust him."

"Good," Devamedha smiled. "If it's like that, then I believe your services are no longer needed."

"What do you mean?"

"You gave me an ally and that's where your journey ends, cousin."

He arched his brows. Her voice had turned distantly cold and she seemed aloof. "What's going on?"

"What you should have seen for a while now." She smiled, pulling herself from him. "I planned to take down Yudhajit, but I didn't know with whom I should.

But now, since I have Satyaki, I don't need you. When I told you, the capital Dvarkvati wants you dead or alive, you didn't ask me how I knew that."

He was taken aback, almost frozen on the ground. "You were in touch with Durgajyoti?"

"When she was there of course, but then we had problems with the messages in between. The messages were being intercepted by Yudhajit and then she disappeared, I heard."

Balaram's spine went cold. He had seen those messages in Yudhajit's room and they were not between him and the Ledger but it was between Devamedha and the Ledger.

"Initially, I thought I would just give you away, but you had good ideas, so I just prolonged it. Surely, the Ledger wasn't too happy." She shook her head. "I was delaying the inevitable but patience has its virtues and its rewards. I got what I wanted and thank you for that. But now I don't need you."

"So, what's next? You will just take over from Yudhajit."

"And kill my ally as well, of course. My scouter had learnt he had attacked my daughter, and while she rests, I will plan Satyaki's demise. The Ledger underestimated me," she said. "It was thought that I would be engulfed with grief and attack Satyaki, but I want him now and I don't want him later. I will take over the Vrishni clan and give it a new birth. The Ledger agreed and thus we both used you and Satyaki for our plans. Unfortunately, Sonja wasn't a part of the plan and I hope she is fine and her health is dandy."

The guards appeared, grabbing Balaram from behind.

"You are allied with Pradhyuman?" He asked incredulously.

"Of course," she scoffed. "He's the king, you idiot boy. You were always an idealist. We all have to look at our own interests, don't we?"

He had been getting it all wrong. It was Yudhajit who was the right person to ally with, not Devamedha. He was done in by all the underdogs around him, he thought they were the right people, but morality was skewered in Dvarka and he should have realised it. He also realised why the Vitihotra wasn't attacking him here. He was, already in enemy territory after all.

Worse, his greatest mystery was indeed solved.

There was a Ledger. And as he was being scampered and being pulled away by the guards from her, his only thoughts were who was the Ledger—his wife or his general.

33

Samva was feeling awkward that his father had saved him—the man who was hell bent on destroying him, became his salvation. It was odd to even think of it. Samva sighed as he was reaching close to the Prabhas Sea and was looking at the wide berth of ocean water that stretched close to the mainline, and the horizon was indeed beautiful in the distance.

He remembered being in extreme pain when he was poisoned. He felt his body was dying and yet he wasn't dead. It was as if he would remain in excruciating pain for his entire life and couldn't do anything about it.

And his father saved him.

Samva glanced at him and he looked older than he had when Samva had met him. He looked wiser too; tougher. The man he had seen, wasn't a coward anymore, it could feel that way. He hadn't spoken to him, just offered him water. Samva wanted to be grateful about it, thank him, but he was feeling embarrassed. He had been cursing his father his entire life and this was the first time when he was actually happy that Krishna was around him.

"Are you okay?" Samva asked.

"Yes," he said.

"What are you thinking?"

"Contemplation towards life," Krishna gritted his teeth.

Samva nodded. He didn't bother to ask more. He remained by himself, till they reached the shoreline where there was a fisherman's community and there were all kinds of fishes being sold, tents being put up, merchant ships being positioned on the ocean while there were dockyards and sailors and tourists too. Samva could see that Pradhyuman's soldiers were here, walking around, looking over the nitty-gritties.

"I'm famous for being the leper and the man in the iron mask," Samva said, as he covered his hood. "I can't be seen here."

On the other hand, Krishna could. He didn't look anything like he used to. He was a different man.

"We are here only for a short time. We need to search for a sailor, who can give us his ship and make us travel south."

Samva nodded. As they dismounted from their horses, and made their way around the community, they began to talk about what Krishna used to do in his spare time. Samva was genuinely interested and as he could see, Krishna was a mighty fisherman himself and he knew all kinds of fishes, especially liking the river water ones. Krishna had a lot of time to himself, so he knitted too and he looked at the horizon in the evening. His life was peaceful, modest but without a purpose. He would reflect on his life, but the purposelessness would get to him sometimes. He would be sad and he wanted to return to his original life.

"Then why didn't you?" Samva had asked.

And Krishna had his reasons. He didn't share them. He felt defensive whenever Samva would ask this. As if it was something embarrassing, something shameful for him.

Samva and Krishna finally happened to find a sailor who was ready to take them in return for Samva's rings that he was wearing—the ones that belonged to his wife Lakshmana, right before she disappeared. Samva was not ready to give them, but seeing he had no choice, he had to relent.

"Are you sure?" Krishna asked.

Samva was looking at the small boat that was waiting for them. The boat would be an important ally in the journey and whatever this journey was, it was greater than anything in this world for him, even the trinkets of gold that he was wearing.

"Do I have a choice? He likes it. It's…uh…it's been a while, even though then I should give it away. Clinging on to the memories and staying in the past is not the right thing. Because the past is what it is…the past… and one has to get over it, no matter how painful or good it was."

Krishna nodded. He didn't want his son to give up like this, but then he respected him for it. He patted him on the shoulder, as Samva pulled out his trinkets and handed it to the sailor, who gave the ropes to the boat in return.

"Well," Samva smiled, "I believe a-hoy."

*

"What did you do all these years when I left?" Krishna asked.

The boat was small, but enough to make space for them. The wind was chirpy and the sound of the ocean gurgling like a bad stomach was coming around them. There was nothing but ocean around them, but for some reason Krishna knew exactly where to go. The sun was about to set and the seagulls up above on the orange flared sky were flapping their wings.

"I sparred and I sparred a lot," Samva said, sitting on the wooden bench of the reed boat.

The waves were tough and they had to continue to balance the boat, whenever they could and felt it was necessary.

"Sparred, why did you spar?"

"Because I wanted to be better," Samva said. "I wanted to be better from the person I was my entire life."

Krishna impassively watched him. "Was it me? Was it because of me?"

Samva nodded, though not denying or feeling ashamed of his feelings. "I often felt I was not good enough for you. I often felt you left because you just couldn't bear the thought of me being your son."

"That's not true," Krishna said.

"But unfortunately, it is."

Krishna didn't know what else to say to him and he felt embarrassed by it. "I'm sorry I made you feel that way." He looked down. The air was whipping hard. "I know I made you and I forced you to train harder than ever. I know I troubled you and called you a wimp, called you a rapist and a murderer. I thought you embodied every evil in this world, but I forgot about you, my boy. If you were evil, you were my evil but you weren't that too and I just misunderstood you."

"You were always an overachiever, someone who everyone looked up to. I wasn't and that's what made you feel the way you did towards me."

Perhaps that could be it. Krishna didn't realise it. But he was held back and he leaned against the ridge of the boat. "We are close," he said. "You asked me something back at the shores?"

"Hmmm?"

"About why I left."

"Yes. Why did you?"

Krishna didn't want to reveal it. It was hard. But then, he had to tell someone, he had to tell his boy. He had to tell why it was necessary for him to do so. "I was scared, boy. I was scared out of my wits. After I gave all my powers away, I realised I was vulnerable. I couldn't sleep. I couldn't walk. I couldn't think straight. I began to feel overwhelmed by my mediocrity. I felt what others felt and it scared me. When you live your life as a god, you forget the simple things that could harm you and I did that. A needle pricked me and I jumped in horror. I saw blood in my life for the first time and the blood hurt me. I was invincible, boy. But not anymore."

"You left out of fear?" Samva asked incredulously, almost feeling his father wasn't the brave man kids were taught about. He was, at the end, just like Samva. He was ordinary.

"I was too hard on you but I became you and I realised you are me. You are the personification of me. We both are ordinary. We both are simple."

"I don't know about you," Samva said. "But I feel, there's beauty in the ordinary."

"Perhaps," Krishna sighed. "Perhaps we don't need great things and we don't need great lives to live. Perhaps mediocrity is something that we should cherish too."

Samva nodded. "It's all right to be scared. I was scared my entire life. I was scared of stuff that I shouldn't even have been scared about."

Krishna smiled. "I guess, we both are on the same boat in this."

He chuckled. "Ah, there it is. I've been told you were quite witty and a wordsmith. Never saw you doing that."

"Oh, I was quite a boy. I used to steal butter and trouble the women in the village. I was young and feverishly excited in my life. I wanted to enjoy it to the fullest."

"Then what happened?"

"I got responsibilities. Too early in my life. It's unfair, I always feel, when you get discomfort too quick and too early."

"And yet discomfort is what makes us who we are."

Krishna wanted to have a glass of mead to cheer on that. He liked having this kind of conversation with his son. It was different. It wasn't the same, world ending kind of vibe right now, but more personal. It's something he would cherish—to have a quick conversation with his son. "I believe we are here and the sun is setting." Krishna announced in a serious tone, getting up, pulling out his mani.

It was wrapped in a cloth, and as he unwrapped it, he could see the mani was glistening brightly. "I still can't believe Kaliya gave me the mani with no hassle."

"There was hassle. My life was dependent on it."

"But he just gave it up. It was odd. I feel this is fake." But it didn't look fake.

"I seriously believe you should trust people more on face value. I know it could be used against you, but sometimes trusting someone blindly can make you have power like no one else. The power of nobility, if I'm allowed to speak," Samva said.

Krishna nodded to himself, agreeing with his son, as he brought the mani in front of the setting sun's rays and the sun reflected on it instantly. Krishna eyeing the reflection and the burning of the stone, used the rays to point to the other direction, to the one he had been eyeing for a while.

And alas, it began to open up. Krishna could see a new land, being formed, becoming visible. It formed right in front of him, and he could see volcanoes and it was as large as an island, thick with canopies and large trees and along a beach. He asked Samva to direct the ship towards it.

"If I stop the deflection, it'll go away. We need to be on the island and then I'll remove it."

Samva began to row further towards it. "How do you know so much about this mysterious, disappearing Antar Dvipa?"

"Because I created it."

"Why?"

Krishna growled. The boy asked too many questions, but he did manage to reach the shores. By then, his arms had gotten dark as they were burning and hurting. The mani was exhibiting great amounts of magic and it was really starting to take a toll on him—but he left it and sighed, getting out of the boat and dipping his hands in the cold water, feeling the pain dissipate.

"I hated doing this," Krishna growled.

Samva by then, was scouring the island and there was no life here, he could see it. "Why did you hide it, sir?"

Krishna sighed, looking back at his son. "Because a friend of mine lives here."

"Who?"

"You know him," Krishna sighed, as he knew there was no point in hiding anymore. "Arjun."

34

Pradhyuman had been meaning to ask Mayavati but he wasn't getting the opportunity. There were no nights or days here. And also, there were people around in cells, who were shouting at each other and sometimes at Pradhyuman too.

One in particular was Jwala. He was the same bearded man he had seen first abusing him.

Pradhyuman had often asked him what was the reason behind it, but Jwala wouldn't tell him. It would make him feel worse, the mystery of it.

There were times when the inmates would sleep off. And then there were times when they wouldn't. They'd stay up late.

Pradhyuman did manage to strike up a conversation once in a while, in solace when there was silence and whispers were echoing, but still not enough to alarm others.

Today was one of those days.

"I'm getting tired of this place. I feel sleepy and I feel frustrated and I feel as if it's not ending. I don't know what kind of a limbo I'm in, but I just want to leave." He clutched his hair, and his eyes looked very sheepish, with black circles underneath. "Please help me, Maya."

The woman in front with black lips said. "You grow out of it. It takes time, but you'll learn to live here."

"Have you accepted this fate?"

"Do we have a choice?"

"You tell me," Pradhyuman said, almost jutting out his face in between the iron bars. "I have no clue. But you have known Shambara for a while. You know how he plays a game, so I'm sure you know with what purpose he had created this. Tell me!"

Mayavati began to contemplate and she went into this closed eye movement, and then she began to hum. "I always felt he was good at experimenting with dreams and nightmares. He had this thing about it. He used to use Maya to tap himself and create dimensions that weren't real but would be a product of your consciousness. He was a scientist."

"You are literally praising him."

"He was a good ruler, Pradhyuman." She protested. "No matter, how horrible he was to me."

"Well, I believe you should stick to the ones who raised him. I'm sure you'll be happy to meet them, whoever they are."

She paused. She didn't say anything but just smiled.

"What?" He asked, irritably.

"You were always a boy with a lot of thunderous anger. You were always someone who would be making quick judgments. I still remember the day when you had returned from breaking your bow and you showed it to me and I promised you that I will mend it. It had been a few days and I hadn't done it, and you got so angry with me. I was busy, that's all."

Pradhyuman didn't remember this episode. But he did remember being quite a frustrating child. "I'm sorry if

I was ever rude. I miss you every day and it's sad you left me."

"I did leave because we are not supposed to be together. I'm a Rakshas and you are not. I am an immortal and you are not."

Pradhyuman wanted to tell her what he felt for her. "You might be my mother, but you were more than that. You were the love of my life.""

"Shut up, boy."

"I never treated you like my mother," Pradhyuman protested as if he wanted for her to hear it, no matter what. "I always treated you like someone I care for, someone I cherish. I want to be with you and we can rule together, we could have, but you rejected all my offers."

She frowned. "You are stupid."

Pradhyuman knew he wouldn't be taken seriously. He knew it was bad to fall for someone who was like a mother figure, but it was something he had thought about often. It was very personal and he wouldn't share it with another person other than her.

"You are ready to be with someone like Shambara but not with me."

"He's a good man. Damaged perhaps, but good. And he's angry with you. You took his kingdom away, his wife. You literally took everything from him. Don't you think that's warranted for, the anger he has towards you?"

Pradhyuman shook his head. His mother had always been like this—someone who would know that the man was bad and yet would care about his positives. Pradhyuman never understood that. "Tell me something else, something you might be able to remember. I'm sure building this dimension would have taken time. The seed of it must have been during the time when he was alive."

"It was," she shook her head. "I often told him it was a horrible idea, to paralyse people in their dreams, and just like any dream, to escape it, I'm sure there is some key, some way to do it." She herself asked but was not able to answer it.

Pradhyuman refrained and remained like this. "These bloody cages. I hate it. I wish I could escape it." He began to push and prod. And as he did, the gate opened automatically.

For a moment Mayavati was confused, and so was Pradhyuman and they both looked at each other in the most quizzical way.

Mayavati instantly tried to open it herself, but it didn't work. It was shut. "How did you do it? And why didn't it work for me?"

Pradhyuman was confused himself and he looked around in the corridor, seeing there's nothing that was standing in his way. There were no guards or soldiers. "This is part of a trick, some kind of a mystery."

"Should I escape?" He asked her, adding to that.

"Perhaps. I don't know. This has never happened before."

By then, the inmates had begun to realise that Pradhyuman was out and they had begun to shout and scream. Jwala in the other cage, tried to open it, hoping he might be able to leave from this place. But it wouldn't open.

Pradhyuman ignored him, but not for long, as

something happened. A powerful reckoning force attacked him, slamming him on the floor and knocking him on the head. He looked at who it was, and he saw Jwala. He had managed to escape as well. Jwala grabbed Pradhyuman's face and began to smash it on the ground, trying to crack open his skull. His face began to bleed and he cried profusely. He was frustrated and he decided to fight back, but Jwala was angry.

"You have no idea what you did. You have disappointed me. You have disappointed the whole of your country. You are a stench. You are a pale reflection of your father. Your father was great and look at you, you are nothing but his spit." He grabbed hold of Pradhyuman's throat and threw him on the ground.

As he went to grab him again, Pradhyuman rolled back with acrobatic flexibility. He came on his feet and looked at Jwala who just stormed at him, grabbing him by the torso and racing him across the corridor while Pradhyuman began to beat him hard. Though he didn't get a long chance, as Pradhyuman was thrown on the ground and they both crashed, while Pradhyuman kicked him in between his legs.

"What did I do?" He was trying to come on his feet, amidst the cheering and the loud clapping in between the inmates. "What did I bloody do? I have tried to live up to my father's ideals."

"And yet you became the worst version of him," Jwala said, punching him on the face. "You know what you did right?" He didn't attack him no more. He was just coming on his feet too. "I had a brother, a young one and he had bought a land for himself, but the taxes that were imposed on him were too much, by your government, by your people. We were frustrated and we tried to make ends meet. Then the bandits came and we realised you allow the bandits too and mooch from them as well. You have a broken-down system that realised local farmers like us. We tried to fight back the taxes but it didn't work out. You know what he did? He attacked your people and you put him in prison, only later to be impaled from the mouth. And he lives in pain, in the valley of the tortures. He still hurts. He didn't do anything but fought for what's right. But you don't get it. You continue to impose such horrible taxes, that it becomes hard for us civilians to live."

"I was just doing right for the empire."

"The empire consists of people. Do right by them!"

And then he went for Pradhyuman and grabbed him by the throat and shoved him against the wall. Pradhyuman felt a jolting pain that coursed through him. He felt a certain horror within him, and most of all, he could see how he disappointed his people. These measures were taken by his ministers and his cabinet and he had no clue it was supposed to be so impactful on someone that they would hurt him.

"And then I got the offer."

A punch appeared on his face. Hitting him hard.

"The offer was simple," Jwala said. "I can come close to you. I have to just accept to sleep. And he told me, I would get an opportunity to meet you, so how could I resist?"

He went straight for him again, and Pradhyuman brought his feet in between them and pushed him back. As his anger flared and he was about to attack, Pradhyuman saw something in Jwala that he thought he would never see. He saw his father. He saw Krishna's face and Jwala had morphed into his father. He couldn't believe it. His father hadn't attacked him. In fact, he remained still.

"I never believed that relinquishing the empire would be a rational decision, but you have proven me wrong. You've made me question if you could truly be my son. You're not cut from the same cloth as I am, as I once was. You come across as weak and feeble. You are someone deserving of harsh treatment. You are someone who perhaps shouldn't have even existed," he concluded, spitting on the floor in disgust.

Pradhyuman gritted his teeth, and said angrily, "I didn't try to be like you because you are a horrible person. You treated everyone wrongly and you made me feel that you were better when you were nothing but an incapable man who was not ready to do anything." He came on his feet and looked him in the eye, facing him.

For a moment, Krishna was surprised. Pradhyuman looked at him and pushed him while Krishna disappeared in a puff. Pradhyuman was confused for a moment, until he blinked and found himself back inside the prison. He had never escaped, he was just facing these damn illusions.

Pradhyuman remained there, heaving.

"What just happened?" Mayavati asked. "What is going on?"

"Nothing," Pradhyuman smiled. "I just found Shambara's weakness."

35

She knew she was going on another journey yet again.

She was being pulled into this vortex of pain and hurt and every cell in her body was feeling a tremor, when she opened her eyes and found herself yet again in a caravan that was very familiar for her. She knew that caravan because the pain that she had felt during the process of this journey was not as worse as the bountiful of pain she would be facing from the caravan.

She looked around, swallowing a lump and Durgajyoti realised that she was back to where it all had begun. She was no more in the forest. She was no more in front of the turquoise-coloured eyed girl who was herself.

She wasn't in front of Pradhyuman. Why was he shown? What was Mayasabha trying to tell her? That Pradhyuman was her true damnation and not Durjay. But how is that possible? Durjay destroyed her life.

And Durjay was in front of her. He was smiling. He had the same curls and same look; a fastidious smile and the beautiful look on him. He was a pretty good-looking man for his age.

"How do you do, darling?"

She wanted to slap him and get rid of him, but she couldn't. She was tied down and her voice was not coming out. She was trapped inside her younger body.

The caravan...she was in it. She remembered the day when she had just married and they were returning to their palace. He had told her how beautiful and grand it was .

"I'm so glad. You are beautiful. You have the most beautiful eyes I've ever laid eyes on."

She was just trying to shout and throw a slap, but couldn't.

"I would shower you with all the gifts."

You took me as a child. I was young, but you forced me to marry you, you old monster.

But he couldn't hear her thoughts.

"Tell me," he smiled in the most clever way, "what do you like about me?"

She didn't say anything. She wanted to scream, but the only words that came out were—"You look good."

"Ah well, indeed I do," he said. "Ever since I saw you in the market, one of the orphans, I was smitten. I had to have you for myself."

Then he planted his large lips on her, she felt disgusted. His tongue felt horrible and his mouth smelled of tobacco. She was trying to know and feel why she was here. He pulled back. "Do you ever think you'll get bored of me?" He smiled, displaying his rotten teeth.

And the person, this alien she was inhabiting, smiled forcibly.

The scene dissolved and she felt herself back into the room. It was a familiar room with the ceilings and the walls. The room was absolutely dark. And she was bound there. She was gagged. She was trying to move. And she was trying to push and prod, but was unable to.

Where am I? She cried under her breath and her voice was tight, her body was tense. Her pupils were dilated and she felt suffocated.

Durgajyoti saw someone entering the room. He moved and swayed like a gentleman, but he was naked from the top, while he wore a dhoti in the bottom. He was holding something in his hand and they were hot thongs. They were warm.

"Do you like pain?" The man asked.

She tried to wither and escape, but it didn't work. The tongs reached her belly and it burnt her. It reached her skin, close to her breasts and it began to burn her there too.

"I like it. I love it when I hurt others. It soothes me, especially the people I love. You know," Durjay said. "My parents had gifted me a bunch of chicks as a child and I used to play with them. I used to love them, but nothing satiated me as much as when I crushed one of them by mistake. It made me feel that pain for me is far more gratifying than love."

And the tongs burnt her skin further, as she began to weep and cry and tears fell from her eyes.

Please help me.

Durgajyoti remembered how he used to torture her always. She remembered how she used to be slapped and kicked and thrown down the stairs. She was pregnant and then she had a miscarriage. He had done pretty awful things and Mayasabha was making her relive it. Especially this moment when he was blazing her body and making her feel as if this was the end. The embers would hurt her and destroy her.

And she closed her eyes. When she opened them, the pain was gone, but there was something else. She was excited. She was in another room now, in a tent. And she looked at Durjay. He was in his battle gear. And he looked frustrated. He was drinking wine.

"How did it go?" Durgajyoti asked, even though she wanted to poison the ale.

"He doesn't like my idea and why would he? He's jealous. He's achieved everything in life, but now he doesn't want any other person to get the limelight."

"What did he say?"

"That we should not indulge ourselves in the dark arts," Durjay fierily said. "This is not dark arts. We are losing men left, right and centre. Imagine if we have a paste, a process that would make the dead reanimate."

"But yours is still a theory."

He looked at her for a moment, as if he was defeated and his wife didn't even believe him, and then he launched at her, grabbing her by the throat. "Have you thrown him off the course? Talked to him. Told him I'm crazy. Because he said, my idea was crazy. Well, he is crazy."

"No—no—no I didn't."

"I don't believe you."

"I believe in your idea," she said, with shrivelling eyes.

"You said two things."

"What?"

"You believe in me and you also think the idea is theory." He smiled. "Then why don't we make it practical?"

The thought scared her. "What do you mean?"

"Ah well, I talked to the shaman. He said it can also work on a live body."

"But..."

"Shut up, bitch."

And then she blinked her eyes, only to open them again and find herself in a dark room, that had a lot of smells floating around. She was lying on the floor, bound by nails stuck inside her soft palms, that bled. She looked in the shadows, there was Durjay with his curls and the crazy eyes, while the shaman was standing next to him, looking ever so threatening as well.

"Now, now, it'll be all over soon."

"This is the fifth time!" She cried.

"You are the subject."

And then the shaman had begun to read some spells and tricks, making her feel like retching but also not. She felt her stomach somersaulting and her body answering to the pain. She was feeling a lot of hurt that coursed through her veins and then her head had begun to shake and shiver, as she started getting fits in a state of delirium. She fell back on the floor and tears came out, as she coughed up blood.

"It's not working. I don't think we should do it on her," the shaman said.

"No, it has to be her. The first subject, try again."

By the time, it was over, she was asked to wear clothes and antiseptic medicine was put on her. She was brought back to wash her face and she realised that he didn't want to just do the experiment, but also hurt her in the process because she had asked him something, revolted and rebelled against his idea. And then she closed her eyes as she saw her own image in the water. She saw her frail face. She had lost all hair on her head and even her brows. She had become this sunken version of previous self. And that made her feel worse. It made her cry and she had never screamed.

Durgajyoti closed her eyes and she blinked again, and as she did, it happened again. She was in a different room. This time, she was sleeping, when she was awakened by the shaman. The same one. He was an old man, and he had round eyes. He was calling out to her.

"Come here," he said.

And she did. She walked to him, like in hypnosis. Durjay wasn't here. Durjay had gone for a campaign for Krishna by then.

"What happened?" She said.

"A lot of things, but most of all I do not want you to go and suffer the way you already are." He was feeling apologetic, a sadness streaked in his eyes. "I want you to be strong and I feel you have already weakened yourself."

"It's okay. It's my destiny."

"We make our own fates, my lady." He handed her a book. "In this holds a spell to awaken a spirit of vengeance, a spirit so dark and so bright at the same time that she can help you and save you from your misery."

"Are you sure?"

"Yes."

"But what if she's not able to?"

"Oh, she will."

She contemplated a lot and she paused and thought, and as she did she grabbed the book and kept it with herself. She blinked.

And then she opened her eyes and found herself in the last place she wanted to be in. She was where she had been earlier. But this time, he was at the table, nailed to the ground.

It was Durjay.

He was sitting right there and was just looking up in the air. He was trying to calm down and yelling at her at the same time. "You are making a big mistake."

"I believe, you should have been tested."

And now, she channelled the spirit that had brought the scenarios where they were right now. The scenario was that because of Baagul, she was able to defeat him as well as the people around him, his guards—and she had trapped him. She had even mind-controlled him for a while to hand off all the assets of the empire to her. And then she executed the masterplan. Which was to take over the crown that belonged to her.

"You are mad! You are a raving lunatic!"

She chuckled. "Speak for yourself."

And then Baagul appeared, out of her, in the form of shadows.

"Torture and kill him for me please," Durgajyoti instructed.

And Baagul listened, as Durjay began to scream loudly. And as he did, his face had begun to melt, and his body had begun to evaporate. The Durgajyoti inside of herself felt proud. She was finally able to conquer her fears. She was finally able to fight it. She was grinning to herself, when everything went blank and she was in this limbo.

Someone was walking towards her. She didn't feel

trapped anymore. She felt liberated, but still she heard the footsteps. She turned to see who it was.

The face was familiar and dark at the same time.

It was Pradhyuman.

"And now, you are going to repeat the same mistake again?" He asked. And the smile, was very much feverishly similar to the one Durjay had on his face when they had first met.

36

Balaram was inside a prison that was burning hot, as the people around him prepared for the major war that was about to happen.

They were preparing to fight Yudhajit, and at the dead of the night, as the ravens cawed and the fireflies danced, Balaram stood in silence, his staff stripped away from him. Balaram had been in there for hours, and if only he knew what Devamedha was up to—he would try to scream out. But he was shocked, suffice to say, that Devamedha was herself not inclined to work with Satyaki. It was the Ledger. She wanted to use Satyaki to get Yudhajit. But who was the Ledger? Was it Revathi or Akoorji? He was still in a dilemma.

Whoever one of them it was, none of them bothered to show up when he was here, all alone, in the dark weather, feeling lonely as ever.

He began to think about the snake and how he had dreamed of it recently where the snake had warned him, that he had been corrupted. He wanted to know how, but the snake didn't answer. It began to consume his counterpart, Lakshman, the brother of Ram.

Balaram was sitting cross-legged and was meditating, when his eyes fell on his paralysed leg. He was born with it. He had some kind of a strange deformity which meant his legs didn't have the power or the energy perform basic duties. It had always made him insecure and because of that he was tired. He rested it and decided he would give it up. He would not be taken seriously until his brother, Lord Krishna, handed him a staff, made from a loose wooden bark and said that this is a gift for him, to support him at times when he would trip while walking.

Ever since then, Balaram held on to the staff, which had matured as he had as well. But the bark remained the same, with gold and silver laced around it, as Balaram had grown up.

"You are in deep thoughts."

Balaram looked up, raising his brows and he saw who it was in front of him.

Satyaki.

He was not grinning and was not his usual self.

"Yes. I'm contemplating my entire journey actually."

"Why?"

"Because I feel, it doesn't make sense. I feel there is no purpose to it. It didn't work out and it really makes me sad."

Satyaki was silent, impassive. Balaram could see he was a little conflicted here.

"Why are you here?" Balaram asked.

"I didn't know she would trap you. But she said you are a threat to our mission."

"She says that because she knows you tried to harm Sonja and she's using you to get rid of your father. Once this happens, she will get rid of you as well."

Satyaki arched his brows. "She said you will say this, to brainwash me."

Balaram shook his head in defiance. She had convinced the foolish Satyaki into believing what she wanted him to believe.

"But you know, it was an honest truth when I said, I wanted a mentor in my life, a guide. I wanted you in my life to help me," he said. "I wasn't trying to bluff or lie and I don't even know how true it is that you are always right in your thoughts about things and people. In fact, it was me who told her that if you got rid of Balaram, I will pull back."

Balaram nodded. "Thank you for that."

"I'll see to this once the war is over."

"You plan to fight your father and then what? You know no one would die."

"We have no choice," he answered, coming closer to the cage in which Balaram was. "My father learnt about our little pact and has decided to move his army."

"How did he get to know?"

"He has sparrows everywhere." He shook his head and mumbled to himself. "I'll make sure he pays for what he did."

"You won't be able to kill him or anyone around. What do you plan to do otherwise?"

"Burn, maim and poison. We are unkillable because of Uncle Krishna, but we are still flesh and bones," he said. "I should go."

And as he left, Balaram called out to him: "I know you won't listen to me and I know you don't want to take chances. You said you wanted me to be your guide, then hear me out. I want you to get me out of this, so we can go to Yudhajit and find a solution that'll end

Devamedha's plans. She works with Durgajyoti and once she's in power of both the kingdoms, it's going to destroy us and all the plans that I had for Dvarka. Durgajyoti is a horrible sorceress and we have to put an end to her."

He looked at him for a while. He wanted to speak, but the rustle of the wind was the only sound that permeated between the silence of the two men, and then he said: "I'm sorry."

And he left, leaving Balaram defeated once again. He knew this would be a problem now, as to how he would escape.

*

He didn't want to sleep but feeling anguished and exhausted for a while had taken a toll on his life. So he took a nap, even though it was hurting him in the chest. He was also afraid of seeing the snake, and as he did so, he could hear something in the background. Some kind of mayhem. It had been happening for a while, and he had thought that perhaps it's the war between Devamedha and Yudhajit, but now the noises came closer. People were scampering. There were a lot of cries and wails and yells.

Balaram instantly opened his eyes, and he found the guards around him were being attacked by black-cloaked men. They weren't soldiers. They looked strong though, powerful in their own right. And they were dozens in number, while explosions happened in the background and people ran for their lives, while some fought.

Was there an internal attack? How did the enemies cross the barriers?

Balaram had no idea, when one of the cloaked figures came to him and whispered: "Let's leave quick." With the staff that belonged to Balaram, the figure burst it through the gate and Balaram was hesitant.

He didn't even know who it was.

"Come, quick! I know a way out!"

"Who are you? I don't trust you."

"Come!" And then the face got revealed, only a tad bit.

It was none other than Revathi.

He grinned and grabbed her hand, as he limped with her, away from the fighting and the yelling. There was a loud blaring of the horns, an emergency signal that there were intruders—but they didn't listen. They made their way out but they were not fast. Balaram was quite slow because of his leg, but he continued to strive forward and not give up. He didn't ask any questions, and he couldn't because the air in him was being sucked out. It was tightening his chest.

"Come this way!" She shouted, as Balaram saw that torches had begun to appear, the sky was lit with arrows of fire and flames, while at the same time chariots were being sauntered and making their way.

They moved in the narrow gap and then out in the open, where the barricades were created and the ascension was there. Balaram used his staff to take support and hop over the barricades, while helping Revathi too.

And as they exited, they saw someone flying over them—a rollicking and a somersaulting soldier, who had appeared out of nowhere, his blade reaching for

Revathi's neck when Balaram deflected it. He twisted and turned his sword around, moving for Balaram, when he deflected it again and shoved the sword, deep inside the heart of the soldier, pulling his organs out and letting the soldier feel the pain for a while, as he fell on the ground and scampered for his heart which Balaram had tossed away.

The horns were louder than ever and the sound of the hooves and the footsteps were heard in the background.

"We should go," Revathi said.

"Where?"

"To the one who ordered me to save you."

"Who?"

"Satyaki."

*

When they had reached a small camp, Balaram saw Satyaki with a band of his men. Not too many. There was a fireplace lit up and guards were stationed around the corners, as if they were expecting someone.

Balaram had been tired of running and the sounds of the horns and hooves were left behind. They moved through the thick tufts of snow and they were exhausted, their body shooting tremors of heated pain and anguish.

As he neared the camp, Satyaki looked up and went to embrace his uncle. "Hope you are doing fine."

"Yes, I am," Balaram said. "Didn't think you would take my advice."

"Well, I had to and, I had to take Revathi, your majesty and Akoorji's help."

"Where's Akoorji?" Balaram asked Revathi who was sipping some hot water, realised he should have asked this earlier.

"I don't know. He was supposed to escape. I just hope he hasn't been caught."

"Indeed." Balaram was worried for his friend, but he had to first consider the situation at hand right then. "Does Devamedha know what you did?"

"I think so," he said. "My men are in trouble. I don't know what to do. I just knew I had to get you out."

He nodded. "It's all right. We will figure something out." He patted the young one on the shoulder. "The question is, are you ready to break the promise you made to Devamedha?"

"I have no qualms." He shook his head. "If she's going to betray me after we win, I might as well stick to the family I have rather than create a new one."

"Good. Then I believe we should call for an audience with Yudhajit."

"And do what?" He asked. "Apologise to my father? I don't think I would do that."

"He's your father. He's not perfect. But he's your father. I'm sure you can find ways to solve the differences."

He paused, almost tearing up. "I don't know what to say. I just don't know what to do."

"I know I got you into this. I made you partner with the snide of a woman Devamedha, but I believe I can rectify this. Let me get back to Yudhajit and let me propose to him a truce between you and him, if everything is right, I'm sure he will accept you."

Satyaki nodded tearfully. He looked confused and sad. “Fine, as you say. I would think that’s the best option for now.”

Balaram came forward and hugged the little kid. Everyone watched him and he could see Revathi being a bit sad as well but a bit relieved at the same time.

“But what’s the plan? I’m sure Yudhajit wouldn’t see us immediately and attack us on sight.” Satyaki asked, pulling back.

“I do have a plan,” Balaram smiled, though he was a bit fearful.

*

The snowy landscape in the background rose like a beacon of hope. The battleground between the Andhakas and the Vrishnis was set.

They were on the opposite side. They were planning and plotting what to do.

Yudhajit was in the front line, looking in the horizon, ready to launch the attack, when he saw…

A figure walking towards them. It had come from the east, and it moved in a steady pace, as his vision cleared up he noticed the figure was holding a staff in his hand, and he knew who it was. But could it be an illusion?

“Fire!” He shouted at his archers. He didn’t want to take a chance.

The arrows slithered across the field, and the snowy flakes hit the bald-headed man, the staff bearer and the brother of Krishna. It smacked him on the chest, burning his skin, but he continued to walk and as he walked, he swiped down his arrows and continued to briskly move with no fear in his eyes.

As he reached close to Yudhajit, whose men immediately got between them, trying to block him away but he stopped there, halted.

"Is it you, Bala?" Yudhajit asked, arching his brows. "Never thought you would side with the enemies."

"Is this how you greet me?" He showed his marks and the blood spilling from his chest.

Yudhajit remained stern and tight-lipped. "You want to talk to me, isn't it so?"

"Yes."

"Good. Then let's talk."

37

Krishna was walking on the trampled grass of the island.

It was a lush, green place and silent and sombre, with not one sign of an animal or a bird around. And yet it was beautiful and rich and filled with all kinds of wonderful flowers, and tall bushy canopies that hid the sun from the ground. There was no reflection and they walked in silence, both of them, not uttering a word even though Krishna could feel Samva's mind was brimming with confusion and excitement.

"You can speak, boy," Krishna said soberly, his mace clinging on to him, while his eyes darted around for any unspoken attack either from Durjay...

Or from Arjun.

"Why is Uncle Arjun here? I know you have always told us about him when we were children. You have always mentioned how he was your best friend and your greatest ally and your student as well. So, what happened? He won the war, right? The last you spoke of him with me, is that he was in Hastinapur. But you lied, didn't you?"

Krishna nodded. Because partially, it was his fault. Partially. Or more so. He looked at the surrounding, scanned it and felt there was a scent of danger lurking around, there was a penance of horror that was permeating through the skins and fabrics of time. He felt the chills and he felt the scares that was grabbing hold of his spine, his blood and his flesh. He could see the volcanos in the far distance, necking through the skies and piercing through the snowy clouds. He could see the trek that would lead to the volcanoes and he could feel the smell of raspberries and gooseberries at the same time, and the dead scent of something rotten.

When they came across corpses.

They were as idle and quiet as if a part of the environment, and they smelled bad, with pieces of flesh dripping from the skeletons. There were arrows across their bodies, stuck on them through their skulls and torsos. But they had also been eaten alive, torn apart, by something.

"What happened to them? And how did they reach here?"

"The island is not impenetrable. It can be accessed by mistake and can be revealed by magic. These must be sailors or pirates who might have ventured, thinking a magical island would hold magic. But it doesn't." His voice was brusque and dark.

"What does it hold?"

"Death," Krishna sighed.

"Are you going to tell me what is going on? Where are we?" Samva asked irritably. "I never liked the mystery about you. I hated that."

"It's not a mystery. It's about your aunt, my half-sister." He sighed. They continued to walk, moving towards the volcano, though confused where Durvasa would be. But he knew if they walked for long, they would find him or worse...they'll find Arjun. "Subadhra was a woman of desires and of sincerity. She was a woman who loved everyone else more than herself. A trait, unfortunately I never possessed."

"Aunt Subadhra, she married Arjun, right?"

"Yes, she did," he responded solemnly. "But then their son died, Abhimanyu. A great lad, trained by your brother Pradhyuman. They told me to rescue him and I couldn't. They don't understand that a god can't resurrect the dead. The god can only protect."

"Then?"

"She became a hermit. In the final days of her life, she left and lived in the woods. Arjun, smitten by her, followed her but couldn't find her." He sighed. "With me, he searched her everywhere but it was in vain. We were afraid that she had no water, no food with her and wouldn't survive?" He shook his head.

"So did you?" Samva asked, even though the last thing he knew about Aunt Subadhra was that she died of natural causes. Now, the truth was revealing itself.

"Yes, we did. She was being pecked by vultures and she looked like she had been dead long back, of starvation and dehydration." Krishna wanted to cry. Seeing a sibling like that brought him so much closer to accepting death as a concept. Death is part of life, he had realised. "I am sorry, the image always troubles me, always haunts me." His chest was heavy and heaving, as if a boulder was pressed against his lungs and was crushing it in the inanest way possible.

"What happened after that?" Samva flared his nostrils, as he listened to the tale of his aunt in disbelief.

"Arjun was dead that day. He lost his soul. He had been numb and he didn't talk to anyone. I couldn't see him like that. But one day he came to me and he told me that he wants me to resurrect her. He lost a son and now he lost his wife and he can't bear the pain anymore. I couldn't lose my best friend, let alone my sister. So I did something stupid."

"What?"

Krishna wasn't walking anymore. He felt lost, not just in the surrounding but in himself. "I told him, there's a way she can return."

"All right, but you just said..."

"No, it doesn't work always and it's stupid to try because the consequences can be dire." Krishna shook his head. "Because you are going against the truth of life, the essential part of life. You are going against the fabric of our existence. Life allows us to be immortals because we are those who are supposed to be immortals. Life allows those to die who are supposed to die."

"What do you mean?"

"Subadra was never supposed to be resurrected. She was supposed to be dead. But I knew who she was in her previous life. She was Trijata, an Asura during the time of Lord Ram's reign. I told Arjun that if he tosses the corpse of Subhadra inside the water that is bestowed by the first ray of moonshine, she will be resurrected. Though there's a chance she might not return as Subhadra, and she could also return as Trijata."

Samva listened intently waiting for something else to happen. "So, she didn't return as expected?"

"Yes. And when I got to know this, I trapped her

here." He said, looking around. "Inside this hellhole and Arjun promised to be with her, even though his life was at risk."

"Oh god!" Samva blurted out in horror. "I'm so sorry."

Krishna shook his head. "We should take a leave and keep our footprints to ourselves. We don't want anyone to know that we are here. These are dark territories populated by those who have faced great tragedy. This place holds my greatest fear, my greatest nightmare."

"And that is?"

"My past."

*

The cowl slithered over him, and the man from the top of the hills, watched them move. They moved like a snake and from far he could realised them, especially the taller one, the older one.

He was his friend, his companion and his ally.

Arjun was in a hood, his bow made of reed and his arrows made of obsidian rested in the quiver that clung on his back.

Why are you here now? What purpose are you here for?

He wanted to ask. But he felt the urge to use his arrows and kill him. Kill Krishna. He didn't know why. He should not harbour such feelings but it was him who couldn't do the right thing. He could have risen Subhadra and Abhimanyu but he didn't. He always gave excuses.

And Arjun didn't.

He had broken rules for the man, for his friend when he had attacked Karna. He had done things in the name of Krishna because it was the right thing to do at that time.

But how would he know?

Anger mixed with the feeling of nostalgia hit him and as he turned, he saw a mist forming, and a figure emerging out of the mist, looking like a pale corpse, with papery hair and eyes that were dead and yet alive.

"Durjay," Arjun said. He knew the man. He had seen him with Krishna a long time ago. "What is going on here? Why is everyone here? What is the purpose of this?"

Durjay had a calm, dancing smile on. "Oh, I'm just following them and making sure they don't reach the end of their odyssey."

"Why?"

"Because I have been ordered." He clenched his jaws. "Because I have no choice."

"Indeed. And why should I care?" Arjun began to move away from the mist.

"Because I know you want Krishna bad. You want him dead. Let me help you in that."

"And how would that work?" Arjun asked, raising brows. "The last I saw, you were dead. How did you rise up again?"

"It was a dash of black magic. It's not pretty though. I got controlled by a woman," Durjay spat. "Horrible, horrible woman. And now if I don't do her bidding, she would not release me."

"Dead coming back...I don't want that anymore,"

Arjun said, realised the mistake he had made once and now did not want that to be repeated again.

"He knew about it," chided Durjay.

"What?"

"How to raise the dead. I told him. I told him the way when Subhadra passed," the misty man said.

Arjun halted, arching his brows. "No, can't be."

"Yes, it is. I did tell him that he can help Subhadra, but he didn't agree to my theories and it made me angry. I tried it on myself but that stupid woman controlled me. But it works. I'm a live example. We can stay immortal like that. Krishna didn't tell even though he could have. But he steered you towards a bad outcome, leading you to be like this for the rest of your life."

Arjun contemplated. He didn't know if he was being tricked or not, but it was still nice talking to someone from the past, even though this someone was dead and asking him to kill someone he had known all along. "What do you want from me?"

"Kill him. I can't," Durjay said. "I'm limited, but you aren't. Do it for me and I shall carry his head back to my bidder and free myself."

"What if I don't?"

"I'll find other ways." He cheekily grinned.

Arjun wanted to say something but before he could he saw what was happening in the forest. Something heavy was moving and it was moving towards Krishna and the young lad with him. He could see it from the cliff, he was standing in.

"Well, I suppose I wouldn't have to do that for you. My wife is already doing it."

Durjay moved alongside, and looked over, a gleeful smile on his face.

*

Krishna knew there was something wrong when the tremors had begun. They were bombastic and loud, and as he turned towards the east, from where it had been coming—he saw the troll, the ogre. It was three times its size and completely naked and it was moving ahead with its elastic skin, large talons and long buckteeth, moving straight for him, as if he was food.

"What the hell is that?" Samva asked.

"My sister," Krishna cursed under his breath. "We should run."

And they did. They moved as quick as possible, away from the ogre which didn't resemble anything like the woman she used to be. It was a different species all together. He had remembered how she had begun to mutate once she came out of the water. It was initially fine, but then she had bumps all across her body and her face had begun to change. And before she would become a threat to the people around her, he found her an island to stay in and hide it, as if it was a guilt he wanted to never face even though it existed.

He sprinted across the jungle, moving as fast as he could, his chest beating hard when he saw the ogre was close and had grabbed on to Samva. There was a shriek and a scream, Krishna skirted and turned, as the ogre had begun to eat his son. Krishna tightened his fist around the mace he had been carrying and he instantly went to hurt it in the knee, trying to break its cap apart, as well as body, but nothing happened.

Samva was still in the process of getting eaten.

"NO!" Krishna yelled, as he saw his son was close to the ogre's mouth.

And then something hit the ogre. It was an arrow. It stung him on the head and then another arrow stung so hard that the ogre let Samva fall on the ground, and began to remove all the arrows from his face that annoyed it.

Multitudes of arrows began to smack the ogre, and Krishna realised he was being helped, grabbed Samva by the arm and shoved him to move forward. They ran quickly and hid behind the foliage, as the ogre made a whining sound and a cry, before moving away, going back from where it had come.

"That was...something," Samva said.

"Yeah. Don't use black magic, boy. One of the most honest advice I could ever give you."

"Who are these arrows from though? Who saved us?"

"I don't want to know the answer..."

And they were interrupted in their conversation when they heard something in the back. Loud footsteps. Krishna turned to see his old, bearded friend, underneath a cowl, white in colour but looking young as ever. He was with his bow but had no arrow in it. Though Krishna knew that he could shoot in a single bat of an eye—he was that fast. Seeing his friend in person, brought back a lot of memories and made his chest heavy. It made him feel happy and at the same time, it made him face his disappointments.

"Thank you, Arjun," Krishna said.

"Why don't you tell me, why you are here?" Arjun said. "And then perhaps, I'll see whether you need to be saved again or not."

38

Pradhyuman was sitting cross-legged and he was calm.

He had never been as composed as he was then. He didn't listen to the noise around him, nor did he listen to the person in front of him: his stepmother. He was, in fact, just calm. The people around him were shouting, and so was his stepmother who was calling him, but he had his eyes closed and he had his face impassively tight. He knew this was an illusion and he had to be the master of it.

"What is Shambara's weakness?" Amidst the voice, he heard Mayavati. "Tell me. I can help you too."

"No," he shook his head frustratingly after being asked multiple times, "you should not get into this."

"Darn it, I should!" She screamed. "You have no idea. And I have not told you this."

"What is that?" He opened his eyes and looked at her.

"I was too guilty for this, but erm..." Mayavati bit her lips, "it was me who brought him to back to life."

He was quiet. He didn't utter a world, though a volcano was erupting within him. "And why is that? Because you missed him?"

"No, no, it was...the Rasatala was in chaos and different clan leaders were fighting each other. I had to find a solution, and so with black magic and Maya that I could conjure, I brought him back. It worked and instead of changing Rasatala, he went on this odyssey to hurt you." She was screaming tears and was on the verge of breaking down. "He made sure I'm in pain too and this led him to put me here as well."

Pradhyuman was listening quietly and when she was done with all the sobs and tears, he wanted to speak, but continued to keep quiet, until there were footsteps heard in the corridor. He looked outside his bars to see that the guards had come to take him. And he allowed himself outside, when Mayavati called out:

"What is it? Tell me! What is it?"

"Nothing. I'm introspecting," Pradhyuman responded to her but didn't even look at her anymore.

He didn't want to.

Because now he knew the truth.

*

Pradhyuman was out in the open, in the same gladiatorial field that he always was. Nothing had changed. The weather was same. The people with no faces were same too. But instead of Shambara being on the top where the king sat, he was down, on the ground and he was in his armour, with his sword and his entire battle gear.

"You know I am beginning to get annoyed by your behaviour. I thought it would be fun to play around with you and make you squeal like a pig, make you hurt," Shambara said, as his armour began to cackle and make sounds. He looked like a rhino, small but wide and ready to pounce. "And now instead of just trying to make you squeal more by bringing blasts from the past, it's best that I fight you. Hand him his weapons!" He ordered.

Pradhyuman was thrusted the weapons that he didn't even use. It was a long spear and a shield. There was nothing else and he felt naked for a moment. But Shambara didn't give him time to contemplate further, as he rushed towards him like a bull.

Pradhyuman dodged him and used his spear to stab him from behind. "What if I kill you in this world?" The king of Dvarka asked. "What would happen then?"

"The same that would happen to you when you are killed. Coma, as I had told you."

"Interesting, so the rules are same for everyone."

"What is a world without rules?" Shambara asked and then jabbed his sword multiple times towards Pradhyuman, but he continued to deflect it using his shield.

"What has happened? Earlier you could snap your fingers and break my spine. And now look at you. You look like a kid trying to win one for the team. What has happened to your powers? Why have you resorted to petty fights like these?" Pradhyuman asked, circling the Rakshas who was just flaring in anger.

"Nothing is wrong. I can still do it."

"No, you can't, you fat little fool." And after such a long time, Pradhyuman could feel he was in control. "You know why?"

"Because you found my weakness, is it?" He asked, as if repeating what Pradhyuman had said when he was in prison. But this was more of a condescending question. "You can't. You can never."

"Perhaps. But I do know that this world of yours is controlled by fear. When you have no fear, you have no control." He smiled. "You know why I don't fear?"

Shambara was confused and he could have jolted and attacked, but he was reluctant. He was afraid, for the first time. "What is it?"

"That you are dead. That you were never alive. And that you are..." Pradhyuman smiled. "Not Shambara at all."

For a moment there was silence, long drawn one and then there was a cackle to which Shambara said—"And how do you think I am here?"

"Shapeshifting. Classic illusion. Done by Meghnad a lot," Pradhyuman said. "It's all right, though. You can show your true self, Mayavati."

Shambara was taken aback. Pradhyuman stood without any defence, the applaud and the loud claps from the audience had gone silent when he said the name of his step-mother.

"I know it's you," Pradhyuman continued.

Shambara didn't smile anymore and then he began to slowly shift its presence. Suddenly, there was indeed a woman but she wasn't wearing a black dirty gown like the one she wore in prison. She was dressed better and had a golden crown. She looked like the Queen of Rasatala...

Because she was one.

"The new leader everyone talked about, who everyone followed in Rasatala. It was you, wasn't it?" Pradhyuman smiled.

"How did you know?" She asked, arching her brows.

"Initially, I thought this world was populated with people like me who are tortured. Then I realised after having my last fistfight with the brute that no…this entire prison is based around me. Not anyone else. Only I'm the one who's sleeping here because your illusions like glass can be broken if they are brittle and I broke them when I showed no fear last time. It destroyed you for a moment and you had to control the illusions and put them back in place.

But I realised that everything here is fake, even you who wanted to use Shambara to instil fear in me so you could puppeteer me here."

She nodded, clapping. "Bravo, my dear. You have solved your case, but do you think getting out of this dream is by breaking through with fear? Oh no. My illusions are stronger than that."

"I don't want to get out. I just want to know why you did it."

She narrowed her gaze. He seemed genuine.

"Why did you bring me here and trouble me with the past? Trouble me with my insecurities. Why?" He asked.

"Do you really want to know?"

"Of course."

She sighed. "Initially when you planned to attack Rasatala, I was pretty disappointed. I created this dream world so I could make you sleep and so you won't be a bother to me. But you see, when I put you here I realised that instead of trapping you here and letting you slip into a coma, I should reform you. Because no mother would like to see his son go astray. And no matter how much of a crazy you are, I still love you."

Pradhyuman wanted to bawl and cry. But he held back. He wanted to see whether she actually meant it and she did. "Have I gone too bad?"

"Absolute power has corrupted you, my child."

He nodded. "I don't know what to do." He felt his knees weaken and he fell on the ground. He was immediately held by Mayavati, who hugged him tenderly. Wrapping her arms around him.

"I'm sorry for making you go through this."

"It's all right," Pradhyuman cried on her shoulder, tightly embracing her. "I know I am wrong here. I have always been wrong. I have not thought about anyone with consideration except for you. I would change for you. I would make myself better. I would do anything for you. But only for you."

"That should not be the case. The world is bigger than both of us and you need to think about the people around you, and the ones who want to be with you and not away from you."

He pulled back and he looked in her eyes and he tried to inch further, to kiss her on the mouth, when she pulled back.

"I'm your mother, son." She said.

Pradhyuman nodded; frustrated. He never thought of her like that, but then it was as it was. "How will I leave this place?"

"By waking up."

"Or by killing you?"

"What?"

"If I kill you, mother," his arms began to tighten around her waist. "Would I wake up from this nightmare?"

"I…uh…you are hurting me."

The arms flexed and they tightened further and it made it hard for Mayavati to breathe.

"You were right about one thing. I was horrible to people because of you. I didn't care about anyone and I should have. So, thank you for making me realise this."

And then he grabbed her throat and began to slowly choke her. When she tried to snap her fingers, he broke them apart making her scream. Veins were popping out, when Pradhyuman realised there was nothing else he could do but just destroy the very thing that was killing him from within. "You have been nothing but horrible to me. You have teased me and you have used me. You only took me in because you wanted me to kill Shambara. And when that was done, you discarded me like a rotten apple. You say you are my mother, but you have abused me. You are horrible in every sense and try to show you are mighty and great. But you are not. You are just a pathetic…"

And he realised the woman wasn't struggling anymore. Her eyes were shut. And she was not breathing any longer. He left her throat and she fell down on the ground, hitting herself on the earth like a loose pelican. He didn't know how to feel about it, but he was afraid and scared for a moment. He swallowed a lump and looked at everyone around him. There were so many people, the audience with unknown faces who were watching him.

And then they began to disappear.

So did everything around him. Everything just began to dissipate and it changed and twisted and the reality that he was in began to create a spitball of him and threw him out of....

*

Pradhyuman woke up.

When he opened his eyes, he could feel there was sand in them. Everything was too noisy and shrewd and his vision was blurry too. He was confused for a moment, and then a smile came, followed with a gurgle of his stomach. He was starving. He turned his head around, smiling even widely , and happy that he was out of the nightmare, out of whatever it was, when he saw Rukmini was on his side, sitting on a chair, half asleep. He went over and held her hand.

She felt it and squealed, waking up from her sleep and jumping to hug him.

"How but...how..." she was choking and crying.

"It's all right," Pradhyuman went through her fingers and her hair. "I'm fine now. It doesn't matter."

She smiled.

And Pradhyuman did too.

He knew it was over now.

39

The fireplace was lit.

Krishna had to explain for Arjun to provide the hospitality that he deserved as to why he was there. And Arjun listened intently though he didn't respond. He just asked Krishna to come with him to the many sheds where he lived on the island because he was not sure which shed would work the best for him, so he had to keep changing as the ogre kept destroying them.

Samva had slept off. He was exhausted and so was Krishna, but he wanted to talk to his friend and know all about how he was.

The shed was close to the cliff, which overlooked the bountiful of water and twinkling stars, and the skies gave a quick rustle of the bristling wind. The water moved at a slow pace, and he was on an edge, lopsidedly hanging his legs from it, when Krishna came next to him and seated himself.

Arjun was having something and Krishna noticed they were some small red berries he was chewing on.

"So you plan to destroy your own clan?" Arjun asked candidly. His cowl was off, and his face was visible, with countless battle scars across his head, his cheeks and the entirety of his skin. His eyes were deep gray, like his father Indra's, and his body was chiselled.

"I have no choice. They have given me no choice."

He nodded.

"How have you been?" Krishna asked.

"Demented." He responded quickly. "What? You know I'm straightforward. It's been a while but I feel so bad. I feel like I want to go back to civilisation but this place doesn't let me go. I'm scared of leaving here, of hurting my wife."

"That's not my sister, Arjun."

He clenched his jaws.

"You are sticking here not for her, but for the memories you had with her," Krishna said.

"I want to run away sometimes, my dear friend," Arjun said. "I do want to escape. I want to hide. I want to live my life."

"And you should," Krishna said. "You know, like you, I hid from the civilisation too. I hid from everything, but I realised it's not where you are, it's where you are going that matters. We are all so victimised by our past that we have just given up."

"I agree," Arjun said. "So, what's the plan?"

"Be a better father." Krishna turned back, to look at his snoring son. "To be a better person."

"You always were, my friend."

"I was perhaps, to you. But not to everyone and it hurts still." Krishna smiled to himself, as if he was just making a sardonic statement about himself. "Have you ever thought of leaving?"

"Every day. And every day I'm afraid. I don't know of what. Perhaps losing more people."

"You know, when I was cursed by Gandhari, I was

shocked and appalled. For years, I didn't take it seriously but fear grew in me in such a paramount way that I decided to do something about it. I made everyone invincible, unkillable. But I should have just let them be. Death is a part of life, Arjun. And just like how we live our lives and do other strange, beautiful things like sitting here at this cliff and looking at the stars—we should also let ourselves, and give ourselves that opportunity to die," he said. "And move on. Because the greatest strength of a human being is their adaptability towards the most tenuous of situations."

Arjun nodded. "You know Durjay approached me."

"Oh really? He's been quite a thorn."

"Told me to kill you."

"So? What did you say? Are you going to throw me off the cliff or..."

Arjun laughed. "No. He told me that he knew how to resurrect life after death and you could have saved Subhadra...but now seeing all of these years later, I realised what happens, happens for a reason."

"In my defence, what he was trying to do was absolutely absurd. That goes against the world, against what fate has decided for you."

Arjun nodded. "Yeah. I don't know what he's up to now, since I rejected him..."

And they soon got to know.

Krishna realised the same tremors that he had experienced earlier had returned now. He shared a glance with Arjun, and they both rushed to wake up Samva. The boy didn't take that much time, but still enough for the creature to return, breaking through the branches.

Krishna could see that the ogre was no more in its senses, in fact its pupils had dilated and there was a certain mist around it.

"It's Durjay. He's controlling it," he said.

"We need to escape. We can't fight it," Samva said.

"I know. But I can," Arjun responded, taking out five arrows from his quiver. "You leave for the south. You'll find Durvasa there. He sits at the foot of the volcano and meditates there, though he has strictly said that whoever breaks his tapasya shall be killed and incinerated instantly, as the volcanoes would burst with his anger."

That sounded like Durvasa, all right. Krishna thought.

The ogre loudly yelled and thumped on the ground.

"Are you sure you want to stay here?" Krishna asked.

"I'll see you if I stay alive," Arjun paused. "But I have to see this through."

Krishna pursed his lips and then he made a run towards the part of the jungle where he was asked to go.

The creature followed him instead of Arjun, but Arjun didn't stop. He used his arrows to divert the attention, but the creature continued to toss rocks towards Krishna, which he and Samva dodged. They were moving at a high speed, sprinting and breaking through the air.

Arjun, meanwhile, climbed on the trees and moved up, before jumping from the tree and lurching over the giant, using his arrows to pierce through the eyeballs of the creature. But the mist was thick and it had grabbed him, almost blinding him, and he was not in his senses.

"I have to end this. I have to."

Krishna couldn't see much of it, as a slope appeared

in front of them, and both Samva and Krishna slipped through it, moving quickly downwards, while behind them the ogre and Arjun were fighting.

*

Krishna and Samva were moving at breakneck speed and they found some solace when they reached a place where they could rest for a while, take a breather and move again. The night was still dark.

"What were you both talking about?" Samva asked.

"Life. Responsibilities," Krishna said.

Samva nodded. He wanted to speak further. They were coming close to the battlefield, to their destination. He had so much to pour out. He had so much to inform him. But perhaps he needed to wait.

Krishna and Samva took hours to reach there, and as the sun was rising in front of them, they were getting closer to the volcanos, almost to the bed of it. They were at the southern gates, and as they came close, Krishna could see something. It was a slithered trunk of a tree, and on top of it sat Durvasa. It was close to where Arjun had said he'd be.

He was an old man, with matted hair and a long beard. He was wearing an orange dhoti and he looked like a speck of oddity in the stillness of the forest.

"We are here," Samva laughed, almost incredulously before he noticed that Durvasa was muttering to himself and was in penance.

Before Krishna could figure out a plan to disturb him, and not make him feel offended, Samva came forward hastily, as he always was, and said: "We need your help."

The old man stopped muttering and opened his eyes, which were red like the volcano that had begun to erupt. There was a kind of power that was radiating from the old man.

Krishna could feel it as well and almost regretted that his stupid son had woken him up.

"Who dares to trouble me?" Asked Durvasa as his eyes fell on Krishna, he arched his brows. "Lord Krishna... how come you are here?" His voice was suddenly stable and he was not showing specks of anger, but still there was something in him, a troublesome delight that was washing over his face.

"I come in peace, Guru Durvasa and we apologise for disturbing your penance," Krishna said, feeling ashamed. "But we have to ask you something that only you hold the answer to."

"And that is?" He narrowed his gaze.

The volcano was about to burst, embers were falling down and the ground was shaking, but not because of an ogre, of natural causes.

"We want to know about the Erakas."

"Ah," a small smile appeared on his face, "The most indestructible weapon to mankind."

"Yes. It could slice through anything and kill anything, right?"

"Yes, that's what I've known," Durvasa smiled. "But Lord Krishna, you didn't have to come all the way to seek this information."

"Why?"

"Because it was you who told me what the Eraka was and you told me that you would want to wipe that information out because if you knew the answer, it would hurt everyone. Somewhere deep down, you have buried it. You could have used penance to bring it out."

"How do I know about the Erakas?" Krishna asked, confused.

"Because it's in your blood, Lord Krishna." He smiled. "A blade anointed in your blood is an Eraka."

"No..." Krishna sighed. "But how...."

Samva gasped. He couldn't believe that the weapon they were searching for, was all this while, his father.

"He doesn't know, does he?" Durvasa asked, signalling to Samva.

Krishna narrowed his gaze realising that he did remember something. He did remember the night where it all began, and the buried memories that he had forgotten about, that he had wiped out for his own sanity, had begun to clamour back to him. He remembered that this was it, this was the moment of remembrance.

"It was the night Samva was born," Krishna said.

"Yes. And I was there."

"He was weak. Maligned. He was about to die."

"Yes."

Krishna was tearing up. "And when I realised what would happen to him, I gave him my powers, some of it, as a way to survive."

"Little knowing that down the road, you would be using those same powers for the entirety of the Yayati clan," Durvasa said.

"I was the first one you made invincible?" Samva

asked. "But I thought you hated me..." his voice trailed.

"And you had told me," Durvasa continued, "that I have made my son as powerful as me. If he ever goes out of hand, use my blood—the Eraka—to hurt him."

Samva shook his head. He couldn't believe that even when he was born, he wouldn't trust him.

"I should have not said that," Krishna admitted, and turned to Samva. "I'm sorry. I know it sounds horrible."

"It sounds way worse than you imagine, father, but it's all right. We finally know the answer, so now we know what we have to do," Samva said.

Krishna was confused. "What do you mean?"

He pulled out his sword and pricked his skin, letting Krishna's blood flow. Krishna instantly grabbed his arm and moaned. "What are you doing?"

"Don't you realise?" Samva gritted his teeth. "I want your blood."

"For?"

"To kill myself, father," Samva smiled with a grin. "All this time, this journey was not about the end of Yayatis—but about the end of me."

40

"Are you sure about this?" Yudhajit asked.

Balaram didn't know whether he was or not. He had been living this entire journey filled with twists and turns, and many more mysteries were yet to be solved. He wanted to go home, see his children, nestle down on his porch and watch the autumn leaves fall.

But here he was—mending relations between a destructive, murderous father and an equally crazy son.

"I don't think there's a choice here, my friend," Balaram said.

"Don't call me that. You betrayed me the moment you thought I had turned. You didn't even bother to ask."

"I was keeping it low," Balaram said. "You got to see it from my perspective. My mission was in a delicate position."

Yudhajit shrugged. They were both inside the tent, and he was sitting on his chair, drinking his ale. There were hundreds of red tents like these spread over the snowy landscape where the cold seeped into the hardened Yayatis. The battle hadn't begun, but it would soon. Balaram had convinced Yudhajit to meet Satyaki and solve their differences. Satyaki had travelled from a safe route and was about to get close.

"I never thought my own son! Gah!" He growled. "If it would have been anyone else, I wouldn't even have listened to you."

"I know that."

"But it's him." His eyes softened.

"He has grudges."

"Then discuss. Not engage." Yudhajit spat his wine. "And now here we are, in a battle yet again with the blind fools. These skirmishes are now becoming troublesome for me."

"It's the Ledger."

"Who is this person?"

He shrugged. "I have no clue. But I plan to find Devamedha and torture her to death, to know about it." He didn't say it in front of Revathi as she was not here, but in another tent getting mended from the cold. Akoorji, meanwhile had disappeared. He was probably a prisoner of war by now, or perhaps he was the one who was working with Devamedha.

"Do you think it's your commander?"

"He could be. He's still at the camp."

"He's quite a loyalist."

"I know. But you can't trust anyone," Balaram impassively added.

And as he did, Satyaki entered with his manacles and two guards behind him, who were ready to strike at him at places which would paralyse him. He stood there with a stern expression, and he looked like he was about to pounce at his father, but chose to remain there.

"The prodigal son returns," announced Yudhajit. "Tell me, my dear son, how does it feel to come back to your father?"

"I'm here because Uncle Bala told me to come."

"What if your Uncle Bala can't help you and you are stuck here?"

"I have a backup army ready to attack you at your most delicate moment."

Yudhajit came on his feet. He wasn't humouring anymore nor was he in that mood. "I am not here to listen to your antics. For doing what you did, inciting a rebellion, you should be castrated, but I listen to you still."

"There's no benefit in you both fighting," Balaram came in between them. "You both are valuable and you both love each other, that's why you are here. Not because of me. Not because I could convince you but because you wanted me to say the stuff to push you over the edge. Satyaki..." he turned to the young boy, "you hate your father, but you also know he's a good man and a good father to you. He has done things, but he can rectify himself. Yudhajit, same with you. I'm sure you won't have a problem, would you now?"

"Why does he hate me though?" Yudhajit came forward with a narrowed gaze.

"Because you killed the woman I loved."

Yudhajit was confused and then chuckled. "Are you for real? Have you no shame? I saved your life!"

"What do you mean?"

Balaram knew the story; as he came forward to speak delicately. "Son, I got to know that she was a wench who was stealing from you. Yudhajit got to know because he was keeping a tab on her. When he got to know, he got rid of her. She was nothing but a destructive force in your life."

"No, she—she loved..."

"Your entire rebellion was based on love?" Yudhajit shook his head. "Never give your heart to a woman. They know how to use it well and then throw it away."

"I don't trust you."

"Then don't! But I speak the truth. I would never..." his voice softened, "I would never hurt you, my son. I wouldn't care who you love, as long as you are happy. But I can't let my son be treated as a fool and that's what she did."

Satyaki remained afoul and confused. Almost teary. "That doesn't excuse you to treat the lower classes badly. You have done that in the most awful ways and people are troubled under your rule. Your regime is worthless and so are you."

Yudhajit shrugged. "Perhaps. But it's a profitable regime."

"Profit is not everything. Compassion matters too."

"To you perhaps. Not to me." He grabbed the crown from his head. "Open his manacles."

The guards did that immediately. Yudhajit walked towards him and he looked as if he had no fight left in him. He could have spat more, but he knew what Balaram had said was the right thing.

"I don't have compassion. I'm a hated man, and a hated king. And that's exactly why you should have the crown." He said, shocking Satyaki.

"Are you..."

"Yeah, yeah, I have been thinking about this for a while," Yudhajit responded, as if it was not a big deal. "But now I feel, this is the moment to do it. To finally take the leap of faith and close it. I don't want my legacy to hate me. I love you, my son." Even though there was bitterness, there were still a lot of unsaid things. "I hope you love me too and enough to honour me by accepting this gift. I do not want the crown. I want to now rest."

Satyaki didn't know whether he should hug his father or kneel and so he knelt, as the crown was placed on his head. "I'm sorry." And he instantly embraced him. They both hugged for long and Balaram had a warm smile on his face, wishing he could be with his own son right now.

And at that moment he realised that Pradhyuman wasn't bad either. The circumstances were not ideal and the lack of his father being in his life is what had caused such an uproar.

"I'm sorry."

"It's all right."

Balaram smiled and came close to both of them, patting them on their shoulders. "I believe we should celebrate."

"Tonight we should and tomorrow we fight with glory."

And before they could all agree in unison, there was a loud horn that was being blown. Balaram arched his brows looking at Yudhajit in confusion, and Yudhajit said:

"The battle has begun."

*

Ideally, Balaram wouldn't have been a part of the battle.

He was one of those who would strategise and stay

back, for his leg was paralysed and he couldn't fight. But he had his chariot. He had his weapon that was the staff and he had attached a few daggers to it, to make it even more lethal.

He knew he was ready.

And he felt confident after such a long time.

The moment he entered the battlefield, everything was chaotic. There were tossing of heads and moving half torsos. People were getting slaughtered out there. Oil was being tossed and they were being incinerated. Balaram had not seen such bloodshed in a long time.

As his chariot was being ridden by a Vrishni, he used his staff whenever he could to swing it across a pair of Andhakas, stabbing them in the head and tossing their bodies apart. Balaram felt good, whenever he did that.

When it hit him.

All the arrows had immediately stung him hard, coming out of nowhere and just grabbing him by the throat, hitting even his driver. It was a volley of serrated projectiles that threw them off course.

Balaram cursed, as he tried to get on his feet, when an Andhaka appeared. He was not wearing his mask because the Andhakas had a tendency of not using them during battles. It eases their sight and helps them to fight better.

As an Andhaka soldier came closer, Balaram instantly hit him in the chest, stabbing him and tossing him on the side. With the help of the staff, he tried to come on his feet. That was when he saw it—another rainfall of arrows coming towards him. He knew they would be reaching him any time, so he leapt and limped towards the shield that was lying on the ground next to an injured soldier, grabbing it and holding it up.

When he pulled down the shield and the rain of arrows was over—something worse hit him. He saw Devamedha's chariot afar, but around it was none other than the...

The wave of mist began to move and slaughter the Vrishnis as it began to move towards him.

"Oh no, the damned Vitihotra is here."

Instead of being injured, the Vitihotra was using the mist and his hardened body made of clinking armour and he had a misty sword, with which he cut humans like butter.

The Vitihotra saw him and lurched, as Balaram deflected his attack with the staff.

Though it didn't work for long, as the tuft of wind and mist smacked him on the chest and he fell back, deep into the slumber of it.

His eyes barely opening...he could feel his chest thumping hard and his mouth going dry...

When his eyes opened...he found himself back in the world of chaos. He found where he was earlier. He found he was in the same place he had been trying to run away from. He was in that dream and there was the snake.

How come I'm here?

"Let me swallow you," the snake asked loudly. "Let me swallow you."

Balaram didn't say anything. He saw Lakshman in front of him. The scene played out the way it always did.

"You are corrupted so let me swallow you."

"How am I corrupted?" Balaram asked.

"You have been influenced."

"What do you mean?"

"The Ledger, it is not anyone else."

"Then?"

"It's you."

Balaram narrowed his gaze and chuckled. "Are you mad? I would have known if it was me."

"You are corrupted. The sorceress," the snake hissed, "had corrupted you, made you forget things, hypnotised you. You go in a trance and work as the Ledger."

"No," Balaram's mouth went stale. "It can't be."

"It is."

"Let me swallow you."

Balaram saw the snake was about to take its favourite leap and moving forward, when he flared his nostrils and gritted his teeth, limping towards Laxman and throwing him off the course...

Allowing the snake to take him in.

*

Balaram woke up. The mist was still around. But he was larger than the mist. In fact, he was so large that everyone was staring at him. They were all shocked and they all were getting scared—even the Vrishnis. He could see his body wasn't his body anymore, but it was a reptile with a long tail and a hood of seven heads.

He was the very snake that he was afraid of.

But he could feel himself. He could feel he was still there, but more powerful and more horrific in its approach. He could defeat anything...

And surely a poor Vitihotra is nothing but a cockroach for him.

As the Vitihotra tried to slash the hardened skin of the snake, Balaram went down and using his fangs bit the Vitihotra's clunky armour then spat the poison within the man, almost burning his body, letting the mist dwindle. It threw him off course and a part of him felt destroyed, but he also loved the feeling of control.

He broke through the armour and ate the man as dinner but felt nothing as he swallowed the body. Seeing this, the Andhaka army began to disperse, as Balaram loudly hissed and said:

"I'm Shesh Naag, protector of Lord Vishnu."

41

Durgajyoti didn't know where she was.

It was a dark, lonely path that was strewn with pebbles and moved towards a dilapidated palace whose debris instead of falling, were moving upwards, being sucked into a vacuum in the sky. Everything was grey and black here, and the ravens had two heads. Durgajyoti instantly felt the chill inside her, and she wrapped her arms around herself.

She began to walk towards the palace, and as she did, her mind raced to the last two visions she had seen, that was provided by Maya. They were clearly trying to tell her something. And she got what it was—that don't repeat the same mistake which she did when she was with Durjay.

But Pradhyuman was different…

Wasn't he?

"All men are the same." The voice within her said.

"You know I hate it when you do that. We have rules, have you forgotten? You can't read my thoughts and I wouldn't read yours."

"I have saved you enough times to break some of these flimsy rules."

Durgajyoti cursed under her breath even though she knew Baagul would know about it. She didn't like how she was not in control of the situation and that there was no privacy when it came to herself. Worse, Baagul was, in fact, someone who had been creating those tremors on her fingers. They were shaking as always.

"Why can't I stop it?" She asked.

"Because you haven't accepted me," Baagul responded, again reading her thoughts.

"That's not true. I have."

"No. Very superficially. But not truly. You still fear me. Why fear something, that's your reflection?" Baagul asked, in a slimy tone.

Durgajyoti knew that Baagul wasn't a reflection, but just an aid. But then she didn't know anything for sure any longer. She wasn't even sure how long she had been here in this Mayasabha. She didn't know whether she's even passing the tests given by the Mayasabha and whether she would get the Maya or not, for Pradhyuman.

As she neared the palace, there was a tuft of wind that reached her face and caressed it.

"I just wanted to tell you, that whatever happens, I'm always there for you," Baagul said, the voice within her boomed with warmth and love, something Durgajyoti thought the voice didn't possess. "And I don't intent to hurt you in any way."

Durgajyoti didn't know what to reason. She did feel slightly happy and comforted even though it was a tad bit embarrassing that someone was speaking to her in this fashion—as if that person genuinely cared for her.

And she hadn't been cared for in a long time.

Durgajyoti moved inside the palace, her eyes drawn towards the centre of the palace where a white beacon of light was brimming with hope and finality. For some reason, Durgajyoti felt that if she touched it, she would be able to feel the Maya within her. She looked up, and she witnessed the debris being sucked inside a wormhole, suspending in air meanwhile. They were being swallowed, and she knew she was feeling lighter and if she didn't reach for the light, she would be taken up as well.

"I should get it," she told herself.

"There's something not right here," Baagul said. "Be careful."

Durgajyoti nodded, moving for the light, as the wind began to blow faster and it was hitting her face, blinding her a bit, but she still continued to move, the face of Pradhyuman in her eyes and the hope he would like her...

But then, she had felt the same way with Durjay. Until she got rid of it, that feeling.

"Are you sure you want to do this?" A voice boomed.

Durgajyoti turned back. And she saw someone surprising—herself. But the one in front of her, was far more confident, her hands didn't shake.

"What is the meaning of this? Who are you?"

"I'm the ghost of the future." The woman in front of her smiled. "Someone not you, but better."

"What do you mean?" She was closer to the light and she could touch it now. She wanted to.

"If you do that, you would gain perhaps a husband, but lose a friend."

"Which friend?"

"The one within you."

"She's not my friend."

"But she will be, down the road. Why go for something uncertain, when you have something certain coming your way?" The woman in front asked. "Why are you doing this? All this while, I wanted to teach you to not do this. You must realise, you are falling in the same trap as that of Durjay. He would treat you horribly."

"But I love him."

"More than yourself?" The woman asked. "If you do so, get the Maya and give it to him, but the energies of Maya would destroy Baagul."

Durgajyoti felt it was a trick and so she asked within herself, but the voice of Baagul was all distorted as if—when she was coming closer to Maya as a source of energy, Baagul was dissipating into thin air.

"Are you...no..." Durgajyoti knew there would be a test. She didn't know it would be this tough.

"You still have a choice, Durgajyoti." The woman smiled. "Choose the one which benefits you, not the people around you. You have been kicked around, shaken and destroyed your entire life. It's time to not give away this pedestal anymore."

"But Pradhyuman is different."

"And he could be. Or he could be not," the woman said. "Baagul was there for you when no one else was."

"She wanted a host," Durgajyoti spat on the ground. She knew Baagul was just a parasite who wanted to suck on someone's blood to thrive.

"No. She wanted a friend. And she had you. She can be quite an uncertain character, but she's the right friend for you," the woman said. "Because of her you conquered the Vitihotras, you hold the Taljan clan. Without her, you are but a simple woman with nothing much to offer. But with Baagul, you are, my dear, a goddess."

Durgajyoti frowned and flared her nostrils.

"Choose. Baagul or Pradhyuman."

"All this time, all the things I've done—were for Pradhyuman."

"Don't let a man decide your fate." The woman came closer and patted her on the shoulder. "You are greater than that. Your hopes, your dreams are greater than any of it. You must stick to your true self and let it win you."

"I know." Durgajyoti was feeling convinced and she felt a little lost for a moment, as she couldn't hear Baagul. Was this all a trick? Or was this something else?

"He wants you because he knows you are powerful. Would he still want you when you are not? The question is that."

Durgajyoti didn't have a response to that. She was unsure about it as well. She always felt that if she did what was right and if she stuck to that, it would work out and things would be better. Pradhyuman would be in love with her and they would have children...

But an uncertain future, at the expense of losing Baagul. That was worth thinking over.

"What do you choose, Durgajyoti? Because your choices define you. Whether you are the person people can look up to, or a person who everyone looks down upon. It's our chosen path that matters and the gravity of it," the woman said. "Touch the source of Maya and you would have something greater than anything in this world and you might lose everything. Your choice."

Durgajyoti sighed, and as she felt the moment, her body began to float. She wanted to touch the source of light, but she didn't and she got drawn away, far away from the source of light, as the voice of Baagul was within her again.

She was being sucked into the wormhole, and her eyes darted towards her doppelganger, who was still on the ground and waving at her.

"What had happened? I lost you, for a while," Baagul screamed from within.

"Nothing." Durgajyoti closed her eyes, letting a tear drop, as the light of the wormhole engulfed her, and her fingers...

They had stopped shaking.

42

"The time has come," said Durvasa.

The volcano burst. And the lava began to float downwards, in a spiral. But the anger and the warmth of the lava wasn't as intense as the conversation between the father and the son who were both made of hot blood and impassiveness.

"The time has come," repeated Durvasa.

"What do you mean?" Krishna asked, through gritted teeth, not even listening to Durvasa, but looking at Samva who had just told him that he wanted to kill himself. "Why would you want to do that?"

"Because I'm worthless."

"No, you are not. You are better than I could ever be. And I'm sorry if I ever made you feel that you are worthless."

"It's too late." And then he brought his sword forward, to cut him and Krishna deflected it with his mace. "You can't make me not do this."

The lava continued to erupt and it had begun to come closer to Durvasa.

"I should have known it was your blood, so I could have done this a long time back," Samva yelled and jabbed his blade close to Krishna, which he deflected swiftly again.

He didn't want to hurt his son, but he was making him do it. Everything had become so hot, and yellow and orange all of a sudden. He knew the lava was getting closer, and he had to grab his son and make a run for it. Surprisingly, Durvasa didn't care, muttering the same thing again and again, closing his eyes.

Krishna's mind had been distracted for just a moment, and it was right then when Samva took the initiative and shoved him on the ground, propelling over him and pulling out his dagger, with which he was trying to stab Krishna, but Krishna was twisting the blade, and making sure it won't happen.

"I came to you...I came to you...because I wanted to go on this odyssey with you and when we had learnt about Erakas, I wanted to kill myself in front of you to know what you did...whatever you did...all this while—was what devastated me, destroyed me and I wanted to give up. But you gave me a curse. You couldn't let me die. You didn't allow me to do that."

"I'm sorry," Krishna was holding on to the knife that was being pushed down towards his chest. "I'm really sorry. I want to make things better between us. Please don't let this happen."

"It was a good last trip, father."

"Samva," he said his son's name, "don't do this."

But Samva didn't listen and he stabbed Krishna, penetrating his blade through his flesh. Krishna didn't feel much pain and as the blade was being pulled out, Krishna saw that the lava had reached the trunk on which Durvasa sat and it had melted the woods as Durvasa became part of the lava and turned into ashes and fire.

Everything was ending, he felt, and the lava was coming even closer to them.

Samva had pulled the blade, and was ready to stab it, when Krishna with tears in his eyes, stopped it—held his hand, making sure he doesn't do it.

"I can't let you do it," Krishna cursed. "The lava is close. Let's stop this absurdity and let's escape."

Samva saw the lava and they both knew they would burn, so he rolled over, away from Krishna so Krishna could leave. Krishna came on his feet to help him...

When he saw Samva. He had the blade right next to his chest. The heart, precisely. And he was on the ground. He had a placid smile on his face, as if he was glad that this happened. And he was looking at the stars.

Krishna rushed towards Samva and bent next to him. "No...no...NOOOOOO!" He yelled. "You can't."

Samva coughed blood. "It's majestic. The feeling."

"What?"

"The feeling that I'm about to die. It's underrated." And he smiled. "I'll meet you on the other side, father." And his eyes closed. "Save Dvarka."

Krishna's tears started flowing and his temper was fiery. As the lava came close to him, it passed him, but didn't affect him, only dissolving Samva's body just like the way Durvasa's body was. Krishna clenched his jaws and felt worthless. He knew he might have given all the powers to the Yayatis...

And yet he had all the powers.

But he couldn't save his son.

The one he had grown to love. He wanted to hug

the body, but there was nothing left, instead it was just hot, flaming lava in front of him.

And just like that—his world had changed forever.

*

Pradhyuman was standing with his council. They had formed a semi-circle in a dark room, where the ministers, the commanders and the generals were. All the high-ranking officials. Even Rukmini was there, by his side. He was in his dhoti and bare-chested, because he had come from a jog around the palace. Sweating like a pig.

Pradhyuman had listened to all the updates. He had heard about Durgajyoti as well, and he wasn't happy with the decision that his wife had taken. He had sent a search party for her, but he had no clue where she was. As for Balaram, there was no trace either and so was the case with Samva. There was no news whatsoever.

"So, what do we do?" One of the councilmen asked. "Now that we know it was the Rakshasas who had consumed you, should we formulate a plan to attack them or should we stick to what we had vetoed in your absence?"

Pradhyuman had learnt about what his wife had made everyone do. And while he would have been angry at her...he wasn't.

"I don't think we should fight Rasatala."

"Then?" Someone from the table asked. "Then what?"

"I don't know." He shrugged, defeated, the feeling of hopelessness was coursing through him. "But I do know I don't want violence anymore. I don't want to fight anymore. I want to have a peaceful land, a peaceful world," Pradhyuman sighed, sitting back. "And I want to change a few policies. I don't think they work in the favour of the people."

Everyone gasped in shock and awe. Pradhyuman remained in his chair, defeated and leaned back, when he saw Rukmini was watching him in horror. He didn't know why he said it. But he knew he had no drive to impress anyone, because the woman he wanted to impress had died…by his own hands.

And perhaps the most beautiful are also the most dangerous, and they have to be plucked out for others to survive.

And that's what Pradhyuman did.

Surprisingly, he did see Rukmini didn't touch the wine in the meeting that followed. She didn't even look at it. The hand that would trace around the bronze goblet, was now tracing the lines of his hand.

*

Balaram didn't know how he had changed back into his normal shape, but he had and he was grateful towards everyone. While everyone from the Vrishni side too were worshipping him for what he had done in the battlefield. They all bowed down and some fell on his feet. It was all very confusing. But Balaram just drifted by.

As the battle was over, and Devamedha and her people had rushed back, they had found a lot of prisoners of war, and they did find Akoorji amongst them, tortured beyond belief.

Balaram was at the infirmary and was taking care of Akoorji, along with Revathi when she asked:

"Did you know who the Ledger was?"

"Yeah, and I personally didn't like the answer."

In the large tent that was dedicated to healthcare, there were a lot of other injured soldiers.

"I'm sorry I second guessed you both," Balaram said. "But I would never again. You are family."

She smiled. "Your plan to combine both the armies didn't work out. What do you want to do now? Pradhyuman still looms large as a threat."

"I don't know." He shrugged. "I don't know what I would do. But I do know that Pradhyuman can change. What I saw between Yudhajit and Satyaki—I realised, that the answer to get rid of my nephew is a flawed one. I should reform him and mend ties. And you know why?"

She raised her brows.

"Because you don't give up on family." He smiled back. "Do you?"

"No, you don't." She kept her head on his shoulder.

They both remained like that, in the humdrum of the battle, realising that they were about to leave this place and change their course.

They both knew it was over for now. And there would be a new chapter, a new hope was ignited in them. The hope for reformation.

*

When Krishna returned, he didn't go where Arjun was fighting the ogre. He went for the boat. He didn't understand why he did that. He wanted to see his friend and cry on his shoulder, but he felt numb. He felt horrible and his chest was feeling the weight of the greatest burden he had ever experienced.

He reached the boat, and noticed it was lopsided, when he saw that the one balancing it—was Arjun.

He was wounded surely, and his quiver had no arrows left in it and his bow was broken, but he was still taking care of the boat. He turned around to look at Krishna.

"Have you met Durvasa?" He asked.

Krishna nodded.

"Where's your son?"

Krishna didn't respond. "Do you know how to move the boat in the right direction? Do you know how to use the waves to our advantage?"

"Yeah." He paused, as they both sat on the boat, and they had began to row, while the sun in the far east was brimming with rays and was dipping down over the horizon. "What happened to your son, Govinda?"

"Let's not talk about it," Krishna said. "What happened to my sister?"

Arjun shrugged. "Did what I had to do. So let's not talk about it either."

They remained silent and stared at the glowing sun.

"You are coming with me. What's your plan?" Krishna asked.

"Don't know, but I know I can't stay here," he answered. "Where to then?"

Krishna touched his wounded chest, and looked at the blood—the very blood that could end the civilisation of the Yayatis.

"Where to?" He said to himself. "To Dvarka, Arjun. To Dvarka."

END OF EPISODE 1

Acknowledgements

I would like to thank Lord Krishna for actually allowing me to write this.

I would also like to thank my parents for supporting me always.

I am grateful to Simon & Schuster India for taking a bet on this story—be it Rahul Sir, Sayantan Ghosh, Himanjali, Abhay, and the list goes on.

Nothing could be possible without Mr Bahri from Redink Literary Agency who has been a pillar of strength during my literary life.

I am thankful for my company Hubhawks and the wonderful team I have with me. This book was written during the working hours in the office, and they were kind enough to be silent when I was in my writing zone.

My wife, Kiran Malik, who has been a champion in supporting the book. And Naghma, my assistant, friend and an avid reader of mine. Always helping me in all the stuff I'm particularly bad at.

And most of all, thank you to the readers. You wanted me to write a book on Lord Krishna. This is my version.